Useful Gifts

Useful Gifts

Gifts

STORIES BY

Carole L. Glickfeld

THE UNIVERSITY OF GEORGIA PRESS
ATHENS AND LONDON

© 1989 by Carole L. Glickfeld
Published by the University of Georgia Press
Athens, Georgia 30602
All rights reserved
Set in Linotron 202 11 on 13 Goudy Old Style

The paper in this book meets the guidelines for permanence and
durability of the Committee on Production Guidelines for
Book Longevity of the Council on Library Resources.

Printed in the United States of America

93 92 91 90 89   5 4 3 2 1

Library of Congress Cataloging in Publication Data

Glickfeld, Carole L.
    Useful gifts.

    I. Title.
PS3557.L514U84   1989   813'.54   88-17099
ISBN 0-8203-1041-7 (alk. paper)

All characters in these stories are fictional, and any resemblance to
persons living or dead is coincidental. "What My Mother Knows"
was published in *The Written Arts*. Earlier versions of "Peola and
Petunia" and "In the Shadow of the Boardwalk" were published in
Permafrost and *West Wind Review,* respectively. "My Second
Favorite" appeared in the *William and Mary Review.* "My Father's
Darling" appeared in *Crosscurrents*.

For Blume Mandelbaum

The publication of this book is supported by a grant from the National Endowment for the Arts, a federal agency.

🐱 Contents

I. Arden Street

🖤 What My Mother Knows

FRANKIE Frangione, standing on the sidewalk, screams up to his ma, up on the second floor in the building across the street from us.

My ma is watching him from the bedroom window. "Scream lazy walk," she says to me. In sign language, cause she's a deaf-mute. Translated means Frankie is screaming up to his ma since he's too lazy to walk upstairs. All the kids scream up to their ma on account of this block having only walk-ups. The elevator buildings are on the next block up Arden Street, across from the church.

We live on the fourth floor. Four double flights, there's nine steps in each half, not counting all the steps in the lobby and the three levels of the stoop. Sixty-six I counted. Which means I have a lot of running up to do if I want something. I can't scream up like the other kids cause my mother can't hear me.

Most of the time my mother's cooking or cleaning. Or iron-ing. She irons all my pinafores. But if she happens to be hang-ing out the window, she sees me usually. She leans out, resting her soft, squishy arms on a pillow so that the gravel stuff on the ledge doesn't scrape. If she's looking the other way, though, like toward Nagle Avenue, I just keep waving my arms till she turns back. Then I tell her what I want. In sign. Like, "Throw ball." Meaning please throw down my Spauld-ing. And she does, in a paper bag, so it doesn't bounce to kingdom come.

I play outside in the mornings and then in the afternoon she takes me to Fort Tryon Park. "For fresh air," she says. The deaf-mutes sit on the benches around the playground sand-box. The way the benches curve is perfect for them because they can see each other across the way to talk. Sometimes they ask me questions in sign language, like what I'm going to be when I grow up. "Teacher," I say. Or they ask if I'm a good girl. I smile and nod. Sometimes they give me a nickel for an ice cream cone. Then I ask my ma for a penny so I can get sprinkles on top, which is extra. She looks at me like she's asking a question and practically kisses her hand, which means did I say thank you for the nickel. I smile and nod.

It's good she has lots of deaf friends she can see in the park. It's a whole other world there from Arden Street, and my mother knows what's going on in both places. All the gossip. More than my big sister thinks she knows, and she can hear, like me.

My ma's the one who told us Frankie Frangione's mother was preg again. The sign for that is done by holding both your hands out in front of your belly, then moving them away from you like your stomach's getting bigger right there on the spot. And she told us that the O'Briens were divorced. "Must," she said, "not see long time." Except she doesn't call them the O'Briens. She says, "Know drunk?" Meaning the guy who's always drunk on Saturday nights. "Unhappy, fight wife, divorce," she said. That just gives you an idea of how my mother's always got her eyes open.

Like when she saw me and Frankie sneak into the alley. We had our eyes on her, too, from across the street. When she looked down toward Nagle, we ran into the alley. Then I told him to touch me. He did. One quick touch down there. He got all red in the face like hives. I said, "Go on Frankie," but he stopped. Just poked real quick like under my underpants and stopped, getting red. "Nah, I'll have to tell the priest," he said.

"WHAT?" I couldn't believe it. That's when he explained about confession. I used to hear kids on the stoop say they had to go, but I didn't know what it was. Imagine. Going up to a total stranger, even in the dark, and telling that you touched someone under their underpants. You gotta be nuts.

"You don't go to confession?" he asks me.

"I'm Jewish, silly," I said.

"So?"

"So I don't."

"How come?"

"Jews don't."

"Then you're gonna go to hell," he said.

"I'm not."

"Betcha."

"Frankie," I said, "Fran-kie!"

He looked kind of funny, so I said we better get out of the alley in case the super came. It was Frankie's building and all, but still. And then we pretended the super was coming and tried to scare each other, running and screaming for our lives till we hit the sidewalk out in front. First thing I did when we got there was look up across the street to see if my mother was hanging out, but she wasn't. She was coming down the stoop, her slippers with no heels flopping open in back. My mother doesn't wear her slippers in the street like Mrs. Frangione. So I knew I was in trouble.

5

Frankie took off and I crossed the street and walked up to her at the edge of the bottom landing of the stoop. I crossed my toes.

"You run hide sneak," she said. "Not like."

She wasn't mad. I could tell by looking. Her mouth gets scrunched up when she's upset, like I hurt her feelings.

I didn't say anything.

"True? Tell," she said.

"Sorry," I said. The sign for "sorry" is a fist facing your chest and then you make the fist go in a circle around your chest, like you're washing yourself with a washrag. I uncrossed my toes.

"Bad girl spank," my mother said, but she's never spanked me. Except once, ages ago. I watched her go up the stoop. She turned when she got to the top landing. "Careful you," she said in sign and went in the house. I got into a game of Kings and then I went home for supper.

Afterwards, when she let me eat a slice of Swiss cheese without making me put it on bread, I asked her why she'd gotten upset. Except I said "mad" because I don't know any sign for "upset." "Why mad afternoon?" I asked.

"Dangerous." She spelled it out slowly. "D-a-n-g-e-r-o-u-s." She meant the alley. "S-t-r-a-n-g-e-r n-o play," she added, meaning that a stranger could be there and it wasn't a place to play. You have to spell out s-t-r-a-n-g-e-r because there's no sign for it. It can take a long time to say things in sign language. Which is why you always try to make things as short as possible. Otherwise it takes forever.

"Who d-a-n-g-e-r-o-u-s?" I asked her.

"Any," she said. "Not know. Maybe happen. T-o-o l-a-t-e. Awful." She washed the knife I used to open the cellophane package of Swiss cheese, even though it wasn't dirty. Then she wiped it with the towel I embroidered, not just cross-stitches, either. She taught me how to do stems and leaves, which are my favorite.

"Listen me, sorry," she said. Meaning I'd be sorry if I didn't listen. "Aunt sister r-a-p-e-d."

6

Sadie, my aunt? RAPED? But I didn't say anything. "Raped" was one of the words I read in the *Daily News* that I didn't know and couldn't ask. The dictionary doesn't explain it good. I just knew it was dirty. I don't know how I knew.

"Sister S-a-d-i-e tell me. Nobody know. Afraid always. Very s-a-d."

I asked her if it happened in the alley.

"N-o n-o n-o." She shook her head and signed both. "Brooklyn, grow up." We lived in Manhattan. "Always remember," she said.

I studied my tooth marks in the crust of the Swiss cheese and then I started to eat the crust.

She shook her head. "Careful sick." But she knew I always ate the crust and never got sick.

It was still light out because it was summer. I didn't want to go to bed but I did. For a while, anyhow. My big sister wasn't home yet from the baby-sitting. I went over and pulled the shade so I could open the window and stick my head out. I couldn't stick it out far since my mother was probably hanging her own head out the window next door and she'd see me.

I stared a long time at Frankie Frangione's windows across the street. All the lights were on and the shades were up. "Waste light," my mother says, if you turn it on before it's dark. The Frangiones always had lights on in all the rooms, at least the ones you could see from our side of the street. Like us, they had windows facing the alley.

I felt sick, but it wasn't the Swiss cheese. I felt like I feel sometimes after I've been on the Whip a few times in Coney Island. Tomorrow I could ask Frankie if I could go to confession because I was scared. But what would happen if I chickened out at the last minute? How could I tell the priest I'm raped? Even in the dark. And then Frankie would get it for sure. They put rapists in jail, that's what the *Daily News* said. Once they said they should electrocute them.

I didn't know it was so terrible when we were doing it. I thought of my Aunt Sadie. "R-a-p-e-d." What if my mother knew I wanted Frankie to poke me some more but confession stopped him? I'd have to tell the police it was MY FAULT. Frankie didn't even want to. He wanted to play jacks. Oh God, I was the one. My sister says Jews don't go to hell, but there were all kinds of ways God could punish you before you were dead.

A funny noise made me jump. My mother's voice. Deaf-mutes don't have real voices when they try to talk. Sometimes while they're doing signs they make sounds like they're crying, but of course they can't hear themselves. Anyway, my mother made a sound to call me. "Rooh." That's how she says Ruth. "Rooh," she called from behind me. It scared me and made me hit my head on the edge of the window over me. Now it was her turn to say she was sorry. She looked it. "Hurt you?" she said. "Sorry." Her fist kept going round and round her chest.

"No," I fibbed.

"Go sleep," my mother said. "Tomorrow shop."

And then I remembered we were going to Alexander's in the Bronx the next morning on the 207th Street trolley. It's a big store, much bigger than anything on Dyckman Street. I like it, even though I don't know why they've got bells ringing all the time. I mean ALL the time. Ding ding ding. Ding ding ding. It's not something I can ask my mother.

Whenever we go, everyone's always grabbing at the stuff on the counters, but not her. She always opens the drawers under them because she wants things f-r-e-s-h.

I got into bed and watched my mother closing the bedroom door. She did it slowly, and when there was just a little space left she brushed the tips of her fingers over her lips (that means sweet) and made her second finger crooked, going in a line from her head toward the ceiling (that means dreams). "N-o watch window," she added, then closed the door. A second later it opened. "N-o think too much d-o-l-l," she said. She closed the door again.

We were going to get me a doll at Alexander's. For my

birthday. I wanted one very bad with blonde hair and real eyelashes. I didn't know yet what I was going to call her. Anna was my favorite name but it was Frankie's big sister's name and I didn't want to think about Frankie. Ever again. His other sisters had those Catholic names—Mary and Catherine and Patricia. I didn't know what they'd call the new baby. "Feel boy s-u-r-e," my mother said. "Another Little Italian." Little Italian is what she calls Frankie instead of his name. But she knows who I mean when I say I'm going to play with F-r-a-n-k. Except now I'd never say it again. Or sign it.

I wouldn't have to see him when summer was over, either. He went to the Catholic school on the next block, like his sisters. On Sundays they went to church there. On Sundays my mother always hangs out the window to see what everyone is wearing when they're dressed up. "How can a-f-f-o-r-d dress many children?" my mother asked. "Shoemaker not wonderful money," she said, about Mr. Frangione. I don't know how she knew he was a shoemaker because Angel's is the shoemaker around the corner from us. She knew Mrs. Frangione had trouble with her feet. "Always tell Little Italian go store," my mother said. Meaning Frankie's mother sent him so she wouldn't have to hurt her feet. I saw Mrs. Frangione when Frankie let me into his apartment to get the jacks. Before we went you know where. Her feet were up on the hassock in the living room.

"See my bird," Frankie said. "Don't put your finger in. Only I can do that."

Then Mrs. Frangione looked me over. I had a red and white pinafore on that my mother just ironed that morning. "You a friend of Frankie's?" she asked. "I seen you," she said. "With your mother, the little deaf-and-dumb lady, right? I really admire the way you talk with your fingers."

"Ma!" said Frankie, and then we got out of there. But he forgot the jacks.

My bedroom was dark finally and my sister Melva wasn't back from baby-sitting. I couldn't tell what my mother was doing because she was so quiet. Maybe looking at the news-paper in the kitchen or ironing. Sometimes at night she hangs out the window, especially when Melva isn't home yet. My mother told me what Frankie's sister Anna and her boyfriend did one night. "Kiss kiss kiss," she said. "Sneak downstairs, can't see, kiss." I could picture them standing in the doorway to Mrs. O'Brien's apartment in the basement. Frankie and I go under there when it rains so Mrs. Frangione can't see us and say Frankie should get upstairs. Anyway, Mrs. Frangione only goes to the window when Frankie calls. It hurts her feet to stand, Frankie says. When they weren't up on the hassock, she was soaking them in Epsom salts. I knew all kinds of things about them that even my mother didn't know.

And then it hit me. I sat straight up in bed in the dark. I knew Frankie had a parakeet and their living room smelled funny and Frankie wasn't so good at jacks. So how could he be a stranger?

I laid down again and watched the lights go across the ceil-ing from the cars outside until it got too spooky. Then I tried to go to sleep. I pretended my new doll was next to me already. I called her Anna, but just for that night, until I could decide.

I told her that after we came back from Alexander's, her and Frankie and me would go up Arden Street and tell the priest. Just in case. And then we'd go to Fort Tryon. If she was good, she'd get a nickel for an ice cream cone. And I'd teach her to say thank you, in sign language.

She wants me to teach her the whole alphabet. "O-K," I spelled out. The "O" is easy but the "K" is hard. "O-K," I spelled again and then I made the sign for sweet dreams.

☙ In the Shadow
of the Boardwalk

"CONEY Island is a dump," my sister said when I asked her how come she wasn't going with us.

"It isn't either," I said, not because I was born there. I love how different the ocean is from where we live now, near the Hudson River in the Inwood section of Manhattan.

"You've never even seen Far Rockaway," Melva said, "where the sand is all white. Ask Sidney if you don't believe me."

Of course, my brother wasn't home. He was at work. Anyway, I tried to imagine a beach full of something that looked like salt but I couldn't. "Is that where you're going?" I asked.

"What you don't know won't hurt," she said, pulling her black off-the-shoulder blouse down to where the top of her brassiere started. I figured she was going to hang around on the corner waiting to see this boy from her high school, Howie Teitelbaum. Unless she was going downtown with her friend Lucille to see a movie and stage show.

She took me downtown to the Roxie for my birthday. It was one of the best times in my whole life. A man named Jack Carson with orange makeup on his face made jokes, and a long line of tall, gorgeous girls wore costumes with silver spangles. They did high kicks in high heels, with nothing on their legs except mesh stockings. From the fifth row we could see everything, even the sweat running down the magician's face after he sawed this woman in half and put her back together again.

When my mother got all the sandwiches wrapped in waxed paper, she and my father and I took the A train on Dyckman Street. Then we changed for the Express, which is elevated when it gets to Brooklyn. The train goes right by the backyards of people's houses, so you can see the bushes and flowers and even people sitting in beach chairs getting sunburned. Some kids waved at the train this time and I waved back like my brother once taught me.

There were thirty-one deaf people at Brighton 13th Street on the beach already when we got there, not counting my mother and father. There's always a lot of them on Tuesdays, on account of the fireworks at night. It was pretty hot, so after I said hello to my parents' friends, I went and lay under the boardwalk where I wouldn't get burned up right away. My sister says it's my fair skin that makes me burn.

Under the boardwalk the sand is different, heavier and real cool. I liked laying on my stomach and digging my toes in, until they reached the wet stuff down below. I did the same with my hands, pretending I could swim through the sand tunnel.

I could see the deaf people on the beach, halfway down toward the water. Their arms were waving in the air, from doing the sign language. I was too far away to hear the funny noises from their throats, like they're barking out parts of words or gargling. I always tell my mother when she's making noises, so she'll stop.

"Not feel," she says, but she can stop doing it if she knows.

I only tell her when we're outside, though, where other people can hear. It's bad enough the way people stare, just because deaf-mutes have to talk with their fingers.

For a long time there was no one else in the whole world except me under the boardwalk, which is all in the shadow. But I could see many of the people on the beach. One woman was buried up to her waist in the sand, like she had no legs. A lot of the other women had giant legs, with thighs bigger than my waist almost. From where I was, I counted eight fat women and six fat men. My sister has a thing about fat people.

When I squinted my eyes, the colors of the bathing suits and towels and umbrellas mixed together in tiny pieces, like a kaleidoscope. The noises mushed together, too, even a helicopter and the waves roaring.

Not too far from me a very pretty blonde girl sat in the sun. The straps of her blue two-piece bathing suit were hanging down in front.

"Don't, Stevie," she said, when the freckle-faced boy next to her started pulling on them. He pulled her closer to him and then they kissed a long time. I wondered if they were going to do petting, which Melva'd told me was a sin. But they didn't. He put white lotion all over her and turned on the radio before they laid down. I recognized the song that was playing: "You Gotta Accentuate the Positive." My brother taught me to do a lindy to it.

All of a sudden I heard some giggling behind me. That's when I noticed a boy and a girl lying way back as far as you can get under the boardwalk. They had a blanket over them, which gives you an idea of how cool it was. The girl started laughing and the blanket was wiggling like crazy, so I figured he was tickling her, until she started making noises like he was hurting her. I guess he said he was sorry because she put her arms around his neck, outside the blanket, and hugged him.

When she saw me looking, she waved and said, "Hi, there," then giggled into his neck.

"Hello," I said, but I didn't know what else to say, so I got up and went down the beach. The sand was real hot. I started running until I saw my mother coming toward me. I asked this lady if I could stand on the edge of her towel so I wouldn't burn my feet and she said okay.

"Where go?" I signed to my mother.

"Pish," she answered.

I pointed to the ocean. "Water?" I asked, meaning why didn't she go pish in the ocean, like she was always telling me to do.

"U-n-w-e-l-l," she said. "Don't want bleed, everybody look me."

I'd seen a bloody rag from my sister once. It was really terrible. That's something I don't look forward to about being grown up. But I know that makes the babies come, so I guess I'd have to get used to it.

I went with my mother to the dressing rooms. While I waited for her, two midgets came out of the toilets. One asked the other if her hair was all right. They couldn't see themselves in the mirror, which was too high. Their hair looked okay, I thought, although they had large heads and real fat legs.

"Spoil born, t-o-o b-a-d," my mother said, when she came out and saw them.

"How born?" I asked.

"A-c-c-i-d-e-n-t, happen," she said. She washed her hands and dried them. "Awful m-i-d-g-e-t," she said, as we started to leave, but she stopped by the door. "Better throw away born."

Outside, before we started back to the beach, she told me the story again about how she wanted to get rid of me when she found out she was pregnant. My sister and brother were pretty big already. "Two enough, Daddy think," she said, explaining it wasn't good to have babies when you were old.

"R-e-t-a-r-d like boy D-o-n-g-a-n," my mother said, meaning that your baby could be retarded like the boy on Dongan Place, who sits in the window all the time, twirling a straw.

"Try inject," she said, meaning the injection the doctor

gave her to get rid of me. "Jump rope, m-u-s-t-a-r-d bath, n-o help."

We went back down the beach but we stopped on someone's towel because she wanted to say something else and the sand burned like crazy. "If f-r-e-a-k, throw away," she said about me, when I was born. She hadn't ever told me that before.

"Me f-r-e-a-k?" I asked, even though I knew the answer.

"N-o, n-o, l-u-c-k-y have brains," she said. "Sometimes, l-a-t-e born, smart."

I knew I did better in school than my sister and brother, but my sister was the beautiful one and my brother was my mother's favorite, but that's because he was first, I figure.

My father was real cranky when we got back. "Wait long," he signed. "Hungry."

My mother took out sandwiches, egg salad, and peanut butter and jelly. She also had some cooked chicken and hard-boiled eggs. I had an egg salad. I liked drinking the milk out of the red plastic thermos cup, even though it smells like the inside of the thermos.

A deaf woman I didn't know asked my mother if I understood sign language, which was real dumb, since my mother and me were signing the whole time.

"S-u-r-e," my mother said. "S-i-n-c-e old two."

I don't remember learning it. It's like I always knew how.

Another woman there asked me, "Hear can?"

I nodded.

"Not deaf born," she signed to the man next to her. Then my mother explained to her about my father getting meningitis when he was eight years old and how she got something as a baby, they think, like scarlet fever, which made her deaf. All the rest of her family can hear. "Can't born deaf," my mother said, meaning I couldn't of inherited it.

None of the deaf people were talking about anything interesting, so I told my mother I was going for a walk.

"L-o-o-k o-u-t," she said.

I collected some seashells, then came back and got my

bathing cap and went into the ocean. The big waves almost drowned me once, so I held on to the rope while I watched a skywriting plane that had done "Coca Co—" so far. The first two letters were already fading. They looked like part of the clouds, the long drawn-out kind with curly edges that were my favorite. Seagulls were flying round and round and the Goodyear blimp was up there like always.

There were so many umbrellas on the beach by then I couldn't even see where the deaf people were. I knew they were near the "Don't Litter" sign behind the lifeguard's high chair. The waves bounced me up and down a lot. The best part was watching each wave splash into the beach, which made some of the kids yell. There were lots of kids yelling. Then I realized something was wrong. The lifeguard blew his whistle and came running into the water, before he started swimming like mad. He swam right past me and disappeared under the water.

When he came back up, he had a little girl next to him. Her skin was shiny like my doll Betsey. He put her arm around his neck and did the sidestroke, dragging her along.

Holding onto the rope, I made my way back to where the beach was. I stood with all the people who made a circle watching the girl, who was lying on her stomach. The lifeguard was sitting on top of her, pressing down on her back with his hands. "Please," he kept saying. "Please." Then water came out of her mouth like vomit.

The next thing I knew, my father was pushing his way to the front of the circle on the other side, across from where I was. He almost got into a fight with a man over it. They yelled at him to get back, which of course he couldn't hear, and then another man tapped him on the shoulder and my father pointed to his ears and shook his head, to explain he was deaf. The man shook a finger at him, pointing to the people. I guess he meant my father should stay back there.

My father said something out loud in his funny voice, which I couldn't understand from where I was. He ran up to the lifeguard and kneeled down next to him, putting his head close to the girl's face. He looked real funny, like he was going to cry.

That's when I ran out so he could see me. He looked very surprised. He looked at the girl and then back at me. "Thought you," he said, putting his hand on his chest. "Thank G-o-d," he signed, and put his hand back on his chest again as he got up and came around. He hugged me while we walked toward the circle of people. I looked back at the girl. Her hair was dirty blonde like mine.

When we were past the crowd, he picked me up in his arms like I was little and carried me all the way to where my mother was. He told her how he thought it was me who drowned.

"Scare," my mother said. "Imagine too much."

When I told the deaf people what happened, they couldn't get over it.

"Mistake think H-a-n-n-a-h daughter," Mrs. Mazzoli said. Then the deaf people laughed because her name is Hannah like my mother's. My father didn't think it was funny though.

I told them there was a siren and we watched the men take the stretcher to the ambulance right on the boardwalk.

By that time my mother was packing up our things. She still had some peanut butter sandwiches and A&P pound cake wrapped in waxed paper left. "Eat nothing," my mother said, meaning I didn't eat much.

My father went into the Men's Dressing Rooms and we went into the Ladies' to change. It was dark in there because the only light came from the windows high up near the ceiling. The floor was wet and muddy on account of the sand that everyone dragged in all day. I watched our things while my mother rinsed off in the shower, then she watched and I rinsed off. Some people did it naked, but we did it in our bathing suits. Anyway, there were no doors on the stalls where you changed, which was the worst part. While we stood on line, we could see people taking their clothes off, though you're not supposed to look.

Finally there was an empty stall and I helped my mother unzip her bathing suit, which she took off and rolled in a towel. Naked, my mother looks huge, even though she isn't much taller than me. Her stomach is like a beach ball and her breasts hang down to her waist, but you can't tell when she's dressed. She looks very normal then. I did all the hooks of her brassiere. Over her bloomers she put on a panty girdle instead of a corset, because she didn't want to be bothered, she said, when it was so hot. Then she hooked her stockings to the garters and put on her shoes and her blue and white polka-dot dress. Then I got dressed.

We went to the counter where the mirror was and she brushed my hair and braided it. Even though she was standing behind me, we could talk because we could see each other's hands signing in the mirror. "C-u-t-e," my mother said, about the baby next to us in its mother's arms. "Like d-o-l-l."

When she got done putting the plaid ribbons around my pigtails, she said, "Like d-o-l-l you born, lot me worry."

"Why worry?" I asked her.

"Think born f-r-e-a-k," she said, explaining she was afraid because of how she tried to get rid of me when I was in her stomach. Right away she asked the doctor if I was okay. He wrote her a note and said I had perfect features.

My mother got done combing her own hair and put on lipstick. She was all red in the face and on her arms from the sun.

My father was cranky when we came out. "Waste time," he said. He complained about the way my mother had folded his shirt. He's always very fussy about how he looks. He trims his red mustache all the time and shines his shoes before he goes to work in the post office.

By the time we got to Nathan's, lots of deaf people were already standing out on the sidewalk, eating and signing. It was so crowded by the counters, it took a while to get my chow mein sandwiches and french fries, plus all the stuff for my parents, which I ordered for them. Nathan's has the best french fries in the whole world, as far as I'm concerned.

We walked back to the boardwalk to Brighton 23rd and waited for it to get dark, so the fireworks could start.

One of the deaf women asked me what grade I was in. After I told her, I knew she was going to ask me what I wanted to be when I grew up, so I told her I wanted to be a teacher. Actually I want to be a hatcheck girl, like my friend Glory's mother, but I never tell anyone that because you have to be real gorgeous and I don't want them to laugh.

"Teacher," the woman said, smiling. "Deaf children?"

"N-o, n-o," my mother answered. "T-o-o hard. Like wild animal," she said about the deaf children. She told me how she went to Fanwood, which was a school, and all the aggravation the teachers had.

"Talk s-i-l-l-y," my father said. "Who know future?" He introduced the lady. "M-r-s R-o-s-e-n. Live B-B," he said, which stood for Brighton Beach. "Husband A-b-e."

Mr. Rosen wasn't there, but my father said they played basketball together at Lexington, which was a different school for the deaf. It concentrated on lipreading, but my father only lip-reads with strangers.

I thought he might tell me some funny stories about being in school with Mr. Rosen, like he told me about Mr. Hurwitz. They poured a glass of water into Mr. Hurwitz's mouth when he was asleep and he started moving his arms like he was swimming. All my father said about Mr. Rosen was that they were good buddies.

"Happy meet you," Mrs. Rosen said to me.

"Happy meet you," I told her.

She grabbed my father's arm. "Like s-u-g-a-r," she said to him, about me.

"Like father," he teased.

But I take after my mother that way because my father has a terrible temper.

Finally, at nine-thirty, the fireworks started. They're all gorgeous but I could do without the ones that sound like cannons. My favorites are the fountains that burst into more fountains. The best part is the end, when the fireworks come real fast, one after the other, with crackling noises like cap pistols. When they stopped suddenly, it was real quiet, except for the waves coming into the beach and the funny voices of the deaf people on the boardwalk.

At the entrance to the subway the deaf people stood around saying good-bye to each other. Some of them lived there, so they just had to walk home. Some of the others were taking a different train. There must of been a hundred deaf people right there.

"Lookit 'em, lookit," I heard a boy's voice say. There was a group of kids staring. They were standing next to the booth that sells saltwater taffy. The girls were pointing and giggling.

"What're you staring at?" I screamed out.

"The deaf-and-dumb people," a kid said. He waved his arms and fingers around, like he was imitating them. His friends all laughed and some started to do the same thing.

"They're not dumb. They're deaf-mutes," I said. "It's not their fault, so what're you making fun of them for?"

"Cause they're freaks," another kid said.

"You're a freak," I said, "because you're stupid."

When he started coming toward me I ran up to where my father was.

"Freakfacefreakface," he yelled, but he couldn't do anything. A girl pulled him away.

Usually it was the grown-ups who stared at my parents and their friends. None of the kids on Arden Street or in Fort Tryon ever did. It made me feel really bad.

Even in the dark I liked the long subway ride to Manhattan. I looked out the window the whole time but I could see what my parents said from the reflection. They talked about what a wonderful president Roosevelt was before he died and how brave Mrs. Rosen was because her husband had a stroke and had to be taken care of.

I couldn't see the backyards anymore but there were lamp-posts and electric signs, and sometimes I could see into some-one's house, if they had the light on and the shades up. I wondered if I'd ever meet any of the people I saw from the train or if my twin lived in any of those windows. My sister told me that everyone has a double somewhere.

I fell asleep and got woken up at Times Square. The lights were real glary. We changed to the A train. I knew all the stops: 59th Street, 125th, where lots of Negroes got off, 145th, where the rest of the Negroes got off, then 168th, where I got my tonsils out at Presbyterian Hospital, then 175th, 181st, 190th, and finally Dyckman.

Even though it was real late, it was still hot, so there were lots of people out on the sidewalk. When we got to Arden, people were sitting on the fire escapes because no one on our block has air conditioners. I saw my sister hanging out the window as we got close to our building and I waved. Melva saw us and waved back. She had the door open for us by the time we climbed up the four flights.

"Boy, did you get a sunburn!" she said when she saw me under the kitchen light.

My mother gave me some leftover pound cake with a glass of milk. Melva sat down at the kitchen table. Sidney was out with Judy, who's his girlfriend now and has lots of pimples, but he likes her anyway, Melva says. Melva thinks it's because she lets Sidney get fresh with her.

"Did you go to the Roxie?" I asked Melva.

"No."

"So what did you do today?"

"Nothing," she said, like she didn't want to talk about it.

"Did you see Howie Teitelbaum?" She was hoping he would kiss her during Spin the Bottle at Lucille's party. I could tell as soon as I asked that she'd seen him. "So what happened?"

"He was with Myron. He didn't even say hello. What did *you* do? I know, you went swimming and then you went to Nathan's, and then . . ."

"If you know so much, how come you asked me? Did you know I saw a drowned girl today?"

I told her the whole story, including the part about my father carrying me all the way up the beach to where my mother was.

"And then you got all burnt," she said.

"What do you mean?"

"Look at you, you're gonna peel like crazy."

"I'm not!"

"Yes you are. Anyway, peeling takes off the old skin. It's good for you."

"I hate it," I said, thinking of the long peels she took off my mother's back and thighs sometimes that were just revolting.

"Wait and see. You'll look exactly like a leper. Maybe your double is in a leper colony."

Melva had told me about the lepers who were so horrible looking they had to be sent away to an island.

"You're the leper," I said. "That's why Howie Teitelbaum won't ever kiss you."

She chased me all the way through the living room but I beat her to the bathroom and locked myself in. After a while she came pounding on the door. "What're you doing?" she said.

"What does it sound like?" I said. I had the faucets on.

"Are you crying?" she asked.

I was putting my hand under the hot water for as long as I could stand, which wasn't very long, then pulling it out and sticking it back in again, but I didn't say that.

"Sidney's home," she said. "He's got lipstick on his collar."

I turned off the faucets. "What color?" I said.

"Open the door and I'll tell you."

I opened the door.

"Borscht color, with the sour cream in it. I don't know why Judy lets him take advantage of her."

"I know," I said. "On account of the pimples." When Melva laughed at me, I slammed the door and locked it again. I turned on the cold water, which wasn't nearly as cold as the ocean, but I kept my hand there anyway and let the water run over it a long, long time.

✌ My Second Favorite

"FULL d-u-s-t," my mother says, when I tell her I'm going
to Glory's to play. She waves her hands in the air like dust
is blowing around. "No good first f-l-o-o-r," she tells me,
meaning that's how come it's so dusty down there. She also
blames Dot, Glory's mother. "Not enough clean," she says
about her. I should never of told her about Dot putting the
glasses of Jell-O on their windowsill, instead of in the frigidaire.

I go downstairs and ring their doorbell. There are names
from all of Dot's three husbands printed real nice under the
peephole. Kamahele is Glory's last name from her Hawaiian
father. Fallon is her stepbrother Roy Rogers' last name. His
real name is Nelson, but no one calls him that. And Rousse is
Dot's name from her last husband, who was French, but no
one calls her Mrs. Rousse.

Even Glory and Roy Rogers call her Dot. That's another

thing my mother thinks is o-d-d about them. She thinks the whole family is o-d-d, including Dot's sister, who changed her name to Nicki. She comes around sometimes to color Dot's hair. One thing for sure, they're not like us.

Glory answers the door and turns off the radio. She doesn't like "All My Children" anyhow. Besides, she's supposed to have all the clothes put away before Dot gets home. We take them down on the hangers from the rope strung across their living room. I don't think Dot has an iron because we hang them right away in the bedroom closet, which Dot painted all purple inside.

It's gorgeous. I mean, who DOES that, paint a closet purple? My mother almost died when I told her about it. I have to agree with my mother that it's o-d-d, but it's wonderful, too. The inside of all our closets are white, of course. My mother has a thing about white. When I grow up, I'll never have anything in white ever again, especially underwear.

"You wanna play Hollywood?" Glory asks, when we're done hanging.

I always say yes, even though most of the time she gets to be Dinah Shore and I have to be Peggy Lee.

"I'll go first," she says. "You sit there."

She points to the corner and throws a pillow down on the floor for me to sit on. My mother would die, seeing this, especially when Glory stands on top of the bed with her patent leather shoes on, pretending like it's the stage.

"Don't kno-ow why," Glory sings. She puts her arms up to the ceiling, like a real singer. Glory knows how to do that. And she sings really good. "There's no sun up in the sky. Stor-my wea-ther."

I hear the outside door open.

"Just Dot," Glory says. She throws up her arms again. "Don't kno-ow why. There's no sun up . . ."

". . . in the sky," Dot sings from the other room. Dot's voice is kind of like a man's, but not really. My sister calls it throaty, if that makes any sense.

"Close the door," Glory says.

I pretend like I don't know what she means. I don't want to close the door because I want Dot to come in. There's something about her. I can't explain it.

"Close the door."

"Is it okay?"

"Ruthie, CLOSE THE DOOR." She stamps her foot on the bed and loses her balance, falling down on it. "You're a dope," Glory screams at me. "You know that?"

"Pretty smart for a dope," Dot says. She's standing in the doorway. She's got bright red hair piled on top of her head with curls hanging down her forehead and some on her shoulders, like Rhonda Fleming in that movie I saw. Very glamorous. Sometimes she wears orange lipstick, but today she's wearing purple. Once she even put some purple lipstick on Glory and me when she made us up for fun.

"Not like," my mother said, when I told her. "T-o-o young."

"I brought some Chinese food," Dot says, "but if you're gonna be an old sourpuss, you can't have any." Dot knows Chinese food is Glory's favorite. She says to Glory, "Stop pouting, you'll get wrinkles before your time."

Dot is very concerned about wrinkles. Glory showed me all these jars of cream that Dot uses so she won't get wrinkles. Glory and I put some on our face once. It was disgusting. But Dot says that's what you have to do when you're grown up to keep your face beautiful. That and a lot of other things. She knows them all. She has a special cream for eyes and one for hands and one for all over your body that smells pretty and this jar of sandlike stuff that she mixes with water and puts on her face to dry. I saw her do it. It's called a beauty mask, which is pretty funny.

"You look like a gray monster," I told her, and then I felt terrible, like maybe I shouldn't of said it. But Dot just laughed.

She also has this stone you rub on your elbows and knees and even a cream to make your cuticles soft. There are almost more jars on Dot's dresser than in the Five and Ten.

Anyway, Dot dishes us out some Chinese food from six different cartons. The only ones I know are chow mein, egg rolls, and fried rice, which is the expensive kind. "Where's Roy Rogers?" Dot asks.

"How should I know?" Glory says. "Probably in the alley."

"Go out and see if you can find him," Dot says.

"Now?"

"Now, young lady, and I don't like your tone. He's your brother, hear me?"

Glory already told me that he's her half brother because they have different fathers, but she tells Dot she's sorry, in a very low voice. I know she's afraid Dot will get out the strap, which she uses sometimes on her and Roy Rogers, but only when she's real mad.

"You're coming?" Glory asks me.

I get up, but Dot says, "Ruthie's staying," so I sit down. After Glory's out the door, Dot smiles at me. "Everything okay, kid?" she asks.

I nod.

"Doing okay in school?"

I nod again.

"Cat got your tongue? Still waters sure run deep."

I half smile, not knowing what to say. I always get real shy around her. But I like it when she calls me Still Waters.

Then she grabs my face between her hands and examines it. Her face is so close to mine I can feel her breathing, very warm. Instead of staring into her eyes, I look at the fake beauty mark she made on the side of her mouth with the eyebrow pencil. She made me one once and I didn't wash it off for days and days, until my sister drove me crazy with her teasing. "All clear," Dot says, meaning there's no pimples. She always squeezes out my pimples with her long nails, which is creepy when I think about it, but when she's doing it I feel all happy inside. It's hard to explain.

"You're looking good, kid," she says, which makes my stomach flip-flop, because in my heart I know I'm ugly. Around Glory and her, I'm even uglier, since they're so beautiful.

Glory is very dark, like she has a tan all over, because she's Hawaiian. She has dark eyes, and her eyelids are long and narrow. Like almonds, my sister says. Glory's body is thin and graceful. She's the best one in acrobatics class. Miss Marguerite said so.

Right now Dot's hair is bright red. She changes color a lot. I like it blonde the best. Once it turned green when she was bleaching it. I didn't believe Glory when she told me, but then Dot said it was true. Dot has blue eyes and she's real tall. I guess hatcheck girls have to be. Dot's sister Nicki is also a hatcheck girl. She's blonde most of the time.

On the wall there's a picture someone took of them at the nightclub where they work. Dot and Nicki have on hats like men wear and halter tops with sequins. They're in very high heels and their legs are naked except for black stockings. Real thin ones. Sticking out from their waist are the boxes, like open dresser drawers, where the cigarettes and cigars go, with the money underneath. The tips go separate. Anyway, you have to be very beautiful to be a hatcheck girl. Dot and Nicki are, that's for sure.

Dot puts a plate down in front of me with Chinese food on it, some from each of the six different cartons. I almost die when she says one is pork. As soon as I start to eat, Dot says, "You haven't put your napkin in your lap yet." God, that makes me feel really dumb, but I had no idea that's what you're supposed to do. Once she told me not to slurp my soup. I didn't even know I was doing it or that it's wrong. I don't slurp my soup anymore but I notice everyone in my family does, especially my father. Of course, he can't hear himself, being deaf.

The doorbell rings then and Glory's back with Roy Rogers. He's only six and he has lots of curly brown hair all over his head and the back of his neck. He doesn't say much but he asks lots of questions. Glory is always telling him to get lost. Roy Rogers' father works for a big company in California, which is why Roy Rogers never gets to see him. Glory sees her father sometimes when he's wrestling at Madison Square Garden. We always watch the wrestling on her TV Saturday nights, but her father isn't famous enough to be on yet.

I eat every bit of the Chinese food—the pork and everything—even though I had lunch at twelve and it's only three o'clock. I don't mention the lunch. "No thank you," I say when Dot asks if I want seconds. We don't have seconds at home. Roy Rogers has seconds.

"You're gonna get as big as Tiger Joe," Glory says, holding out her arms to show us how big her father is. Tiger Joe is his stage name. His real first name is something Hawaiian I can't pronounce. Wrestlers have to be big. The bigger the better, Glory explained.

"Is my father big?" Roy Rogers asks Dot.

"Well, Mr. Fallon's not fat like Tiger Joe but he's sure tall. Six two." Dot stands up to show us how tall that is. She keeps on talking about Roy Rogers' father. "He's a real handsome guy. I can remember the first time I met him. The way Mr. Fallon tipped his hat to me, I was a goner."

"What's a goner?" Roy Rogers asks.

"I was gone, done for, I fell for him. That was some mistake," she says, laughing. "Cheap bastard. If he paid up his alimony we could move and buy a house."

I want to ask what "bastard" means, but I don't dare. I only know it's a bad word. Dot uses lots of bad words. She always laughs when she does. I think she thinks I understand more than I do because I laugh when she laughs. I can't help it.

When we're done eating, Glory and I put the dishes in the sink on top of the other dirty dishes. When they get stacked real high or when there are no more clean ones, Dot washes them, but not before. That's another thing: my mother washes dirty dishes right away and dries them. "R-o-a-c-h crawl," she says, meaning that if you don't wash and dry, it makes the roaches come. Dot doesn't even dry the dishes when she washes, but leaves them on the drainboard. "I have better things to do," she said when I asked her how come once. It's true she's always busy, either painting closets or walls or her face. She's always fixing things up, including me.

"You know what?" she asks us, when the dishes are in the sink. Dot goes over and gets a pair of long scissors. "I'm going to cut Ruthie's hair," she announces. My stomach flips over. I think first of having to explain it to my mother and then I worry that I'm going to look like a freak. I always look like a freak after I get my hair cut in the beauty school my mother takes me to. I want Dot to cut my hair but I also don't. At least I'm used to how I look now. Anyway, I'm stuck. I can't move. Then I see Glory's eyes get big all of a sudden, like she's jealous, but I don't know why. Her shiny black hair is short and real straight the way Dot cut it, with very straight bangs across her forehead. It's too gorgeous.

Glory pouts when Dot tells her to get the towel, but she does, and puts it around me, using a bobby pin to hold it together in front. Roy Rogers sits down on the floor, prac- tically at my feet, to watch, which I think is real strange for a little boy, but Roy Rogers is strange anyhow. He puts Dot's cream on his face and takes his dog Pluto to bed with him. Pluto's not a real dog, of course, but a stuffed animal. Once he cried because Dot wouldn't let Pluto take a bath with him and then she let him and Pluto got all wet and when he dried he was all wrinkled up forever, but he still sleeps with Roy Rogers. They sleep in the same bed as Glory, the one we use for our stage, because there's only one bedroom. Dot sleeps on the couch in the living room. That's where the kitchen table is because they don't have a separate kitchen like us. Dot made a curtain to put over it, but most of the time it's open.

Anyway, I'm sitting on one of the kitchen chairs, so scared I want to run out of the house, but if I do, I know I can't ever come back.

"You have beautiful hair," Dot tells me. "Really," she says, like she's trying to tell me she means it. "Don't you know you do?"

I shake my head. My hair is like nothing. It's not red and it's not blonde. I'd give anything for it to be blonde. I use the barrettes to hold the sides back and it just hangs there on my back and shoulders.

"I wish I could give you a perm," Dot says. "When I have time, I will."

I can't explain it but that makes me feel funny inside. Which is how I feel when she's squeezing my pimples, or when she makes me look in the mirror and then tells me to pull my blouse down in my skirt. My mother doesn't even like it when I look in the mirror. "Make funny face," she says, meaning that you get ugly if you look at yourself in the mirror too much. Dot has a head-to-toe mirror on the inside of one of the closet doors, and almost every time I go there we end up looking at ourselves in it for some reason. Sometimes it's because we're trying on different clothes or hats. Other times we're playing Ballerina.

Dot takes the barrettes out of my hair and makes me a new part. The comb she's using is dirty but I don't say anything. My mother would die. "Can get l-i-c-e," she told me, "from dirty comb." I pray to God I don't get lice. I know Glory had it once and Dot used the kerosene on her. It had to be the worst smelling thing in the whole world. Glory cried, but Dot just laughed. "That's the price of living, kid," she said. Whatever that means.

It takes Dot forever to cut my hair. Glory gets bored in the middle and reads a Super Woman comic. Roy Rogers never stops staring the whole time. With his curls and blue eyes he looks like he belongs on a Christmas card. Even his mouth is all scrunched up like he's a singing angel. That's what Dot made him at Halloween, an angel costume, with wings and everything, and a halo that was on a wire that stuck up above his head. She made Glory a cat costume with a long tail that dragged on the ground and whiskers on the face. Glory and Roy Rogers went out trick-or-treating, but I couldn't go with them. "T-o-o d-a-n-g-e-r-o-u-s," my mother said. "Maybe p-o-i-s-o-n candy. Many s-t-r-a-n-g-e-r-s."

Anyway, Dot made me a bag with some of the candy they got but I couldn't take it home because you know why. Dot keeps it in a special place in a kitchen drawer for me and I can eat some whenever I'm here.

"Relax," Dot says, making me bend my head so she can shave the hairs on my neck. She says, "It looks great. You're gonna look like a million bucks, kid."

I know she's saying that just to make me feel better. As far as I'm concerned, I'm hopeless. At least in looks. I know I'm real smart and good in school but I'm ugly, ugly, ugly.

When she's done, Dot tells me to go look in the bathroom mirror. You should see how bright it is in there. Dot put in a string of fifteen light bulbs all around the mirror so she can see better to do her makeup. I go in the bathroom but I don't get up on the stool to look at myself. I wait a second and then I come out and say, "Thank you, it's very nice."

"Nice?" Dot laughs. "Nice? You look pretty snazzy, kid. Such gorgeous skin. I'd kill for those eyelashes."

Maybe she can read my mind because she explains what she means without my asking. "No one has eyelashes like that. A yard long," she says. "Your new 'do' frames your eyes. When you're my age you're gonna break a lot of hearts."

I look up to see Glory looking at me like poison. I want to tell her that Dot is just saying those things to make me feel good, but of course I can't.

"Let's go outside," Glory says.

"I can't," I say. "I gotta go upstairs for supper."

"Supper?" Roy Rogers says. "You just ate."

"I'm gonna be a big fat lady wrestler in Madison Square Garden," I say.

"Fat lady," Roy Rogers says, and we all start giggling.

"Fat lady," Glory says, but she can hardly say it, she's laughing so hard.

Even Dot is laughing. Soon we are all rolling on the floor laughing and tumbling around on each other. When we stop we are in one big pile of bodies on the floor, with Dot at the bottom, Roy Rogers and me on top of her, and Glory on us. My mother would die if she saw.

Dot fixes my hair a little before I go. "I hope your mother likes it," she says, handing me my barrettes.

On the stairs going up I feel my hair carefully to get an idea of what she did. The sides are too short to put back with the barrettes, so I put them in my pocket. I pray to God that I don't look like a freak.

My father opens the door when I ring the bell, which is good, because he doesn't notice my hair. While he's turning out the light that goes on when the bell rings, I dash to the bathroom and close the door. Then I climb up on the sink so I can see myself in the mirror. It's different than I thought. My ears are sticking out a little because the sides are so short. There's a side bang in front, like Dot said. I look at my eye-lashes and wonder if they really are long. Then I wash my hands and go to the kitchen.

"Look at you," my sister says. "What happened?"

"What does it look like?" I say, starting to feel sick.

"Cut?" my mother asks. "D-o-t cut hair?"

I nod.

"Why?"

"Don't know," I say. "Feel like."

Everyone at the table is looking at me now and my toes are crossed real tight. My mother tells me to turn my head around so she can see the back, which I do.

She nods. "Have time," she says about Dot, "why not clean house?"

"You look like Dinah Shore," my sister says.

Inside I'm dying when she says that. "Dinah Shore?"

"You know, the singer?"

I know but I pretend like it's no big deal. I take the napkin from the table and open it up, putting it in my lap.

"What are you doing that for?" Melva asks.

"Just because," I say.

"F-a-n-c-y," my mother says to my sister. Even though she can't hear, my mother's figured out what we're talking about. She's real smart that way. "D-o-t teach you polite?" she asks me, meaning about the napkin.

I nod. I notice Melva has her elbows on the table and my father is reaching right across me to get the salt to put in his soup. My brother is mashing the crackers in his soup with a fork.

"You're too serious to be the Dinah Shore type," my sister says, "but it's a cute haircut. C-u-t-e," she spells out to my mother. My mother doesn't say anything.

"Anyway, Dinah Shore isn't even my favorite," I say to my sister, with my toes crossed. I don't tell her she's my second favorite, after Jane Powell. In my heart I'm wondering how Dot knew. Slowly I put my spoon in the bowl and then I put it up to my lips and blow on it, like Melva is doing. Then I slurp it off the spoon. I slurp every mouthful real loud after that and I'm bursting because no one at the table even knows I'm doing it on purpose.

✿ Useful Gifts

MY mother believes in useful gifts, but when I saw the marionette hanging in Schiffman's Toys on Dyckman Street, I knew what I wanted for Chanukah. She was dangling in the middle of the window, wearing a pink net tutu over a pink satin slip. Her strings were fixed so that she was doing an arabesque, her arms reaching out in front and one leg stuck out in the air behind her, a little crooked. Her hair looked soft, like orangey red cotton, pulled back into a bun that dancers wear. Right off I named her Mitzi, like the girl in the movie I saw with Gene Kelly.

Mrs. Schiffman surprised me coming out of her store all of a sudden. Her arms were folded, but not quite, because they were too fat. "What are you looking at?" she said.

That's how come I dropped the quarter for the rye bread I was supposed to get.

"No s-e-e-d-s, sliced," my mother told me when I left the house.

She also told me to be careful about the money. How did she know something would happen? The quarter rolled under a car.

Mrs. Schiffman went in her store and came back with a broom so I could push the quarter to where I could get it. I was sorry for thinking she was fat, but all I said was "Thanks a lot."

When I looked one last time at Mitzi, Mrs. Schiffman said, "Tell your mother it's thirteen ninety-five."

I didn't bother, because I knew it was hopeless. But I thought about Mitzi and even prayed to God, just in case. I told Him I'd never ask for anything ever again if I got what I wanted.

For Chanukah I got three cotton dresses for summer from the wholesale factory my father took me to. They were all alike but in different pastel colors. Then my mother took me to Miles, which has the machine that sees inside your shoes and makes your feet look green. I wanted the black patents with the T-straps, but my mother said if I was going to wear high heels when I grew up I had to get the brown oxfords. She got a pair of oxfords, too, in black, with a fat heel, not very high.

The day after, my friend Iris Opals, who lived across the court before they moved to downtown, invited me to celebrate Christmas morning with her family, so my mother and I had more shopping to do. We went to get Iris's present at the Five and Ten.

Right away I figured out what Iris needed: a set of jacks. We always played with mine, since she didn't have any. But my mother headed straight for children's clothes. "N-e-e-d socks," she said. "U-s-e-f-u-l wear out," she told me, meaning that socks wear out, so more socks would be useful to get.

My mother picked up a package of three pairs of socks from the counter in my size. Iris is a year ahead of me, but she's not as tall. The socks were white because white is my mother's favorite color. I swore that when I grew up I'd never have anything in white ever again, except my wedding dress, of course.

My mother was looking over the socks in case something was wrong when I tapped her on the arm. "Don't want," I signed. "Socks awful."

"One dollar, enough," she said.

"Not go," I told her, meaning that if we got the socks I wouldn't go to the Opals' for Christmas. For some reason she didn't look upset. She just put the package down and asked me, "Idea?"

I got her over to the toy counter and showed her the jacks. When she looked at the price on the back of the cardboard, I was sure she'd buy them. She took out some money, but all of a sudden she remembered the birthday present she had bought for my sister's classmate, Ellen Pruzan. Ellen lived in a fancy building across from Fort Tryon with air conditioners and a rug in the lobby. My sister said she'd rather die than take handkerchiefs to Ellen's party, so she got a stomachache and stayed home. The handkerchiefs were sitting in a kitchen drawer.

"Left waste," my mother said, meaning the handkerchiefs should go to Iris. That's when I ran out of the store.

My mother came out after me, calling my name, except she can't say "Ruthie," so she said, "Ru-ta, Ru-ta," in that funny voice that deaf-mutes have. People always looked when she did that.

Next thing I knew, there was a man grabbing her arm. "Lady, you didn't pay for that," he yelled, about the package of jacks in her hand.

"She's deaf," I told him.

He yelled even louder. Now everyone was staring.

My mother tried to give him the dollar, but he wouldn't take it. "You'll have to come with me," he said, and we went back into the Five and Ten. He held onto my mother's arm till we got to the back room. All the time we waited there it smelled like pencils.

"S-t-e-a-m hot," my mother said, about the radiator. She made me take off my coat and she took off hers.

Then a man with a thin mustache came in and said he was the manager and his name was Mr. Gary. Instead of sitting in a chair, he sat on the wood desk so that the corner stuck out between his legs. "She your mother?" he asked me.

"Yeah," I said. Then my mother nodded at him after I interpreted what he said.

"Ask her if she knows it's wrong to shoplift," Mr. Gary said.

"Know wrong take?" I asked her.

"Funny, many p-e-n," my mother said, about the pens sticking out over both his ears.

Mr. Gary was staring real hard, waiting for me to tell him.

"Can trouble," I said to my mother.

"Fault follow you." She looked at Mr. Gary and then pointed to me, waving her arms like I was running toward Dyckman. She made a sign as though she was going to spank me, but I knew she didn't mean it.

Mr. Gary got up and came over, so that he was standing between my mother and me. "She saying you did it?" he asked me. "Tell me the truth."

"It was an accident!" I told him. Except I yelled it.

"Kid's got moxie," the other man said. He meant some nerve. He laughed like I was a liar or something. I wanted to die.

When I looked at Mr. Gary again, he was running his finger over his mustache. He said they'd let my mother go this time if she paid for the jacks but next time they'd call the police.

"S-i-l-l-y," my mother said. She kept shaking her head.

On Christmas morning, when I woke up, I knew it had snowed during the night because I heard the sound of the shovel on the sidewalk. I didn't want to take the jacks to Iris's, but I was stuck. I wanted to forget the man's face who laughed, but it kept popping up in my mind. I figured that every time we played jacks from then on I would remember how I almost got my mother put in jail.

After breakfast I put on the new oxfords and the dress I got with my father at the wholesale factory the summer before for my birthday. The plaid was brown like the oxfords and there was a ribbon around the waist.

Since Iris lived just across the court, I didn't have to use my galoshes. The super already made a path. Her building was exactly the same as mine, but everything was backwards, like in the mirror. I counted the seventy-two steps up to the fifth floor and rang the bell. There was a sign on the door that said "Merry Christmas from THE OPALS."

"Merry Christmas!" Mrs. Opals said, half giggling when she opened the door. She smelled funny, not like White Shoulders, which my mother bought off Mr. Opals sometimes. He sold perfume and scarves on the side, my mother said, because he had to pay for all the lessons Iris and Ivy were always taking.

"What's that?" I asked Mrs. Opals, about the thick yellow stuff in the cup she was holding.

"Schnapps," she said. Then Mr. Opals came in with a bottle of liquor in his hand and poured some into the yellow stuff. It smelled like cough medicine. "Oh, you-u-u," she said.

As I was walking into their living room, I heard Mr. Opals behind me say, "Now I've got you!" I turned and saw him kissing Mrs. Opals right on the lips. My parents only did it on the cheek, but we never had mistletoe. It was like in the movies: their arms were around each other and their eyes were closed.

"You can put my present here," Iris said, pointing to a place under the tree where there was a lot of torn-up fancy paper and ribbons. The package of jacks was in paper my mother saved from the year before, and the green string came off a cake box, so it looked pretty bad.

The tree was very beautiful anyhow and took up the whole corner of the room, right up to the ceiling where there was an angel in foil. Red and green and gold balls dangled from the branches, along with candy canes and something called angel's hair, said Ivy, who is Iris's sister. Ivy might have been fibbing. She's only in the third grade in the parochial school where Iris goes.

Then Ione, who wasn't even two years old yet, came running in and stood next to Ivy, who was standing next to Iris.

They were like the three bears in my baby book: small, medium, and large. They all had on blue velvet dresses with organdy collars, light blue knee socks and patent leather shoes with straps. I felt so ugly I could of died.

Iris and Ivy showed me all their presents. The best things were the red hatboxes for carrying stuff like leotards and makeup to their acting and modeling lessons. Across the top, their full names were written out in gold: Iris Dawne Opals and Ivy Deanne Opals. The "I" was for Mrs. Opals' first name, Irene, and the "D" was for Mr. Opals, whose name was Donald. I don't have a middle name, which is bad enough, but then my parents had to name me Ruth. I have two cousins and two classmates named Ruth besides Ruth Silberman in 42 Arden, which is between Iris's building and mine.

Iris showed me how to put my arm through the strap on the hatbox and walk back and forth like a model.

"Chin up," Mrs. Opals told me, before she asked what I'd gotten for the holidays.

I pretended like I didn't hear and walked over to see the figurines sitting on top of the radiator cover.

"Isn't the crèche gorgeous! Couldn't you simply die!" Ivy said.

Everyone was quiet after I asked what a crèche was. Then Ivy explained it had to do with religion. She was taking catechism, along with acting, dancing, and ice skating.

"Very nice," I said about the figurines, but they looked faded, like the plastic flowers we had in our living room, on account of my mother always washing them.

"You should have been with us at midnight mass," Iris said. "It was like a stage show at the Music Hall." Mr. Opals looked at her kind of funny but he didn't say anything. She showed me the different parts people played, even the boys in the chorus coming down the aisle and how the priest waved his arms around.

Mrs. Opals was smiling like she was in heaven. "You're a natural mimic," she said to Iris. "A son couldn't be nearly so talented," she said to Mr. Opals. Then he said, "That's my girl!"

Ivy must of gotten jealous because she put her toe shoes on all of a sudden to show me how she could stand on *pointe* on one leg. Her arabesque was like Mitzi's, because her leg wasn't straight in back either, and then her blonde hair fell out of her French twist, flopping down her shoulders like a horse's mane. Mr. Opals caught the tree as it started to fall over when Ivy lost her balance.

"Useless clumsy fool!" Mrs. Opals yelled at her, but Ivy acted like she didn't mind. Her mother was always yelling at her because she wasn't as graceful as Iris.

I went into the kitchen with Ivy so she could show me her pirouettes on the linoleum. When Ione crawled in behind her, Ivy's foot whopped her in the arm. Ione screamed. Mrs. Opals couldn't stop Ione from crying, which made Mr. Opals mad.

"Well, you're the one who didn't want Mrs. Zimmer to baby-sit," Mrs. Opals said to him about my mother. Mr. Opals gave her a look like he wanted to kill her.

Iris came in then. "I'm dying to open our presents," she said. "You?"

"Yeah," I said, crossing my toes.

We went back to the living room. "You first," I told her.

Iris ripped off the paper. "Jacks!" she screamed. "How divine!" She whispered in my ear that she'd said ten rosaries to get more games for Christmas.

"No whispering," Mrs. Opals said. "And, please God, you're not going to fritter away your time when you have more important things to do." She turned to me and smiled real big, so I could see a lot of the teeth she got capped because she used to model. "Tell your mother, dear, she's thoughtful," she said. "I'm afraid, though, Iris has to make the best use of her God-given talents."

Before I could help it, I told them the jacks were my idea. She and Mr. Opals looked at each other and he shrugged. "As ye sow," he said, which I knew was from the Bible, but I didn't know what he meant.

"Now you," Iris said.

I knew it was a book. I opened the paper without tearing it hardly. It was *Pollyanna*, which I already read from the library, but I said, "Thank you very much."

Suddenly Mrs. Opals started singing like a soprano. I thought Mr. Opals said something about a marionette but Mrs. Opals explained that *Naughty Marietta* was a play she was in once. The next thing I knew, Mr. Opals was blowing into a harmonica and we listened to Iris and Ivy sing Christmas carols. Then we all sang "Away in a Manger." I didn't sing the words about Jesus but just mouthed them, which Mr. Opals must of noticed because afterwards he said, "Jesus gave us the gift of His life and we must never forget that."

"Enjoy?" my mother asked me when I got home. She was real surprised by the present Mrs. Opals gave me to bring her. There were three big pictures in black and white of Iris, Ivy, and Ione in different modeling poses. Each one was autographed.

On the back of Iris's picture she'd written: "To Mrs. Zimmer With Love, Iris Dawne Opals."

Ivy wrote: "To Mrs. Zimmer, U R 2 Nice 2 B 4 Got 10, Love Your Friend, Ivy Deanne Opals."

Mrs. Opals wrote on the back of Ione's picture: "From the Opals Family with fond rememberance to dear Mrs. Zimmer and her lovely daughter Ruthi." She left off the "e" from my name and I looked up "rememberance" in the dictionary and found she spelled that wrong, too.

When I got back to the kitchen from looking up the word, my mother was still sitting there staring at the pictures she laid out on the table. "Not natural beautiful," she said. "Show-off, like actress." My mother was always saying that when Iris and Ivy were going to charm school. I still thought they were gorgeous, even without being made up. I wanted to look like them, take their lessons and be famous someday, which my mother said they were going to be.

Finally my mother put away the pictures in a dresser drawer. "What present?" she asked, about what to give Mrs. Opals back.

My mother made three pot holders for Mrs. Opals, which she took over when we went there on the Sunday before Christmas vacation ended. I was supposed to go skating with all the Opals, excepting Ione, who my mother was baby-sitting. But right off Mrs. Opals acted very strange. First she kept thanking my mother for the pot holders, telling her how beautiful they were, when she knew they were just made with loops on a loom. The blue and yellow didn't even match their kitchen. Then Mrs. Opals took a long time to tell me that Iris and Ivy were taking figure skating at Rockefeller Center, instead of Wollman Memorial, where I thought we were going.

It dawned on me that Mrs. Opals didn't want me with them because of what I was wearing. Ivy had on a pink outfit with a very short skirt, standing out like a ballerina's. Iris's was green and had sparkles and she wore matching gloves up to her elbows but without hands. I had on my brown corduroy pants and navy pea jacket. I didn't cry until after they left.

Not long after that my mother noticed Ione had a bad case of diarrhea. As soon as she changed the diaper, she had it again. "Must something eat," my mother said, meaning it must have been due to something Ione ate. She looked in the frigidaire, opening and smelling the milk bottle. "Sour," she told me. She couldn't find anything in the medicine cabinet to give her. Chernak's Drugs on our corner was closed, so she sent me to see if the big drugstore on Dyckman was open. That's when I saw the "Going Out of Business" sign at Schiffman's Toys, but Mitzi was still in the window.

When I got home I told my mother the drugstore was closed, so she said we were going to take Ione to the Jewish Memorial emergency room. It was so crowded we were there all afternoon. My mother brought along the milk bottle to show the doctor, which I thought was silly, but he smiled at her and tapped the side of his head, like he was telling her she was smart.

Mr. Opals must of found the note I left him on their kitchen table because he came running into the emergency room, yelling that he had to talk to a doctor in private. He got in with a doctor and they closed the door, but I heard them anyhow. Mr. Opals said, "My wife should never of left her in the hands of a deaf-and-dumb lady." Then the doctor said that if it hadn't been for my mother Ione would be critical. I didn't know exactly what that meant, but figured it meant very sick, maybe dead.

When Mr. Opals came out, he was quiet and he put his arm around my mother's shoulders. By that time Mrs. Opals was there, with her fur muff, which she kept waving around on one arm, when she talked. She kept saying to Mr. Opals, "Ask him, go ahead, ask him." Mr. Opals gave her one of his looks. "Well, I'll ask him myself then," she said. She asked the doctor if Ione could do some modeling the next day.

I didn't bother to tell my mother because I knew what she'd say. "First important baby" is what she always said when we passed by the baby carriages outside the bars on Nagle Avenue. My mother carried Ione in her blanket with the initials IDO on it all the way back to our stoop, then Mrs. Opals took her. She invited my mother and me for a ham dinner, but my mother mouthed, "No thank you."

Mr. Opals took money out to pay my mother, giving her five dollars extra, besides the two he owed her for four hours. My mother didn't want to take it, but he made her. "U-s-e-f-u-l, b-r-a-c-e-s," she said to me, meaning she was saving for the braces the dentist said I'd need in junior high. I went up with the Opals to get my skates and then went home for supper.

After we ate, my mother told me to telephone Mrs. Opals to see how Ione was.

"I was just about to call you. Ask your mother if she can baby-sit Ivy tomorrow after school. Iris has elocution and I have to take Ione to a modeling job. Cribs," Mrs. Opals said. "A national company."

"C-r-a-z-y," my mother said, about Mrs. Opals, but she said okay. Then Mrs. Opals asked if I wanted to talk to Iris. I didn't, but Iris got on the line anyhow to tell me about Linda Lindemann's party.

"You'll get invited," she said. Then there was a long quiet and she said, "Ruthie, can I ask you a favor? I want to give Linda the jacks."

I felt nauseous listening to Iris explain about auditioning for a play called "McDonald's Farm." She was trying out for the milkmaid part and for the goose, in case she didn't get the milkmaid. It was a smaller part. Her mother said she'd have to practice both every day. "Then, when I get a part," Iris said, "performing will take all my time, so I can't play jacks anyway."

"Okay," I told her.

"You're not angry?"

"Why should I be angry?" I said.

After I got off the phone my mother thought I looked sad on account of not going ice skating, but I told her I was thinking of what to get Linda Lindemann. Especially because Alan Goldfarb, who I had a crush on, would be at the party, but I didn't tell my mother that. Linda had practically everything, even a room of her own and a clown marionette. "Have many t-o-y-s," I told my mother.

For a few minutes my mother and I sat at the kitchen table without saying anything. Then she waved at me to get my attention. "Know," she said, looking real happy. "N-e-e-d handkerchief." She went over and pulled them out of the drawer. Of course, they were white.

Linda needs handkerchiefs like she needs more jacks, I thought. She already had two sets of jacks, one silver and one in mixed colors, red and green. I was sure Iris didn't know that, which made me feel a whole lot better.

The next week Mr. Opals came up to our apartment for the first time. He gave my mother two packages wrapped in paper that had tiny purple flowers. He kissed her, but it was on the cheek. "Thank you," he mouthed, and then she showed him how to blow a kiss with his hand to say "thank you" in sign language.

He told me Iris was going to be a milkmaid in the play and Ivy was going to be the goose because the other girl got sick. Then he asked me if there was something special I wanted. Even if Schiffman's wasn't already gone, which it was, Mitzi would of cost too much. So I said a hatbox.

He started to ask me what I was going to do with a hatbox, but he changed his mind. "It'll be a pleasure," he said. Before he left, I reminded him about the "e" on "Ruthie."

When he was gone, my mother opened the packages real carefully. She wanted to save the fancy wrapping. The little package had a necklace with a gold chain and the initial "H" for my mother's name, Hannah.

"How know?" she said, about Mr. Opals.

The other package had a big bottle of White Shoulders, which she opened and kept smelling. "Like flower," she said, putting a dot of it behind each ear and on her neck.

She stuck the bottle under my nose.

"S-t-i-n-k," I told her.

She smiled so that her dimples showed. "Not c-h-e-a-p, real perfume," she said.

"Waste money," I said.

She shook her head. "N-o, n-o. U-s-e-f-u-l," she said. "Keep long time."

Fort Arden

THE thing about Glory and Roy Rogers was that they weren't too chicken to play on the roof.

I got the idea when we were at the bottom of the stoop playing Johnny-May-We-Cross-Your-River. I was Johnny and the kids were trying to cross over. "Johnny, may we cross your river?" they yelled out.

Usually I gave them colors. They could cross if they were wearing the color I said, but when I saw a balloon disappear over the top of my building, I said, "Yes you may, if you're willing to come up to the roof."

Right away my friend Glory crossed, and so did her step-brother, Roy Rogers. The rest of the kids, though, just stood there in front of the little brick wall that separated the stoop from the garden.

"No fair," said Tommy, the eldest of the Shanahan kids.

"What'sa matter?" Glory called out.

"Yeah, what'sa matter?" Roy Rogers said. He was only seven but he always did everything Glory did.

"Too dangerous," said Tommy.

Glory snorted. Roy Rogers tried to snort, but it sounded like he was trying to keep his nose from dripping.

Then Pat Shanahan yelled, "We can't, because our ma wouldn't like it."

"So, don't tell her," Glory said, rolling her dark eyes.

"You don' know nothin'," Tommy said. "We'll have to tell the priest, so nothin' doin'."

"That's rich!" I said, pretending to belly-laugh.

Robin Reinstein was just standing there, next to the Shanahan kids, twirling her brown hair around her finger. I gave her a look.

"Can't. My mother will see I'm gone," she said, letting go of her hair to point to her windows up on the third floor.

I looked up. Mrs. Reinstein was standing at the stove next to the open window in a red and white checked housedress. She waved at us.

Then I remembered what we'd done on Memorial Day. "That didn't stop you from coming to the alley with us to do you know what," I told Robin.

I watched her turn a funny strawberry color, starting with her ears, then spreading over her cheeks like hives.

"She's blushing!" Tommy Shanahan said.

"Am not!"

"Am too!"

"You're all dumb," Robin said, "like Ruthie's mother."

"My mother's not dumb, she's a deaf-mute. So there! You're so dumb you don't even know the difference."

"Awww, she's too chicken to play with anyhow!" said Glory, tossing her head, which made her dark bangs crooked. She linked arms with Roy Rogers. They came over and got me. I linked arms with Glory on her other side. We marched up to the first landing of the stoop, then turned around.

"Big chicken!" Roy Rogers yelled.

We marched up to the second landing, stomping our feet hard on each step.

"Biggest chicken!" Glory yelled.

On the third landing I yelled, "Great biggest chicken in the whole wide world!"

When we got up to the roof the balloon wasn't there. We looked over the edge of the wall. Down on the sidewalk the Shanahan kids were playing Green Light with Iris and Ivy Opals.

"What're we gonna do?" asked Roy Rogers.

"Stop scratching!" said Glory, knocking one of his hands away from his curly head.

"I don't know. What?" I said.

"Let's play Dare You," said Glory. "I'll go first."

"Uh uh, Choosey," I said, meaning we should play Choosey to see who went first.

"Odds!" Glory shouted, before I could pick. She knew odds was my favorite.

Glory and I put our fists behind our backs. Roy Rogers did the calling out. "Once, twice, three, SHOOT!" he said.

Glory stuck out two fingers. I stuck out one. So she got to go first.

It didn't take her long to think of something. She went right to the washlines where clothes were hanging to dry. "You have to make a switch," she said, "from two different lines."

"Ha, ha," I said, switching a black sock on one line with a black sock on another. "No one's gonna know," I said. Then I looked around for something to dare back. I pointed to a pair of blue polka-dot boxer shorts. "That for the bloomers," I said.

Roy Rogers and I almost died when Glory jumped up and pulled the pink bloomers off the line. When she dropped them, we collapsed in hysterics. Glory picked them up and dropped them again, she was laughing so hard. Then she couldn't get them back up on the other line because she was too short, so I held the line down while she stuck the clothespins on the bloomers.

After we did the boxer shorts, she and Roy Rogers started yelling and rolling around on the tar. We didn't hear Mrs. Krakowski open the door, which usually creaked a lot, but we heard her booming voice. "Gott!" she said, seeing the three of us in a big heap. She put a big basket under the washlines. We watched her take off the sheets and fold them, slapping and poking each other when she took down the boxer shorts.

"Ants in her pants!" Glory said. "See them crawling?"

"Ants in her pants!" Roy Rogers said.

I started giggling, pretending I saw the little blue dots moving around.

We could hear Mrs. Krakowski muttering to herself, but we couldn't hear what she was saying. She looked over at us when she took down the bloomers. I could of died. "Such a hot day, no?" she said.

Glory kicked me. I kicked her back. "Real hot," I said.

After that, Mrs. Krakowski talked only to herself. When she left we were hurting so much we couldn't laugh anymore.

"What now?" I asked.

"It's my dare," said Glory, doing a backbend all of a sudden. With her head upside down, she said, "All the wash is gone, so I have to think." She stood back up, then went leaping across the roof, doing jetés, stopping like a statue with her arms out in front of her when she got to the other end. "C'mere," she yelled.

When I got there, she was pointing with her chin to the wall that separated our roof from 26 Arden, which didn't come up as high. Smiling with her lips together, Glory said, "I dare you to jump."

"That's rich," I said, "and if I kill myself . . ."

"Aw-w-w," Glory said.

"Aw-w-w," Roy Rogers said.

I figured that even if I could climb up the wall I'd get all bloody jumping down the other side. I could see my father saying, "I'll break your neck." Then I looked into Glory's dark eyes and got an idea. "Here goes," I said.

I went over and knelt on the stone top of the little wall at the edge of the roof that came halfway up the dividing wall. I kept my head turned away from Arden Street, which was six stories down.

"What're you doing?" Glory asked.

"I can't look, I can't look," said Roy Rogers, putting his hands over his eyes.

"It's my stepladder," I said, standing on the ledge and reaching up to the top of the dividing wall. I kept my back turned to the street. Holding on with all my might, I pulled myself up. Then I sat up there, my feet dangling near where Glory's head was. Roy Rogers was peeking at me through his fingers. When my heart stopped pounding like a drum, I turned so that my feet hung down the other side. But the little wall at the edge of 26 Arden didn't come up as far as I thought.

Roy Rogers was yelling behind me. "She's gonna do it."

"Shut up, stupid," Glory said.

If only someone would come up to the roof now, I thought, even Mrs. Krakowski. I was sorry we'd made fun of her.

"Change your mind?" Glory said.

I held on as I lowered myself down, but I had to let go for the last few inches. As soon as I felt my feet touch the ledge I pushed off toward the roof and went tumbling. I scraped my hands and one knee.

I heard Roy Rogers clapping and yelling. "She did it, she did it!" When I looked up, he and Glory, who were both terrific at climbing, had gotten up on top of the dividing wall. They were in the middle, though—not at the edge.

Glory's almond eyes were like little slits. "So, go ahead," she said to him.

He bent forward, like he was getting ready to jump, but all he did was keep rocking back and forth.

"What're you waiting for?" she asked.

"Want me to catch you?" I said. I saw Glory was about to say something. "I dare you to jump into my arms," I said to Roy Rogers, "but you have to sit down first."

He plopped down and I got under where his feet were. Then he leaned forward. "T-i-i-m-m-b-e-r-r-r," he shouted, coming at me like a bomber pilot. He knocked me down, with him on top of me, which he thought was real funny. I scraped my other knee.

"Now you," I said to Glory, "but I'm not catching you."

"No fair, no repeats," she said, making up a new rule.

"Chi-i-i—" I bluffed.

Her eyes got like slits again. She started walking on top of the wall toward the edge of the roof. "If *you* can do it . . ." she said. All of a sudden I knew her feet wouldn't even get close to the ledge on my side, because she was a lot shorter than me.

I ran over to the edge and looked down at the sidewalk. "The Shanahan kids!" I yelled. Just then, Tommy looked up, even though he couldn't of heard me.

"Get him!" I said to Roy Rogers.

"Bang! You're dead," Roy Rogers called out, firing on him.

And that's how Fort Arden was created.

"Keep a lookout for more enemies," I ordered Glory, and then Roy Rogers and I ran down five flights in 26 Arden and six flights back up to the roof of 38 Arden. When we got there, Glory said sarcastically, "What took you so long?"

Right before the Fourth of July I stuck a flag that Glory had made with all forty-eight stars into a hole at the edge of the roof. "Now everyone on Arden Street will know we've taken the fort," I said.

I had learned about the flag when Mrs. Landau took our class to the other two forts in Inwood: Fort Tryon and Fort Washington. She told us about uniforms also, but it was too hot, so we only tied bandannas around ourselves.

That day Glory was on the cannon and I was right next to her, looking out for enemies down below. Roy Rogers was marching back and forth at the other end, carrying his broomstick over his shoulder like a rifle.

"Look!" I said to Glory, as he tried to twirl it. He hit himself in the side of the head and dropped the rifle.

"He's hopeless," Glory said. "Remember when we taught him to say, 'Who goes there?'"

"Yeah," I said, even though I was the one who taught him. He kept giggling until Glory smacked him in the head and said, "Nelson, this is real serious. It's not like playing cowboy, Nelson."

"Don't call me Nelson," Roy Rogers said and then he was okay.

"I hope he doesn't come over," Glory said. "I want to ask you who you think's prettier, Doris Day or June Haver?"

"Doris Day. But she's not as pretty as Jane Powell."

"You think *she's* pretty?" Glory said. She made a sound like she was trying to throw up.

"Mrs. Reinstein!" I said, pointing down to the sidewalk. "Fire the cannon!"

"BO-OM! BO-OM! BO-OM!" Glory thundered. She was very good with sound effects.

Mrs. Reinstein disappeared up the stoop. Then the Old Clothes wagon pulled up. The Old Clothes man got down from the seat behind the horse.

"Fire the cannon!" I yelled.

"Ruthie, I told you. Not anyone with horses." Her bangs got crooked when she tossed her head. "Soon you'll be telling me to fire on Irish Rose." That's what we called the tenor who came to the back alley to sing for money. Once we threw him down a penny. "And don't tell me to fire on the coal man, neither."

Next thing I knew, Roy Rogers was waving his red ban-danna. We signaled him over.

"How come I'm all by myself?" he said, pouting.

Glory mussed his curly hair. "Because you're the sentry."

"Says who?"

"I do," Glory said. I gave her a look. "We do," she said, meaning me and her.

"But . . . you're girls," he said. "Only boys can be in the Army."

"Roy Rogers, if you weren't so dumb . . ." Glory started, raising her shoulders to show me how aggravated she was with her stepbrother. "First of all, we're bigger than you. Secondly, what do you know about anything? And last but not least, you are a dumb, dumb bunny." She turned her back, but he just stood there.

"There are too girls in the Army," I said. "They're called Waves."

"See?" Glory said, looking at him again. "So git. You can't play Fort today."

Roy Rogers's face scrunched up like he was going to cry. He walked slowly to the other end, picked up his broomstick, and came running back. He pointed his make-believe rifle at her. "Bang! You're dead, dead, dead."

"Oh yeah?" she said, pretending to swing the cannon around.

Roy Rogers leaped at her. "Bang, bang!"

"Bang! I got ya!" said a deep voice behind us. It was the milkman, coming from the doorway of 42 Arden, in the middle of the roof. He was carrying two crates of empty milk bottles, one on top of the other, so that you couldn't see his face, but you could see his white pants.

"Bang!" Roy Rogers said.

"Bang, bang!" I said.

"BO-OM! BO-OM!" said Glory.

The milkman dropped the boxes down on the roof. The noise was like thunder. "Eheheheheheheheh," he said, machine-gunning us.

Roy Rogers fell down on the tar.

"I'm dy-ing," Glory said, falling on top of him.

"Good-bye," I said, doubling over, then collapsing.

"See ya," said the milkman, laughing as he picked up his crates and headed across the fort to 38 Arden.

"Ugh! That stuff stinks," I said, about the tar. "It's all mushy, too." That was because of the hot sun.

"Who cares? We have to have a different plan," Glory said.

"An enemy got through our lines. From now on, I'll be General."

The next time we went up, Glory put Roy Rogers on the cannon. I had to laugh because she made her and me sentries at different ends of the fort. We couldn't even talk to each other except by yelling. I was sorry I didn't go to the park with my mother where the pool was. Robin Reinstein had gone right after lunch. It was so hot out I was dripping. Glory was waving her red bandanna.

When I came over she said, "We'll be rovers now."

Together, she and I walked back and forth, guarding the fort. Each time we got to the middle, we talked to Roy Rogers so he wouldn't get lonely. It was so hot our sneakers stuck to the roof as we walked. I was glad when the sky started getting gray.

"Dare you to stay out when the rain comes down," Glory said.

Right away I said okay, since my father was downtown playing cards at his club.

The sky became an even darker gray and then there was a bolt of lightning. Giant drops of rain splashed our clothes and the roof, making big puddles. When we heard the thunder, Roy Rogers ran for the door.

"Go down and get the bucket!" Glory yelled after him.

The rain came down like Niagara Falls. In a few minutes she and I were drenched. I could see Glory's underpants through her dress.

When Roy Rogers came back with the bucket, Glory let it fill up with rain. "The next person who crosses the stoop will get drowned," she said.

There was another roar of thunder. Roy Rogers started running. "Don't drown anyone till I get back!" he yelled.

No one crossed the stoop while he was gone. It was only drizzling when he came back. Then Mrs. Krakowski came up the sidewalk.

"Don't let her see you!" Glory warned.

We ducked down behind the little wall.

"Get the bucket!" she ordered Roy Rogers.

Mrs. Krakowski started up the stoop.

"Ready, aim . . ."

Before Glory could say, "Fire!" Roy Rogers shoved the bucket of water toward the stoop, but then he lost his grip on it. Out sloshed the water, curling like the top of a waterfall, before we heard it go splat on the ground. The bucket came bouncing and crashing after. Face down, we dived onto the tar.

"Is someone crazy?" we heard Mrs. Krakowski shouting. "Vot, have we got lunatics living here now?"

Glory and Roy Rogers kept hugging each other as they lay next to me, giggling into each other's necks and sometimes into mine. I saw the whole front of Glory's pastel green dress was smudged from the black tar. Roy Rogers's face and hands were black. I looked down at my pinafore, because my mother had a thing about dirt, but I couldn't see any on the red and blue flowers.

Then I peeked carefully over the wall. Mrs. Krakowski had gone. The drizzle had stopped. Half the sky was blue again, and over the gray half was a gorgeous rainbow.

"Close your eyes and make a wish," I said, closing my own eyes to wish I'd be as pretty as Doris Day when I grew up.

"What did you wish?" Glory asked Roy Rogers, trying to trick him into telling.

"Give me a nickel and I'll tell."

"Then you won't get your wish," I said.

"I don't care."

"Okay," Glory said. "A nickel."

"A nickel," said Roy Rogers.

"So, what did you wish?"

"Told ya. I wished for a nickel," Roy Rogers said, bursting into hysterics.

Glory's black eyes looked like they were trying to kill him. Then they turned on me. "What's so funny?" she said.

I almost fell down in stitches. She stomped off the fort, leaving Roy Rogers lying at my feet, sloshing around in a puddle.

Soon my side ached from laughing and my teeth were chattering, because it had cooled off and I was still soaked. Roy Rogers and I went downstairs. Glory was in the hallway outside their door. "What are we going to do?" she asked him. "The bucket's not there." She didn't look at me the whole time.

"Ask Mrs. Krakowski?" said Roy Rogers, like he knew it was the wrong answer.

"I dare you," she said.

"Dare *you,*" he said.

"You know Dot's gonna get the strap out," Glory said, about their mother. A few times Glory had showed me red welts on her back. My mother said Dot had a really bad temper, even though she was always so nice to me.

"*I'll* ask," I said. I figured Mrs. Krakowski wouldn't say anything to my mother or father because she always told me how she felt sorry for them.

Once Mrs. Krakowski came up to me on the stoop and said, "Too bad."

"What?" I asked her.

"Your parents being deaf-and-dumb."

"They're not dumb," I told her. "They're deaf-mutes. They're used to it because my mother got that way when she was a baby and my father got meningitis when he was eight years old."

She clucked her tongue. "Never to hear your own child . . ." She tried to hand me a dime. "For candy," she said.

"I'm not allowed," I fibbed.

"For something else, then."

"No thanks, Mrs. Krakowski," I said politely.

"Ruthie's gonna ask Mrs.-Ants-in-Her-Pants," Roy Rogers said, jumping up and down.

56

"Stay here," I told them, afraid they'd make me laugh right in the middle. I went across the stoop.

When she opened the door, Mrs. Krakowski screamed, "Gott! A drowned rat!"

"I dropped the bucket by mistake," I said. "Could I please get it back?"

"You?" She slapped the side of her head. "Vot to expect?" she muttered to herself as she went inside. She came back with the bucket. "Your parents, Gott bless, don't know any better. Such a mess!"

I thought she was a mess, with her blouse hanging half out of her skirt and her stockings bunched around her fat ankles, but all I said was, "Thank you very much, Mrs. Krakowski," and took the bucket. I ran across the stoop to where Glory and Roy Rogers were waiting.

Glory took one look and said, "Oh cripes! We'll have to hammer it!" One side was all bashed in.

Dot wasn't home, so I sat under Dot's hair dryer and Glory started hammering. Then Glory sat under the dryer and I hammered.

"Let me, let me," said Roy Rogers. Glory gave him the hammer. She and I took off our clothes and put on robes so she could iron our things dry. She did her own dress okay but she burned the ruffle on the shoulder of my pinafore. The spaces between the red and blue flowers were brown instead of white. Roy Rogers thought that was hilarious, but he stopped laughing when he hit his foot with the hammer.

When it was time for supper I went upstairs. My shoes squished on each step. It didn't matter, since my mother couldn't hear them, of course, but next time she ironed she would see the burn.

When she saw me, my mother signed, "Like Negro." She stood in the doorway of the bathroom while I washed my face and hands. "Hear happen?" she asked, meaning did I hear what'd happened.

I shook my head, wondering if she meant the bucket. She looked real serious.

"Milkman," she signed, then spelled out "m-u-g-g-e-d."

"What m-u-g-g-e-d?" I asked. I'd seen the word in the *Daily News* but didn't know what it meant.

She made signs to show me how the milkman had been knocked over the head and was laying unconscious when Mrs. Shanahan found him. That's what she told my mother after the ambulance came.

My mother and I went into the kitchen and she put a bowl of blueberries and sour cream on the table.

"Where happen?" I asked.

"Up r-o-o-f. D-a-n-g-e-r-o-u-s."

Suddenly I wasn't hungry, even though I loved blueberries.

"U-p-s-e-t?" my mother asked, but I pretended I ate at Glory's.

Later Mrs. Shanahan phoned us about the milkman. "Tell your mother Jewish Memorial said it was a concussion," she said. "He'll be okay. But I wonder what the world is coming to when someone almost gets murdered on our own roof."

"Milkman almost k-i-l-l-e-d," I told my mother. "Will b-e all right." I didn't know what a concussion was, so I didn't bother spelling it out.

"N-i-c-e man," my mother said about him. "Feel sorry." She got a hairbrush and started brushing the knots out of my hair. That's when she noticed the burn on the ruffle. "Stupid me, careless iron," she said.

For a second I almost didn't say anything. But then I said, "G-l-o-r-y iron, b-u-r-n," explaining we got soaked in the rain. I didn't tell her we were on the roof.

When my mother didn't get angry, I put my arms around her waist and hugged her. Her stomach and breasts were like big soft pillows. She squeezed me and then she let me go. "S-o-r-r-y spoil dress," she said, smiling so that I could see her dimples. That's when I realized Glory had never told me she was sorry for burning my pinafore. But that was Glory. She hadn't even thanked me for the bucket.

After my mother braided my hair, I got out my library book, but I couldn't concentrate. I wanted to talk to Glory about moving Fort Arden. I figured the brick wall at the top of the stoop would be perfect. There were lots of long, skinny spaces between the bricks, so we could hide behind there and still see who our enemies were.

One thing for sure, I decided: from then on I was going to be General, because Glory and Roy Rogers owed me plenty for saving their lives.

🪻 Peola and Petunia

"SHE was homely as sin," my big sister told me. "So plain if
you passed her in the street you'd never dream she was a Hollywood star."

"How come?" I asked, not sure whether to believe her
about Jennifer Jones. In the *Photoplay* magazine we had open
in front of us on the kitchen table, Jennifer Jones looked
pretty gorgeous to me. My sister, though, had gotten to see
her close up, right in our neighborhood that afternoon, because they were making a movie at the top of Fort Tryon Park.

She slid the magazine over closer to me. "Look at all that
makeup. In the movie she doesn't have lipstick or any eyebrow pencil. Besides, she probably had a lot of plastic surgery
to begin with."

"Did you read that?" I asked.

"They all do. You think they're born so perfect?"

I didn't know. Dot, my friend Glory's mother, was gorgeous.

I knew she didn't have any plastic surgery, but I didn't say that. I had a feeling Melva wouldn't like it.

"Help me write an absence note," she said, because she'd played hookey to watch them make the movie. She opened her loose-leaf notebook. "What should I say?" she asked, even though she was in high school and I was still in grade school. My teacher had said I was advanced for my age in English. Melva wrote down what I told her:

Dear Mrs. Hornbaker,
    Please excuse my daughter Melva Zimmer for having a very bad stomack ache so she couldn't go to school today.

Very truely yours,
(Mr.) Albert Zimmer

"You spelled 'stomach' wrong," I told her.
"Wanna bet?"
"Sure?" I said.
"What?"
"Who's ever right gets a tickling?"
"Okay," she said.
After she looked it up, she changed the spelling, then copied the letter onto a blank piece of paper. She practiced my father's signature over and over in her loose-leaf, until I couldn't tell the difference between hers and his. She wrote it on the letter. "I owe you a tickle," she said. "Let's go in the bedroom."

We passed my mother, who was sitting in the living room knitting a sweater for me. She stopped us so she could measure it, from the bottom, up to my underarm, where she was going to start the sleeve.

"Why make for her, not me?" Melva asked her.
"Will," my mother said.
"Never. R-u-t-h your f-a-v-o-r-i-t-e," she said. "Same old s-t-o-r-y."
"N-o, love same," my mother said, shaking her head.

As we went into the bedroom Melva said to me, "I'd like to take the knitting and rip all the stitches out."

I felt really bad when she said that. Sometimes I thought my mother loved me more than her, but I was sure my brother was her favorite. "Sidney's her favorite," I said.

"And you're Daddy's favorite," Melva said. "So whose favorite am I?"

"Mine," I said. I started to hug her until she pushed me away and told me to take my pajamas off. She closed the bedroom door. I was wearing only underpants when she had me lay face down on the bed.

Holding the open end of the bobby pin, she drew the rounded end up and down my back for a long time. It felt like heaven. There was no talking, since we were both concentrating very hard. Then she started on my left leg, from the thigh down to the ankle, and came up the back of my knee. A funny feeling went all through me, like the one I got when I played with myself sometimes, in bed, after she was asleep.

That feeling had always scared me, because I didn't know what it was. Sometimes my heart pounded so hard I thought I was going to die and I swore I'd never touch myself again. But then I'd end up doing it.

When I jerked suddenly, Melva asked me, "What's the matter?"

"Nothing."

She started on the other leg and as she ran the bobby pin over the back of the knee I felt it again. I sat up real quick. "I don't feel like being tickled," I said.

She looked at me suspiciously. "Why?"

"Just because." I got up and put my pajamas back on.

"If you don't tell me why, I'll get Peola after you."

"Mama's home," I reminded her. Peola never came out when my mother was home. Sometimes I thought Peola was only make-believe, but I wasn't totally certain. And even if she was, Peola was very, very scary.

"Well, Mama won't be home tomorrow night," Melva said,

"and Sidney's got softball practice." She cackled, just a little like the way Peola did. "Ee ee ee, ah ah ah."

"I hate you," I said, and ran to my mother before Melva could smack me.

The next night, as my mother was leaving with my father for the U.L., which is short for Union League of the Deaf, I begged her not to go.

"S-i-l-l-y," she said. "Come back tonight."

"Be good," my father said out loud, in that funny gruff voice he has because of being a deaf-mute. And then they were gone.

"Wanna play Chinese checkers?" my sister asked.

"Sure," I said. Usually we played a twenty-five game series. That took a long time, which meant that Peola wouldn't be around for a while. We played at the kitchen table, crossing our legs under us and mashing them into the new oilcloth my mother had put on the chairs. It kept going back and forth: she'd win one and then I'd win one. I bit my nails the whole time and she kept picking her nose.

Then I got a couple of games ahead of her. That's when the roach came out from behind the stove. A big one. "Get it," she said, so I hit it dead with my slipper.

The game looked different when I sat down again. "You didn't cheat me, did you?" I asked. Sometimes she'd tell me if she had, but she said she didn't.

I beat her anyway. A couple of games later she said, "This is boring. Let's look at the new *Silver Screen.*"

I was afraid to make her mad, so I said okay, even though I thought movie magazines were silly. Who cared who Mickey Rooney was going to marry or where John Derek went on a date? I loved going to movies, but the stories were almost never about real people, unless they were dead.

First Melva drooled over Montgomery Clift, then over Elizabeth Taylor, who she thought was the most beautiful girl in the world. "Isn't she just gorgeous! Monty probably falls at her feet," she said.

I liked blondes better but I didn't say anything.

"Here, what do you think's the most beautiful thing about her?" she asked, pointing to a picture where Elizabeth Taylor was looking at her poodles.

Since Melva had dark hair, I said, "Her hair?"

"Guess again."

"Her eyes."

"Again."

"Her figure?" She was wearing a really tight sweater.

"That's very dumb. She's short-waisted."

"So, what then?"

"Her nose. See?" Her fingernail traced the outline. "Perfect!" She stared real hard at me, after I didn't say anything. "What do you think?"

"I don't know," I said.

"You don't know? You *are* real dumb," she said. "So we're gonna have to ask Peola."

"Please," I said, "I don't want to."

The next thing I knew, Melva pulled the cord on the overhead light and grabbed my arm, sort of dragging me to the bathroom. On the way she said, "Peola's been around for thousands of centuries. She sees everything, hears everything, knows everything, and she likes little girls like you. But only in the dark." And then I heard Peola's terrible cackle.

In the bathroom Melva said, "We're in Pe-o-la's cave. Silence!" and locked the door behind us. I didn't dare say a word. It was dark in there, except for some moonlight from the narrow frosted window.

She stood me up on the rim of the bathtub, my back propped against the tiles that came halfway up the wall. As my eyes got used to the dark, I could make out a figure, but it wasn't my sister's. It was smaller, sort of hunchbacked.

"I am Pe-o-la," an odd crackling voice said, very slowly. It was both higher and lower than my sister's, sort of like an old woman's. "How is my Pe-tu-nia?" she croaked, drawing out

the syllables. "Don't be frigh-tened," she said, starting the
cackling that terrified me.

"I'm not Petunia, I'm Ruth," I told her.

She stuck her face in mine. The jaw was twisted to one
side, and she was toothless. Her lips curled over her gums. "If
you're not Petunia, I will have to put you in the dungeon with
the roa-ches and spi-ders . . ."

I knew what I felt crawling over my body were only her
fingers, but I could imagine the real thing.

". . . and mice!"

As something went up my leg I jerked away, slipping off the
rim of the tub. Peola caught me in her arms, cackling like
mad. "Hee hee eee eee ah ah ah, I've got you, Petunia." The
arms wound tightly around me, pressing me to her body.

The shape of the breasts felt familiar. "You're Melva!" I
said. "Stop pretending!"

The hands grabbed my shoulders and yanked me backwards. "You—you can't ever see Melva again!" The twisted
face pressed up against mine. "Look at me!" it ordered.

I looked at the right eye, or at where the right eye should of
been. There was nothing there. No pupil, just white stuff. I
started screaming.

"Who are you, lit-tle girl?"

"Petunia," I said.

"And who am I?"

"Peola."

"And who is the most beautiful girl in the world?"

"Elizabeth Taylor," I said. "Because of her nose," I added,
knowing what was coming.

"And who's the ugliest?"

"You!" I said.

"Eee eee eee! You're such a good girl Melva will tell you a
secret when I bring her back. Now close your eyes and say ab-
ra-ca-dab-ra ten times." While I said it, Peola limped over to
the light switch. When the light came on, Melva was there,
smiling at me with both dimples showing.

We went back into the bedroom. This time we sat on her bed, under the autographed picture of Montgomery Clift. I could see the crease, from the time she slept with it under her pillow.

"Swear you won't tell anyone," Melva said to me.

I made my pinkie into a "J," letting the end touch my bottom lip, then move upwards in an arc. I swore to God I wouldn't tell anyone.

In a real low voice, she said, "They're talking about me."

"Who?"

"The tramps in my class."

I didn't know what to say.

"You don't believe me?" she said, kind of angry.

"Of course I do."

"They're laughing at my nose," she whispered.

"Why are you whispering?" I asked.

"So they won't hear me," she said, obviously exasperated.

I knew it had been too good to be true, escaping Peola so quickly. Usually she made me promise to do something awful, like call up Morty Schulman, a boy Melva had a crush on. Once I had to buy Chesterfields at the grocery store and pretend they were for my mother. After that I got an ingrown toenail, which I knew was for lying.

Melva got up and went over to the dresser. She held up a hand mirror, turning sideways to study her profile in the big mirror. "See? That's why I wear a pompadour, to take attention away from this." She grabbed her nose between her fingers and started twisting it.

"Stop," I said. "Don't!"

"I can't stand their laughing at me. I want to kill myself. What would *you* do with a nose like this?"

"Like what?"

A wild look came into her eyes. "LOOK AT IT!" she yelled. Then she banged the mirror down and came over to the bed. She shook my shoulders. "See how it's hooked?" She grabbed my finger and pressed it hard over the bones of her nose.

"Then why don't you get it done?"

"I'd have to baby-sit a hundred years to get the money." She started sobbing, which made me feel real bad. I tried to think.

"What about the drawing contest?" I asked. She had been practicing drawing the face in the movie magazines where it said, "Draw Me." There was a one hundred dollar prize for the best one.

She looked through the movie magazines until she found the ad. "Illustrators earn a good income," it said. "Enter now and learn how you can become a professional illustrator."

"Even if I don't win, I could still be an artist," she said.

I looked over the ad. "You have to go to school, I think."

"So?" she said. "You think I'm too dumb?"

"Drawing doesn't take brains," I said. For some reason, she smacked me. "I'll tell Mama," I said, and went into the kitchen to wait for my parents to come home.

A little while later Melva came in to show me the faces she'd drawn, like nothing had happened. "Which one is best?"

"They're all pretty terrific," I told her. "I can't even tell the difference."

She picked one and put it in an envelope. She said she was going downstairs to mail it, but she wouldn't let me go with her. "If you're afraid, you can hang out the window and watch me. Just yell if anything happens."

I hung out the window, watching her walk past the lamp-post up Arden Street to the mailbox on the corner. When I heard a key turn in the lock, my knees almost buckled. It turned out to be my father.

"Where M-e-l-v-a?" he signed, right off.

"Mail letter."

"Think herself," he said to my mother. "Leave alone," he said, meaning me.

Even though I was still mad at her, my father had a pretty terrible temper, so I told him, "Come back one minute, I not baby." That made him smile and he went into his bedroom.

My mother gave me some cookies she had brought in a napkin from the U.L. and then Melva came back.

"Daddy's real mad at you," I told her.

"Who cares, as long as he doesn't take away my allowance," she said.

"Uh oh," I said. "I think that's what he's going to do."

She looked me in the eye. "Are you fibbing?"

I started to laugh. "He was mad but I talked him out of it."

"That's because you're his pet." She threw her cookie at me, before she stomped out of the kitchen.

For weeks afterwards she drove me crazy every day after school, wanting to know if she'd gotten any mail from the International Artists Institute. Sometimes she said my mother and I were hiding the letter from her. "Not, swear," my mother told her. A couple of times I had to swear, too.

When the letter finally came, she read it over and over, a few times out loud. It said that she'd done very well but she hadn't won the contest. "You have talent, Miss Zimmer, but it needs developing," Melva read with a lot of excitement. "Talent! I have talent!" The letter also said, "A bona fide representative will be telephoning to discuss your talent and to explore the opportunities of a professional artist, without obligation."

After that, every time the phone rang she drove me crazy. "Answer it! Answer it! Tell them 'Miss Zimmer is home, one moment please.'" One Saturday night she didn't go baby-sitting because she thought they might call.

"Funny telephone Saturday night," my mother said.

"She's just hoping I'll miss the call," Melva told me. "God forbid I should be something besides a secretary."

Late one afternoon the phone rang. My sister picked it up, forgetting to answer, "Zimmer residence, Melva speaking," like she'd been practicing. She picked it up and said, "Hello?"

When she got all flustered, I could tell right off who it was. She made an appointment for the man to come when my father would be working on the night shift at the post office.

Before the man came that night, Melva made my mother take the slipcovers off the couch, which she'd never done before. She turned all the living room lights on: the ceiling fixture, the four wall sconces, the floor lamp, and the lamp on the end table.

"What is this, a blind man's coming?" my brother said. "Jesus Christ, I need sunglasses in here."

"If you say anything, anything at all to Mr. Johnston . . ." Melva warned.

"This may come as a great shock but I have bigger fish to fry. Me and Moe're going to the Trocadero," Sidney told her, which was the ballroom on Dyckman Street. "Va va va voom!" he said on his way out the door.

Mr. Johnston was panting really bad by the time he got to the fourth floor. Right away he asked for a glass of water. "T-o-o f-a-t," my mother signed, after she brought it.

She and I sat on the armchairs. Mr. Johnston and Melva sat on the sofa. When he put his glass down on the coffee table, my mother picked it up and put it on a napkin. His brown suit and tie shone under all the lights. He laid his large brown briefcase, which looked like elephant skin, down on the sofa. My mother made a face. "Dirty," she signed to me.

Mr. Johnston showed all of us a binder full of letters from students who had graduated from the school and pictures of drawings by them, which he said had been in magazines. He read some letters out loud from famous senators and artists, saying the school was professional. I could spell "professional" but I didn't know what it meant.

From the briefcase he took out my sister's drawing that she'd mailed in, but it was in a frame now. "Miss Zimmer," he said, "you should hang this somewheres, so you can look back on it when you're a professional artist. You have talent, but frankly, it needs developing."

The words sounded familiar. Then I realized he was saying what the letter said. I tried to catch my sister's eye, but she was in another world. I told my mother, "Good draw," about what Mr. Johnston said.

My mother nodded. "Heavy body, dent chair," she said.

"Any questions?" the man asked, drinking up the water. He had talked for a long time.

"Question?" my sister interpreted to my mother.

"How much?" my mother said.

The man told us about making a down payment and sending in payments on the installment plan, which my sister explained to my mother.

"How much?" my mother asked again.

"She wants to know how much," I told Mr. Johnston. Melva gave me a look like she could kill.

"A hundred and twenty-five dollars. A small investment to make in your professional future," he said.

"One hundred twenty-five," I told my mother. Her face didn't change.

"I'll have to talk to my father," Melva said.

"Oh," Mr. Johnston said, looking disappointed. "I wish he could have been here, but I can come back."

"He's deaf," my sister said, "so I'd have to explain it to him anyhow."

The man stood up and came over to my mother. He shook her hand. "I really admire you, Mrs. Zimmer," he said to her. Melva interpreted it as "Think you wonderful."

My mother shrugged. "Think me stupid?" she signed to me. Even though the man couldn't understand what my mother was saying, Melva waved at her to stop.

We all walked him to the door and watched as he went down the stairs. "Nice to meet you," my sister called out.

After closing the door, Melva started screaming and jumped up and down so hard that the people downstairs banged on the pipe. I went into the kitchen and tried to read my math book, but I couldn't concentrate, thinking what a dope my sister was, even though she was so much older. No way was my father, the world's biggest cheapskate, going to give her the money. I felt sick because my sister couldn't go to art school and she didn't even know it.

I could see her asking my father for the money, my father saying no, my sister talking back to him, my father smacking her. Trying to forget it, I turned on the radio. "Mystery Theatre" was on. I brought my Pickup Sticks over and sat on the linoleum, dropping the sticks in front of me. I wanted to get better and beat Melva.

Right before lunch on Saturday, I came upstairs from a game of Johnny-May-We-Cross-Your-River on the stoop. No one was in the kitchen. As soon as I started across the foyer I heard my father yelling. Melva screamed, "You bastard! You bastard!" I knew it was worse than I'd even imagined.

Outside the bedroom I could see a reflection in the dresser mirror of my father's back and Melva's pompadour. He had her up against the wall and was hitting her, I guessed, from her screams and my mother's cries. My mother was in the bedroom, too, although I couldn't see her from where I was. I sat down on the floor, closed my eyes, and covered my ears, begging God to make my father stop. The next thing I knew, I felt someone walk by me. It was my father, hurrying to the kitchen. Next, my mother came rushing into the living room, but she went the other way, to the bathroom, making crying noises.

I went into the bedroom. My sister was on the floor near the corner, bleeding like crazy. There was blood all over her, her face, her clothes, on the wall. My mother came back with some wet washcloths and towels, which she put on my sister's face.

"Call doctor," she told me.

"Come here?" I asked.

She nodded. "D-o-n-t think," she said. She could tell thinking about Melva made me sick.

I found Dr. Hellman's number and dialed it. It took me a

while to explain it to the nurse but I did. When Dr. Hellman finally got there, my father had left the house. It was the only time I can remember that we didn't have lunch.

Dr. Hellman asked me to ask my mother who hit Melva. "Say fall," my mother told me. I said I didn't know. He patted my head. "You're a big girl now."

My mother went with Melva and Dr. Hellman to the hospital. She told me to tell Mrs. Opals to mind me. I went down to the stoop and played with Robin first. Anyway, Mrs. Opals came down and put her arm around me. "What happened?" she asked me. "I saw your sister with all the bandages."

"My father hit her," I said.

"You shouldn't make up stories." She shook her head.

I said I was sorry because I knew I shouldn't of told her. My mother wouldn't of liked it. "She fell and broke her nose," I said.

"She's going to get a new nose, then."

"She is?"

Mrs. Opals smiled, like she was telling me something I should of known. "If you break your nose, they try to put it back together, but it's never the same." She clucked her tongue. "Too bad!"

I couldn't believe what I heard. A new nose for my sister? I said thank you to God under my breath and promised I wouldn't be fresh to Melva anymore. But I didn't tell Mrs. Opals to mind me.

My mother and sister were gone a long time. I played a lot of Pickup Sticks and a long game of war with myself, dealing the two packs and pretending I was two people. Sidney called and I told him what happened. *"Paskudneh,"* he said about what my father did, meaning really disgusting. He said to tell my mother he had to work overtime on account of doing inventory for Mr. Fleishmann.

I turned on the radio after it got dark. I kept hearing funny noises which scared me until I decided it was only the radiator making steam. I was very excited about seeing my sister's new nose, but when she walked in with my mother, all I saw around her face were even more bandages.

"I'm starved," she said, even though it was ten o'clock at night. My mother warmed up the lunch we didn't have, except she wasn't hungry, so Melva ate two lunches. She said she was supposed to stay in the hospital but my mother told them we didn't have the money. Melva tried to tell me what they had done to her there. I had to put my hands over my ears when it got too gory.

My mother saw me. "Operation?" she asked. I nodded. "Awful," she said. "Feel like faint."

After Melva got done eating, she tore out pictures from her movie magazines and Scotch-taped them on the walls of the bedroom. They were all of actresses, mostly in profile. "If I can't have Elizabeth Taylor's nose, that's the one I want," she said, pointing to Jean Simmons.

"I hope you get it," I said, starting to worry.

"Peola told me I would."

"When?"

"When they put me under the anesthesia. Why, don't you believe me?"

"Of course," I lied. "I thought, though, she only came here, to our apartment."

"She goes everywhere. She came to say good-bye to me, in fact. And she's taking Petunia with her." Melva smirked like she had some big secret.

"Where?"

Melva ran her fingers over Elizabeth Taylor's hair. "To haunt Montgomery Clift. He's too stuck-up for his own good. Peola told me."

My mother came in to say good night. "D-o-n-t awake, imagine," she told Melva, meaning she shouldn't stay up imagining too much about her nose. But Melva fell right asleep. I was the one who stayed up worrying. What would happen if the new nose was worse than the old one?

I heard Sidney come home. I got scared when I thought he

might be the one to tell my father about the operation, but when I peeked out the bedroom door the living room was dark, which meant Sidney was already in the sofa bed. My mother'd said Melva's nose would cost plenty. Behind Melva's back she shook her hands like they were wet, which meant really a lot of money. My father was going to have conniption fits.

When my father came home he went to the kitchen for a while, like he always does, then to the bathroom. The sink water ran and ran, before he came out and stopped by our door, where the mezuzah was nailed into the frame, as high as the tips of my fingers could reach. I could hear him muttering the Hebrew prayer. Once I had prayed under the mezuzah and asked God to get rid of Peola, but He didn't listen to me, maybe because I did it in English.

I crept out of bed and tiptoed over to the windows. The shades were up and I could see the moon and lots of stars. All the lights were still on at the Frangiones across the way. I don't think they ever went to sleep. By moonlight I could see my sister lying on her bed. She looked like one of those mummies in the Metropolitan Museum, her whole face wrapped in white gauze, with just slits for eyes, and her arms straight down by her sides. She looked dead.

I watched Melva for a long time, hoping she would move. When she turned her head so I could see her new profile, there was a strange little sound. And then the room got quiet again. But I wasn't fooled. I knew Peola was right there with us, hiding under the bandages, waiting.

🐦 Talking *Mama-Losh'n*

THE siren sounded just as my mother and I jammed together in the window, leaning out over the fire escape, our elbows on the sill. Melva had the next window over to herself. Across the street, apartment windows got black as lights went off, one after the other. Within minutes the lampposts were out. It was completely dark, except for tiny flares of matches lighting cigarettes or the glowing embers of those already lit, from the people who hung out across the street from us.

Down the block a shrill whistle blew. "HEY! YOU! Turn that light out!" boomed my brother's voice. "This is your air raid warden speaking."

"Oh God!" Melva said.

It was my brother's first night as an air raid warden. Sidney's loud voice came through his megaphone like thunder in the dark. Since there was enough moonlight, I told my mother in sign language what we heard.

"Like b-o-s-s," my mother said, meaning that Sidney liked being a boss.

For a long time Melva and I didn't hear anything else, except the voices of our neighbors from the windows above and below us. We didn't even know where Sidney was, until we saw the beam of his flashlight shining into the front window of a car in the middle of the street.

"Pull over," Sidney's voice boomed. "I mean NOW!"

The car rolled slowly to the curb and turned its lights out. Sidney's flashlight went out, too, and then we lost track of him again.

It was hard for me to believe that my very own brother was out there in charge of Arden Street. Even if he hadn't told me about the Japs who could fly over our block and bomb us if they saw the lights, I would of been impressed. I knew he felt proud, because when the notification came he'd said, "They wouldn't have given any old *shmuck* such an important job." I didn't know what *shmuck* meant but later Melva said it was a really bad word.

After a while the all-clear siren sounded. Apartments across the way lit up again and the streetlights came back on. We put the screens in the windows and went into the kitchen to wait for Sidney.

"Listen to this!" my brother said when he came in. My mother held out her hands, like she wanted to take his helmet. Sidney waved her away.

"S-i-l-l-y," my mother said. She brought him iced coffee and sat down with us at the kitchen table. The whole time Sidney was telling us what'd happened, he kept his helmet on.

First he told us about Mrs. Sheehan, who lived just two steps down from the sidewalk, in the next building. She had run outside during the first siren. "I told the buttinsky to get her ass off the street . . ." my brother said.

"Sidney . . ." my sister interrupted.

He looked over at me. "Sorry," he said.

He took a long time telling what he'd said to Mrs. Sheehan

and what she'd said, back and forth, and how she kept standing on the sidewalk, letting him know which lights were still
on, in case he couldn't see for himself.

He imitated her Irish brogue: "Mr. Zimmer, sure and I'm jes
tryin' to help ya." My brother was terrific with accents, even
though he hadn't taken any languages in high school, like my
sister was doing.

"Then what?" Melva asked.

"I told Mrs. Sheehan she could help the U.S. of A. by
getting her goddam ass inside."

Melva kicked me under the table. I kicked her back. Then I
told my mother about Mrs. Sheehan, except I cut it short.

"Irish, nosey," my mother said.

"What else? What else?" Melva asked Sidney, like she was
real curious, even though when she was mad at him she used
to say he was full of hot air.

Sidney told us about the man who lived over on Sickles and
was walking his schnauzer on Arden. "I instructed him to get
the hell back to his own block," Sidney said, "because I wasn't
putting my neck on the line to have his dog crap in my
territory."

I started giggling.

"This is goddam serious," he said. "There's a war going on.
You don't have your dog take a crap during an air raid."

I bit the inside of my cheek, but when Melva kicked me
again, the giggles burst out. Soon she and I were in hysterics.

"Jesus Christ! Girls can be so damn silly," my brother said,
taking off his helmet and slamming it down on the table.

Being an air raid warden wasn't my brother's first choice.
When he was seventeen he tried to join the Army, but they
told him he had to get his G.E.D., since he'd dropped out of
high school. Up until then he was happy-go-lucky, going out
with his friends all the time, dating Lori Steinfeld and giving
her lots of presents with the money he made as a stock boy at
Greenblatt's Grocery. But he became real serious, staying

home nights to study, which made Lori mad. When he got his G.E.D., though, she said she was pleased as punch. She was two years older than him and already in nursing school. She didn't want him to volunteer for the Army but to wait till he was drafted. He went down to the recruiters anyway, only it turned out he was 4-F, on account of his flat feet.

"I'm not gonna take no for an answer," Sidney told us.

My father thought he was crazy, spending all his money on the foot doctor and on special metal arches they made to put inside his shoes. Every night before he went to bed Sidney did his exercises, grabbing pencils between his toes and walking on tiptoe. But when he tried again to join up, he was still 4-F.

Then Mr. Greenblatt sold the grocery to retire and my brother lost his job. After that, Sidney, who was tall and skinny, got even skinnier. His nose stood out like a parrot's and I hardly ever saw his big dimples anymore. His friends, who used to call him Smiley, started calling him Slim. "Disappointed, s-o-u-r," my mother said about him, behind his back.

The whole winter he was looking for work. He left the house when I did in the morning to go to school, and sometimes he bought me chocolate-covered raspberry jellies or dots (the kind that are stuck to paper) at the corner candy store where he bought the *New York Times* for the want ads. He got my sister to type his applications because she was taking the commercial course at George Washington and was a terrific typist. But most of the places wanted someone with college.

My brother spent everything in his savings account before he asked my father if he could borrow some money. My father had a fit. I could see them in the living room from where I was, sitting on the floor in the foyer, reading my library book. My father was in the big chair, in his undershirt and slacks, and my brother was lighting up a cigarette, standing by the lamp table.

"Smoke too much!" my father said right off, about the Lucky Strikes. While he signed he made barking sounds that deaf-mutes make when they're angry, kind of a cross between a person and a growly dog.

"When take t-e-s-t?" my father barked. He meant the Civil Service exam, so Sidney could get a job in the post office, where my father worked the night shift on the New Jersey table.

"Not interested," Sidney told him again. He'd told my mother the p.o. was okay for my father, since he was a deaf-mute and couldn't do any better, but for him it would be a dead end.

My father got up from the chair, smiling real sarcastically. "Fine, fine!" he said. "Who s-u-p-p-o-r-t you?" He poked my brother in the chest when he made the sign for "you."

"Please, n-e-e-d money," my brother said, "J-u-s-t loan." He stubbed out his cigarette in the ashtray, looking like he was about to cry.

"Money? Go take t-e-s-t, you," my father said. He poked him in the chest again.

"You go h-e-l-l," my brother said.

That's when my father hit Sidney in the face. I started screaming, though my mother couldn't hear me and my sister wasn't home. He kept hitting Sidney, but Sidney didn't move away. All he did was cover his head with his arms, the way he'd shown me to do when he taught me how to box because, he said, even little girls needed to defend themselves sometimes.

Finally my father stopped hitting. He stomped across the living room, almost stepping on me before he saw me. He kicked my book by mistake but all he said was "D-o-p-e" about my brother, then he went in the kitchen.

I didn't see how my father could mean that. Sidney was always reading the encyclopedia for fun and memorizing things from the almanac. The only reason he had dropped out of high school was to get a job, because my father didn't give him enough of an allowance.

My brother came over and picked me right up off the floor, holding me in his arms. "Don't cry," he said. "The sonofabitch isn't worth it." He had to put me down, though, because he started crying himself.

Not long after the big fight with my father, Sidney came home and told us he'd gotten a job as stock clerk for Baum Fabrics, a linen store downtown on Fifth Avenue. He was real happy about it at first. Then, for some reason, he wasn't so happy anymore. Every night he came home from work tired and sweaty, took off his shoes, lit up a Lucky Strike, and waited for the cup of coffee my mother always made him. He would read the *Daily News* without saying anything, have his supper, and then tell us stories that made fun of Mr. Baum, who he called the *tsadik*. "That means a good guy," he explained, except whenever he said it he meant the opposite.

Every so often, he would have Melva and me in stitches, imitating how Mr. Baum waddled up and down the store holding a pencil behind his back to make his fat arms meet. Then Sidney would change into another sport shirt and different pants and go see Lori or some of the guys he hung around with. When my mother would tell him not to spend all his money, he'd say that he planned to enjoy himself before buckling down. He was thinking about going to night school at NYU to study retail management.

My mother invited Lori for supper on Sidney's birthday. My father was at work, but we had a cake with candles and my mother made my brother's favorite, potato pancakes. I thought Lori was real pretty, with shiny black hair, kind of wavy to her shoulders, a big pompadour in front. She had a tiny nose like Jane Powell, which my sister called a snub, and she wore a big red flower over her ear. Not a real one, but the kind that came with a bobby pin attached.

My mother said she was stuck-up, after she tried to teach Lori to spell her name in the sign language alphabet and Lori pretended she was too dumb to learn. "Think high c-l-a-s-s," my mother said, meaning that Lori thought she was too good to talk with her fingers. When they broke up on Memorial Day, my mother was glad.

Lori wanted to get engaged right after she graduated nursing school, while Sidney wanted to wait. Breaking up with her made him sick. He stayed home from work, saying he had stomach pains. When the phone rang, he jumped out of bed to get it, but it wasn't her. I felt really bad. Later I was playing with my dolls in the living room, which was where his bed was, folded out from the couch, and I heard him sniffling. When I turned around, he was wiping his eyes with the sleeve of his pajamas.

"You know what? You're a natural teacher," he told me, about how I was teaching the dolls to spell. He made me promise to go to college and become a teacher, but I kept my toes crossed when I promised, because I'd wanted to be a nurse, like Lori. "You can make a good living teaching," he said, "until you get married and have babies."

The week after, Sidney came home and said, "You'll never guess, I've been promoted!" He said Mr. Baum gave him a job as a salesman in the front of the store. He would have to start wearing a shirt and tie with a jacket to work. My father raised his room and board from ten dollars to fifteen.

From then on, when Sidney came home at night the first thing he did was tell us how much he had grossed in sales for Baum Fabrics. It was always in the hundreds of dollars. He was still tired and sweaty, though, and my mother put Johnson's baby powder in his shoes. She said it would stop his feet from smelling. I never smelled anything, probably because of my sinus trouble.

He still didn't smile much, except the day he got his instructions and equipment to be an air raid warden (a megaphone, a whistle, and a flashlight) from the Fort Washington Armory. He came back grinning from ear to ear, with the deepest dimples, and put his new helmet on my head, laughing when it covered my whole face. For a moment he got serious, warning Melva never to touch it when he wasn't around. I asked him why he had to wear a helmet walking up and down Arden Street. That made him double over laughing. "She's such a card," he kept saying to Melva, but he never answered my question.

The night the inspector was supposed to see him during the air raid, Sidney was a bundle of nerves. When he came home from work, he didn't read the *Daily News* or tell us how much he'd grossed. Instead, he kept trying his helmet on in front of the mirror, finally asking Melva which way was best. He made me feel his cheeks to see if he needed a shave and even combed his hair twice in front with the Brill Cream. Then he got out his instructions, reading them over and over while he paced around the whole apartment.

I guess he got tired of pacing because he said to me, "Hey, cutie pie. Let's go someplace and talk *mama-losh'n,*" explaining it was Yiddish for getting down to business. He liked using words he had to explain.

"Where are we going?"

His face lit up. "Guess!"

"You mean it?" I said, getting the idea we were going to Schillingman's on Dyckman Street, two blocks over from Arden, where they had the best ice cream.

When we got there he said I could have anything I wanted. I got two scoops, cherry vanilla and pistachio, with sprinkles on top, which was extra. My brother got a single chocolate. He put four dimes on the wooden counter while we waited for Mr. Schillingman to scoop the sugar cones. It was pretty dark in there, with the lights way up on the ceiling where the fans were spinning.

Mr. Schillingman gave him seven cents change and wished him a good evening, except he said, "Goot," because of his accent.

Instead of saying thank you, my brother said, "*Danke schön.*"

Outside the store it was hot, in the 90's probably. Usually I sucked the vanilla off the cherries, then chewed them, but the ice cream was melting pretty fast, so I had to lick my cone like mad.

"See those bums?" my brother said, pointing with his cone to some high school kids leaning up against a parked car. "They'll never amount to anything."

In front of Nick's Fruits the sidewalk was jammed with baby carriages and strollers every which way. Lots of ladies were standing around the crates waving their arms, yelling for Nick. He looked up when we passed by and said, "Sid, how'ya doin'?"

"The best," my brother said. "You?"

But by then Nick was weighing something on one of the scales.

When I finished my cone, Sidney said, "Now, let's have a *tête-à-tête.*"

"A what?"

"Something between you and I," he said, just before a kid on roller skates almost crashed into us. "*Nudnik,*" he shouted, so that people outside the fish market stared. Sidney didn't seem to notice. He looked at me, putting his big hand on my shoulder. "What you should do when you grow up is go into sales."

I didn't know what to say. Ever since he told me I should be a teacher, I thought that's what I was going to be. I had even learned to pronounce words like Mrs. Landau did, especially "dance" and "idea," after she told our class most of the world didn't appreciate a Bronx accent. We lived in Manhattan, of course, but it was pretty close to the Bronx. And when people asked me what I was going to be when I grew up, I'd been telling them, "Teacher."

I kicked a bottle cap on the ground, waiting for Sidney to say something else. He said I was smart enough to be a salesgirl, since I'd skipped a grade, and what with his influence Mr. Baum would hire me right away when I graduated high school. "Your big brother's looking out for you," he said.

"I know," I said.

I liked being out after supper, even if it was hot and muggy. The sky was orange and peach, with dark gray clouds that came sometimes before a thunderstorm.

At the top of Dyckman my brother said he was sweating like a pig, so we went inside Nedick's, which was one of the few places in our neighborhood that was air-conditioned. Everything was so white in Nedick's it hurt your eyes: the tile walls and floor, even the kid behind the counter. He wore a white shirt and apron and a white pointy hat, like the kind you make by folding up paper, except it was cloth.

The kid looked at my brother as if he was crazy when Sidney asked how business was. He put the orange drink down without saying anything. That made forty-three cents so far that Sidney spent. He was always telling my sister he was broke, but Melva said it was on account of the Lucky Strikes. After he and Lori broke up, he started smoking two packs a day and was up to two and a half.

When we got outside, Sidney said, "Sales is 90 percent personality. That *nebbish* has zip. He'll always be a soda jerk."

We turned the corner onto Broadway. Outside the park, old people sat on the benches fanning themselves. I knew their buildings didn't have air conditioners like those downtown, where I wanted to live when I grew up.

Glory was on the stoop when we got back to our building, playing Double Dutch with the O'Brien kids. They were twirling and she was jumping, but I felt her eyes on Sidney. Sweat was running down his face and his shirt was all wet under the arms and down the middle of his back. He stopped on the first landing to turn around. "The U.S. of A. is a land of opportunity," he said to me, "and don't you ever forget it." He said it so loud I wanted to get out of there real fast.

"Promise me you'll go into sales," he said, still too loud.

I crossed my toes, then nodded, making sure not to look at Glory. Finally, he said he'd race me and we ran up the stairs. Near the fourth floor he slowed down to let me catch up, then he beat me to the door.

Once we got in the apartment, he rushed around, wiping himself off and changing his shirt. He didn't let my mother powder his shoes. He got all his equipment and then he was gone.

We didn't have to watch long that night before we heard Sidney's voice booming out to someone up near the corner. "HEY! YOU! Lights out!" After that, it was real quiet until just before the all-clear. "Get off the street," we heard him say to someone, but we couldn't see anything.

When he came back, he was real excited. The inspector told him they might make him supervisor of the other air raid wardens in the Inwood District. "Lori will be sorry," Sidney said. "I'll show *her*."

The week before school started I went with my mother to Fort Tryon Park where she always met her deaf friends in the afternoons. I got real bored so I told her I was going home to play on the stoop, but instead I went up to the top of the park and got on a bus that goes all the way down Fifth Avenue. I only had one nickel on me. Still, I wasn't worried when I put it in the box because I decided to visit my brother at Baum Fabrics.

I knew the route pretty well, since I'd taken the bus lots of times. Up by the park there were brown brick buildings with kids playing outside. Along Riverside Drive there were white stone buildings and people walking big dogs. Then there was the section that wasn't so nice. Garbage cans were lined up along the curb, and sometimes spilled into the gutter.

At 110th Street it changed again, because that's where Central Park began. The trees were so beautiful I could never get tired of seeing them. On Fifth Avenue there were gorgeous places with awnings and doormen. I watched very carefully for 57th Street, where Sidney worked.

The store was little, with a big sign, BAUM FABRICS. I stood outside, looking at the white and beige lace tablecloths hanging on cords strung across the window like washlines. I liked the kind we had at home better: a green and yellow plaid oilcloth.

Finally, I made myself go in. The store was air-conditioned, which I didn't expect, since Sidney always told us how hot it was. I expected to see fat Mr. Baum, but the short man with the white mustache who asked if he could help me was skinny.

"Is Mr. Zimmer here?" I said, like a grown-up.

"Who?"

"Mr. Zimmer? Sidney Zimmer?"

"Oh, Sid. Sure," the man said. "He's in back. I'll have to get him."

But then a woman came in and asked about a tablecloth. They went outside and she pointed to one in the window. He ended up taking out a big pile of tablecloths from under the counter before she bought. When she left, the man went to get my brother, but he came back without him. "Sid is unloading a shipment. Since the truck can't wait, you'll have to," he said.

We stood around without saying anything. I'd never been in a store that was so quiet. The man wrote something down on a pad by the register, then hummed "Begin the Beguine," which is a song my brother sang when he was teaching me to foxtrot.

Just then my brother came out from behind the curtain. He was all sweaty and wearing strange clothes: a brown shirt and pants that matched, instead of the white shirt and gray suit he left the house in that morning. When he saw me, he said, "Jesus! What's wrong?"

I told him I took a bus ride and needed a nickel to get back. He stared at me for a moment like he didn't get it. Then he turned to the man. "Hear that, Mr. Schinkel? This is the genius sister I've been telling you about."

"Pleased to meet you," Mr. Schinkel said. "You got a real nice brother there." He turned to Sidney. "Well, I won the bet with Baum. Lady comes in off the street and pushes my gross over the record." Mr. Schinkel smiled at me. "Sid's working his way up to sales. Someday he'll be behind the counter here. I wouldn't be surprised if he broke my record." He winked. "But it might take him fifteen, twenty years."

My brother walked me to the bus stop, but he couldn't wait with me. He made me promise never to take the bus again by myself.

On the bus I felt sick and my side was killing me. I hardly noticed the scenery. Then we were at Fort Tryon and I ran down the park and back to Arden Street.

I was in the kitchen when my brother came home from work. As usual, he had his cigarette and read the *Daily News.* My mother put baby powder in his shoes. After supper Sidney told us how much he had grossed that day. "Over a thousand," he said, like nothing had happened. We played some gin rummy until it was time for him to go on air raid duty.

Right after Labor Day my mother and I ran into Lori Steinfeld on Dyckman Street. She was looking in the window of Miles Shoes when she saw us walking by and came up to us. She was in a white nurse's uniform and you couldn't see her pompadour anymore because of the white cap.

"How's Sidney?" she said. "What's he been doin' with himself?"

She was surprised to hear that he was an air raid warden. "Tell your mother I'm working up at Presbyterian," she said, meaning the hospital at 168th Street.

"Good l-u-c-k," my mother told me to tell her back.

"You can tell your brother you ran into me," she said. "Lori Steinfeld."

"I know," I said. Then, before I could help myself, I said, "Sidney got a big promotion at Baum Fabrics. He's in sales now."

"Really!" she said, putting her hand on my mother's arm. "I always knew he had it in him."

As we walked away my mother said to me, "H-o-p-e not telephone," but I wasn't sure which was better, if he called her or didn't.

Until we got back to Arden Street I kept going back and forth over it, knowing in my heart he was going to anyhow. But then I figured Melva would tell him to wait and not call Lori right away, which is what she used to tell him after he and Lori argued. I didn't think Sidney would call her before the weekend. Definitely not before he was done with air raid duty that night, unless, of course, he thought Lori would want to come over our house and watch the air raid with us.

🦷 Plastic Flowers

MY whole spring vacation from P.S. 152 my mother spent getting ready for Passover. She redid the foyer closets, vacuuming the back corners and putting in a fresh bunch of mothballs. She laid down new oilcloth on the kitchen shelves and washed the whole inside of the frigidaire. Roaches came out half dead from behind the stove where she had put a lot of roach powder.

One morning, on account of the garbage truck, I woke up early and found my mother kneeling on the kitchen floor with my father standing over her, yelling the way he does, which was real scary.

I saw them from the foyer. My mother couldn't see me because my father stood between us, but I saw her hand spelling out, "B-u-s-y l-a-t-e-r."

My father exploded. "NOW!" he barked, signing at the same time. "R-u-t-h sleep now, l-a-t-e-r t-o-o l-a-t-e!" When he moved to one side, my mother saw me. She waved her arm, making him turn.

I explained about the garbage truck, looking at the giant freckles on his shoulders. I wondered why he didn't have his shirt on yet, since the rest of him was dressed. He didn't say anything, just walked out of the kitchen.

I sat down on the linoleum where the soup boxes and cans of vegetables were all spread out. My mother let me help her dust them off. Usually I had to beg her to do anything, such as dry dishes. At my best friend Glory's, it was just the opposite. Her mother, Dot, always made long lists of things for Glory and Roy Rogers to do. Once, when I asked Dot if I could help her water the plants, Glory got mad and almost stopped speaking to me.

When the things were put away, I had cornflakes and milk, then I got dressed. My mother changed her slippers to shoes and put her raincoat on over her housedress. We took the shopping cart with us to the A&P to do the Passover shopping.

My mother knew just what she wanted, even though she never made lists because her writing wasn't very good. We got two of the ten-pound boxes of matzo, six of the big jars of gefilte fish, two jars of herring in sour cream, and six cans of macaroons, half almond and half chocolate. There was more to get but that's all we could fit in the cart. Going up the four flights of our building, she held the front end. I had the back end.

My parents didn't talk to each other during lunch, which was our main meal because my father worked nights at the post office. The only sounds were of the forks and knives on the plates and my father's chewing.

When my mother was done with the dishes, she said the plastic flowers needed a bath. That didn't surprise me. She washed them right after we had bought them at the Five and Ten, before school started, and then again before Chanukah. I went and got the flowers from the vase in the foyer and the three vases in the living room, tiptoeing so I wouldn't wake my father, who was taking a nap in his chair, like he always did before work.

While I sat at the kitchen table reading the Inquiring Photographer in the *Daily News*, my mother swished the flowers around in the soapy water in the deep sink next to the regular one. "Full dirt," she said. "Look black." As she signed she accidentally spritzed me with suds. "Sorry," she said, smiling with her lips closed and her dimples showing. She let the water go down and then put more Vel in and filled up the sink again. The third time, she didn't put soap in. When she held up the flowers to shake the water off, I hardly recognized them. Instead of the loud reds, oranges, and blues we had picked out at the Five and Ten, there were only pastels.

"Wash make f-a-d-e," I told her.

She shook her head. "Sun f-a-d-e. Wash make bright."

But the flowers looked sick. The green plastic leaves had yellow spots as though they were about to die.

"T-o-o f-u-s-s-y," she said to me, but she was always saying that, like when I put the flowers in the vases according to the colors. I couldn't stand colors clashing, which I learned about from Mrs. Drucker, my art teacher in school.

My mother put the flowers on the drainboard to finish drying and said she was going to get dressed. It always took her a long time to put on her good brassiere and corset and nylon stockings and a real dress (instead of her housedress). I asked if I could get the rest of the Passover things at the A&P while she got ready. I could hardly believe it when she said okay.

At the A&P, I got the matzo meal, Kosher coarse salt, and farfel, then stood in line with my cart, looking to see what everyone else was buying. I could tell a lot about someone from what was in their cart, like if they had a dog or a bird, or if they were Catholic, since Jews didn't eat bacon or pork chops.

I was straining my eyes to see what the label said on a package in the cart over on the next aisle when I heard a voice say,

"Is your mother all right?" I looked up and saw Mrs. O'Meara, her freckled face and a bit of red hair sticking out from her white kerchief. "I never seen you alone in here before," she said.

I told her my mother was getting dressed to go out.

"Passover's almost here," she said, looking at my cart. "Easter is this Sunday already." In her cart there were two packages of hot cross buns. My mother always got cake at Goldin's Bakery on Dyckman, which didn't have stuff with white icing on them. I asked her what was in the package that looked like a giant sponge.

"Tripe," she said. "Pig's stomach."

I giggled. Once Glory had tried to tell me that the tongue my mother cooked was a real animal's tongue. That wasn't as silly as a pig's stomach, though.

Mrs. O'Meara and I walked back to Arden Street together. On the stoop she made a big sigh. "I'll be doing the windows this afternoon," she said. Then she smiled. "If it wasn't for Easter, the O'Mearas'd be living in a dirty pigsty."

That surprised me. I didn't know that people who weren't Jewish did extra cleaning. I wasn't even sure that all Jewish people did it, because I thought my mother had a thing about it.

Mrs. O'Meara went up to her building, across the stoop from us. I ran up the four flights three steps at a time. As soon as I opened the door I heard a funny noise, like a strap hitting something. My father was yelling, "Never, never," while the thwackthwackthwack got louder. Then I saw him hitting the edge of the sink with the plastic flowers.

"Spoil," my mother said.

My father shoved the window open and threw the flowers out. He slammed the window down so hard I could feel the floor shake. My mother made a funny sound, like deaf people make sometimes, like a doll saying, "Ma-a-a-a."

Not knowing what else to do, I went in and put the bag on the table. My father came up to me and hugged me with his right arm. Out of the corner of my eye I could see his left hand spelling out to my mother, "A-l-w-a-y-s b-u-s-y." Then he let go of me and went out of the kitchen.

"Think himself," my mother said. "Never help." She meant he never helped her around the house.

"Go down flower?" I asked, meaning should I go down and get the flowers from the alley, but she wrinkled up her nose. "D-o-g pish," she said, meaning dogs pished down there.

"Buy new?" I asked.

"A-l-b-e-r-t fault," she said, meaning it was my father's fault we didn't have enough flowers now and she wasn't going to do anything about it. I followed her into the bedroom and watched her put on lipstick, first making the outline and then filling it in, before she rubbed her lips together and blotted them with tissue. The lipstick was too orangey for her dress.

I waved good-bye to my father and we went out, first to Fort Tryon Park, where the deaf people met around the sandbox in the playground. "Things d-o," my mother told them, so we didn't stay long.

At the Kosher butcher's on Dyckman we got two chickens. I was hoping we'd go to the Five and Ten for something, but we crossed Dyckman and went to Goldin's and got a rye bread, sliced with seeds.

"Last bread," my mother signed to me, while they were slicing, meaning it was the last rye we'd be getting before Passover, when we had matzo instead.

At Nick's Fruits we got some bananas and apples, then we turned the corner onto Nagle. Right away we both noticed there was a new store where the glove store had gone out of business. We went up to the window. There was a cardboard sign with black letters: MAHMOUD'S GARDEN. There were also vases in the window with flowers. Plastic flowers. A woman came out of the store with red roses sticking out of a brown bag.

"O-n-l-y look," my mother said, starting to go in. "J-u-s-t look," she said again as soon as we were in the door.

It was dark inside, probably because the lights on the ceiling weren't spaced close together. Lots of ladies were crowded next to each other, bending over the barrels of plastic flowers lined up against the walls. Each barrel had a different kind and color flower.

When I started signing to my mother, I realized she wasn't next to me anymore. Then I saw her down the aisle, digging in a barrel of red tulips. The chickens and fruit were on the floor between her legs. She looked up. "Ask how much," she signed.

I went up to the man at the cash register and asked him. He stared for a moment like he didn't hear me. His face was large and the color of a Nestle's bar. He had thick black eyebrows and a mustache much bigger than my father's. My father's was a reddish blonde.

"Is that your mother?" the man asked me. "The deaf-and-dumb lady?"

"She's not dumb," I said. "She's a deaf-mute."

"Don't get me wrong. I didn't mean nothing," he said. "Explain to your mother that because she's so beautiful I give her the flowers twenty for a dollar and five for free. For everyone else, it's ten for a dollar."

I didn't tell her the part about being beautiful. I wondered why the dark man said that. My mother was short, only four feet eight inches. Already I was taller than her. She had light brown hair pulled back from her little round face, made into large pompadours on both sides, which she stuck big combs into. She had to hold in her huge bust and stomach with a brassiere and corset. Otherwise the front of her was like two stacked beach balls. But in a dress she didn't look fat. She was wearing her red and white checkered two-piece and black laced oxfords with medium heels from Red Cross Shoes on Dyckman.

We took our time, walking up and down the store, looking into each barrel. All around us ladies were grabbing at the flowers and calling out to each other. Then the dark man came up to us and whispered in my ear, "Tell your mother she is the most beautiful flower in my garden."

My mother was curious what he said. "You pretty," I told her.

She smiled at him with her teeth showing. She had a funny look on her face, like she was trying not to show her feelings. I don't think she liked him. "Clever make friends," she signed to me.

He asked me what she'd said.

I shrugged my shoulders. "Nothing."

"Come on, little sweetheart, what did your mother say? Does she like me?"

"P-e-s-t," I told my mother.

He tried to talk to her himself. Without saying it out loud, he mouthed the word "beautiful" and pointed to her eyes.

My mother has brown eyes, nothing special.

"What is her name?" he asked me.

"Hannah Zimmer," I said. "Know your name," I signed to her.

She smiled.

"You German?" he said. He looked kind of funny. So I said, "My mother's Russian. She was born there."

"My name is Mahmoud Abdullah," he said. "I spell it for you, so you can tell your mother."

When I got done spelling it, my mother said, "T-o-o long, can't remember."

That almost made me giggle.

A lady yelled from the cash register about who was going to take her money. "Sweetheart, I'm coming," he yelled, walking away from us. I could see him watching us as he rang the register. By the time he came back we had picked out three yellow tulips. He sort of pushed his way between us and reached into the barrel. He stuffed a whole handful of yellow tulips into a brown paper bag. "What else? What else?" he asked. "What does she like?" he asked me. He walked up the aisle, grabbing handfuls from different barrels and putting them into the bag, then he gave the bag to my mother.

"How much?" My mother asked him herself, mouthing the words.

He waved his hands.

"Think f-r-e-e?" my mother signed to me. She was smiling so that all her teeth showed.

I don't know why but I felt squirmy inside.

Another lady was yelling by the register, so Mr. Abdullah excused himself. My mother and I just stood there. "See ring," my mother said, pointing to her wedding band. "Know me married," she said.

When Mr. Abdullah came back, he gave my mother a card that said "Mahmoud's Garden" on it. He mouthed to her, "You come back tomorrow morning."

My mother nodded. I could tell she didn't get what he said.

He pointed to the shelf. "I give you a vase tomorrow. Any one you want."

I told my mother.

"Maybe feel sorry, me deaf," she said, blowing him a kiss with her hand to say thank you.

I looked at the shelf to see if there was anything nice. There was a vase with a Chinese Lady on the front of it. Her blue and pink dress had lots of material so there were waves at the bottom of the vase and around the sides. The top of the vase was green and orange. A lot of different flowers could go in it.

He saw me looking. "Tell her she should come back in the morning," he said.

Halfway up Arden Street my mother said she had left the bread at the flower store, so I ran down the block to get it. Mr. Abdullah held up the bag when he saw me. "Where do you live?" he asked.

"Sickles," I lied. "22 Sickles." I wondered if he'd find out, because that was where Marilyn Jaffe lived and I went to her house sometimes after school to help her with long division.

"I'm saving the vase," he said, before I took the bread and
ran up the street.

When I told my mother he wanted to know where we lived,
she shook her head and closed her lips so you could hardly see
the lipstick.

I asked if we were going to get the vase tomorrow.

She thought for a second. "Handsome man," she said.

I didn't see how she could think he was handsome, but then
she thought my father was handsome. That's why she married
him, she told me once.

As soon as we got upstairs I counted the flowers. There were
fifty-seven, more than five dollars worth at the regular price.
My mother washed them, while I had milk and rye bread with
butter. My father had already left for work. When the flowers
were dry, I laid them out according to the colors and put them
in the vases. I had a lot left over, which made me wish for the
Chinese Lady, but I didn't know if I wanted my mother to see
Mr. Abdullah again.

Still, when I woke up the next morning the first thing I
thought of was how to make her. I went to the kitchen but she
wasn't there. She wasn't in the bathroom either, so I went to
the other bedroom where my father was probably still sleeping. I figured she was in there, cleaning drawers or something.
I couldn't believe my eyes when I opened the door. My father
was lying on his back and my mother was sitting on the edge
of the bed next to him. His hands were on top of her breasts.
She jumped up when she saw me. "Go k-i-t-c-h-e-n," she
said.

I poured my own cornflakes and milk in a bowl and read the
Inquiring Photographer. The question was about what people
were giving up for Lent. I knew Glory was giving up desserts.
Then my mother came in and I asked her why my father was
touching her bust, but she said he wasn't.

"Saw," I said.

She shook her head. "Know too much. Like grown-up."
That meant she wasn't going to tell me anything.

It was ten-thirty. Mr. Abdullah said she should see him in

the morning, but she was still in her housedress. She never went anywhere in her housedress except the A&P with her coat on over. She never put her real dress on till the afternoon. I wondered if he would wait.

After lunch, though, my mother didn't get dressed. When I reminded her about the vase, she said, "B-u-s-y, see l-a-t-e-r." I went down with her to the washing machines in the basement. We sat on the folding chairs waiting for the bedspreads to get done. Then we pulled them through the wringer, my mother standing on one side and me on the other. We carried the cart upstairs after that.

Just as I was done handing my mother clothespins to hang the bedspreads out on the washline, my father came in looking for a toothpick. That's when he noticed the flowers. "Buy new?" he asked my mother.

"F-r-e-e, man give," my mother said. "Crazy."

"True?" he asked, like he thought she was lying.

I waved at him. "Man like Mama, give flower," I said.

For some reason, that made him even madder. He grabbed my mother's arm and pulled her out of the kitchen. "I-n-n-o-c-e-n-t," she spelled out to him, before they turned the corner.

Since I knew my mother was going to wash the kitchen window and curtains, I climbed up on the windowsill and got down the rods, then put the chintz curtains into the big sink. I listened for angry sounds from my father, but I couldn't hear any.

Soon my mother came back. She noticed the window right away. "Thank help," she said.

"Daddy mad?" I asked.

"Cool," she said, meaning he had cooled down. She handed me some money, but not for shopping. "Go movie," she said.

"Today?" It was Thursday and usually I went on Saturdays. She gave me thirty-five cents, even though the movie only cost a quarter and I never got more than a nickel for candy.

"E-n-j-o-y," she said.

When I got outside, I started toward where the Loew's was, but on Nagle I crossed the other way and went into Mahmoud's Garden. Mr. Abdullah came running up to me and asked where my mother was. He called her Mrs. Hannahzimmer like it was all one word. I pretended to smile and said she was busy. Then real quick I asked how much the Chinese Lady was, holding out my hand with the quarter and dime in it.

He looked kind of funny all of a sudden and then I realized he was looking outside the store. A dark woman with a brown scarf around her head and some dark children with her were crossing Nagle toward us. It had to be Mrs. Abdullah.

He took the money out of my hand and put the vase in a brown bag and kind of shoved it at me. "Tomorrow," he said, and went to the back of the store.

I held the door open for Mrs. Abdullah. The kids were all fat but she was real skinny. Beautiful and dark, like my friend Glory, without being Negro.

I sat in the library all afternoon, looking at the magazines and trying to read a book, but I kept thinking about Mahmoud Abdullah. I wondered if he was looking for white slaves. Marilyn Jaffe's big sister had told us about white slaves and she wasn't kidding. I tried to imagine how he would get my mother and me into the back of his store to chain us up, before he took us away. I got real mad at him because he must have thought my mother was dumb, just because she was deaf.

At three-thirty, when I figured the movie was over, I went home. My father was napping in his chair, even though he was taking the day off from work. My mother had done the kitchen window, top and bottom, and was washing the curtains. Right away she asked me what was in the brown bag, so I opened it up and took out the Chinese Lady.

She put her fingers over her lips. "Tell A-l-b-e-r-t," she said, meaning I shouldn't say anything to my father. She looked like she was going to say something but she started rubbing the curtains against the washboard. I put the leftover flowers, as many as I could fit, in the Chinese Lady and waited for my mother to turn around. But when she did, she didn't notice.

"Not t-r-u-s-t," she said, meaning Mr. Abdullah. "Touch you?" she asked.

She had told me before about letting men touch me. "Me not stupid," I told her.

"Careful," she said, then took the rubber plug out of the sink. She wrung out the curtains and pointed to the overhead drying rack, which I let down because the washline outside was full. When she was done hanging, I pulled the rope until the rack was close to the ceiling again. My mother still hadn't said anything about the vase.

"Pretty?" I asked her.

"Give f-r-e-e?"

I told her it cost me thirty-five cents.

"N-o movie?"

I shook my head. "L-i-b-r-a-r-y read."

"Devil," my mother said to me, but I could tell she wasn't mad. "Help rug last," she said, meaning I should help her with the rug and that was the last thing we were going to have to do before Passover. First, though, she made me put the Chinese Lady in my room.

We rolled up the rug from the living room, careful not to wake my father, who was snoring. She took one end and I took the other and we carried it up to the roof. She took out a rope from the pocket of her housedress and strung it across, like a washline, between two posts, and we put the rug over it. Then my mother went and got the brushes.

She showed me how to beat on the rug to make the dust come out. Soon we were almost choking and my eyes were burning from the dust. The sky was a bright pink and way above there was a dark gray cloud which I pretended was made from the dust that came out of the rug, to keep from thinking about how my arms were killing me. Switching the brush from one hand to the other didn't help.

The wind started to blow and things were creaking all

around us, which of course my mother couldn't hear so it didn't scare her. I heard a noise like someone was opening one of the doors to the roof. What if it's Mr. Abdullah, I thought, coming to take us away? But it was only Glory and Roy Rogers. She was going to show him her secret hiding place for special rocks, which I already knew about.

"Haven't seen you all week," she said. "You angry or something?"

"I've been helping my mother," I said. "A lot."

"Big deal." When I didn't say anything, she asked if I could come down after supper.

"Okay," I said. I was dying to show her the Chinese Lady before my mother washed it.

"What'cha doing?" Roy Rogers asked.

"Getting the dust out," I said, beating harder to show him.

"A poison cloud!" Glory screamed. Both of them went running across the roof to get away.

My mother stuck her head around the rug. "Give e-x-t-r-a flower G-l-o-r-y," she said, meaning the four red tulips and two white carnations I couldn't get into the Chinese Lady.

I nodded, thinking that maybe I could trade her for a chocolate Easter egg, the kind that had flowers on top in different colors of icing.

Soon the dust stopped coming out. The cloud above was gone, too, and the sky was almost purple. We got the rug off the line and started rolling it up, when I heard a lot of creaking, then heavy footsteps. I told my mother, but I was too scared to look myself. Behind me the footsteps were getting louder. My mother got an expression on her face like she saw something she didn't expect. I was dying.

"S-i-l-l-y," she said. "Daddy."

"Daddy?" I turned around.

"N-e-e-d help?" my father said.

While my mother got down the rope and wound it up in a ball, my father gave me one end of the rug to hold and he took the other. Then we carried it downstairs. Behind us I could hear the heels of my mother's slippers flopping open on each step. I was glad they had made up with each other while I was gone. But I was sure my mother wouldn't let him touch her again you know where.

❦ My Father's Darling

BEFORE Labor Day, Melva asked my father for some money to buy some clothes for school. I was sitting with the cards on the floor in the living room, playing war with myself, and I saw her follow him into the bedroom to ask. I didn't expect him to reach into his pocket and give her the money right away, but he did. So what did Melva do? She told him ten dollars wasn't enough.

"Think me rich?" my father signed.

"You cheapskate," she signed right back, maybe because she couldn't help herself.

In two seconds flat he had her up against the wall and was twisting her arm behind her. She was screaming as I ran to get my mother from the kitchen. "Afraid break arm," my mother said before she rushed to the bedroom.

When we got there, Melva was holding her arms crossed in

front of her face. My father was smacking the side of her head. He sounded like he had a terrible sore throat, yelling, "Honorfatherhonorfatherhonorfather."

My sister sank down to the floor when my father waved my mother away. "Misermisermiser," Melva said, but not in sign language, hardly moving her lips. Like one of those ventriloquists on Ed Sullivan.

My mother tried to stick her arms between my father and Melva, making noises like she was crying. When he turned around, I looked away because I knew what was coming. He pushed my mother so hard she fell down.

Melva didn't get to keep the ten dollars. "He'll get his," she told me. "Everyone gets what's coming to them." She told me it had to be true because she read it in the Old Testament. And then she cried.

After lunch my father said he was going for a walk. Melva was supposed to do the dishes but she said, "I'm getting out of this hell house." That meant she was going to see her best friend, Toni. So I said I'd do the drying. For some reason, Melva gave me a look like she could kill.

My mother filled up the deep sink with suds and put the dishes in. She rinsed them off in the little sink and handed them to me, one by one, until she stopped to talk to me. "Fine, fine, present necklace M-r-s K-l-e-p-p," she signed, shaking her head. She said all the deaf people were gossiping about it. I guess that's how she found out. "Not think first o-w-n daughter," she said.

"Daddy present M-r-s K-l-e-p-p?" I asked. "Why?"

She scrunched up her face like she was going to cry. "Clever, try make like. Understand?" She said my father was probably going to see her on his walk.

I nodded. I didn't really understand why my father was trying to get Mrs. Klepp to like him. She was deaf and lived over on the next block from us.

My mother put her hands in the soapy water. When she

took them out to sign again, she sprayed me. "Sorry," she said, taking the dish towel to brush off some suds from my hair. "Think high c-l-a-s-s. Real t-r-a-m-p."

A tramp was what Melva called the girls in her high school who smoked in the bathroom. I knew Mrs. Klepp was always smoking, but I don't think that's what my mother meant.

"D-o-n-t tell M-e-l-v-a, S-i-d-n-e-y," she said.

Even though Melva and Sidney were much older than me, my mother talked to me like I knew better than they did.

"Shhhh," I told her, hearing the key in the outside door.

My father stuck his head in the kitchen but didn't say anything. I heard him go into the living room where he always took his afternoon nap.

My mother smiled a funny smile. "B-e-t no one home," she said, about Mrs. Klepp.

The next Sunday, when we were all having dinner in the kitchen, my brother asked my father for money to get a catcher's mitt so he could play on the Sluggers. That was the team that was sponsored by O'Hanlon's Tavern on Nagle Avenue.

My father dropped his fork and knife down on his plate on purpose. "N-o play b-u-m-s, Catholic," he signed.

"Not b-u-m-s," my brother signed back. "J-u-s-t play baseball."

"Catholic, no good," my father said, getting a very angry look on his face.

Melva did her ventriloquist act again. Without moving her lips, she said, "Sidney, take it easy."

But by that time my brother was real angry. "I-f Catholic no good, why you friend M-r-s K-l-e-p-p?"

Right away my mother tried to tell my father that Sidney didn't mean what he said. My father told her not to butt in. He told Sidney to go to the bathroom. That meant he was going to get a strapping. For a few seconds we all sat there like stone.

"Go!" my father yelled in his hoarse voice. As he got up he

banged his fist down on the table, hard enough to make the plates jump. My mother stood up in front of him but he pushed her down in the chair. He grabbed Sidney by the arm and pushed him toward the door. A few seconds later my mother went running out of the kitchen after them.

"Why did Sidney say that?" I asked Melva.

"He saw them go into a movie together. Downtown. But don't tell Mama. It would hurt her feelings."

"Why does Daddy like Mrs. Klepp?"

"She's a tramp," Melva said.

When we heard Sidney screaming, we went in the living room. We could even hear the belt every time my father hit him. My mother was crying outside the bathroom door.

"I could murder him," Melva said. "He doesn't deserve to live."

I went back into the kitchen and put my hands over my ears.

That night I heard my father come home from the U.L., which is short for Union League of the Deaf, where he went to play cards on Saturdays and some afternoons before going to work at the post office. I would wake up sometimes when he came home and listen to him go through his routine. I could hear him hang up his jacket in the hallway closet and open and close the frigidaire before he sat down in the kitchen to read the *Daily News* with a snack, probably pumpernickel with prune butter, which was his favorite. I saw him once through the hallway mirror, but he didn't see me watching him, and he couldn't hear me, of course.

After he got done in the kitchen, I heard him praying outside the room I shared with Melva, beneath the mezuzah. He made smacking sounds. I knew he was kissing his palm and then the shiny gold case that my sister explained has the parchment with writings from the Bible. I could even hear him mumbling in Hebrew. He made more smacking sounds before he went into the bathroom. Like always, I heard the toilet flush and the sink water running for a long, long time (which I could never figure out), then his footsteps back past our room and into the bedroom where my mother was already sleeping.

"Do you think he was sorry?" I asked my pretend-friend Mary, who was lying next to me. Mary said if he was really sorry he would stop making everyone so miserable.

"I hate him," I told her.

Mary said that was terrible, especially after how nice he was to me. I was the only one who didn't get into trouble with him. I told her that when she was bigger she would understand, and then she fell asleep. I tried to think of something to do that would make my family happier but I fell asleep before I thought of anything.

On Saturday morning I went roller-skating. Robin Reinstein and Tommy Shanahan came around the corner with me, so we could skate in the street without anyone seeing, but at the last minute Robin got chicken and stayed on the sidewalk, so it was just Tommy and me, out in the middle of Sherman Avenue. The street is a lot smoother than the scratchy sidewalk and doesn't have all those cracks, so it's a lot more fun to skate.

I was coming down real fast toward Arden when I heard my brother's booming voice calling, "Ruthie!" I stopped so fast I fell, and before I could get up I heard a car screeching on its brakes just a few inches from where I was. The next thing I knew, my brother lifted me right up and put me down on the sidewalk where Melva was. They were both dressed up because they had just come from Temple.

"What the hell are you doing in the street?" Sidney yelled, so that everyone could hear, including Tommy Shanahan. When Tommy saw me looking at him, he disappeared around the corner of Arden Street. Robin was gone by then.

"Daddy would kill you if he saw," Sidney said.

"Her? He wouldn't lay a finger on her," Melva said. "She's her father's darling. Aren't you!" she said, smiling real sarcastic like.

"I don't ask for trouble," I said. "That's why I'm around the corner."

"Well if I ever see you skate in the street again . . ." Sidney threatened, but he didn't finish because when I looked down at my knee and saw it was all bloody I started to cry. "Go upstairs and put iodine on," he said.

I skated ahead of them, took off my skates, and ran upstairs. My father woke up from his nap and came in the kitchen while my mother was putting Mercurochrome on, since iodine hurts so much. I told him I fell skating, but not where.

"You not watch right," he said to my mother, practically standing over her.

"Can't know what d-o-i-n-g, every minute," she said to him. She put the Band-Aid on my knee.

"Not f-i-t mother," he told her.

"Why me, me? You never watch," she said. "A-l-l t-i-m-e m-e."

I got out of there and went to tell Mary what happened. She said it wasn't my fault, and then my father came in.

"Want go U-L with me?" he asked.

"Now?"

He hadn't taken me to his club for a long time. I always liked going, especially because of the subway ride downtown. I said okay.

"First change dress," he said, because he liked me to look nice when I went with him.

He dressed up, too, in his brown suit. I saw him brushing his hair with the brush my Aunt Lois gave him for his birthday. It had a real silver back. He combed his mustache with the matching comb. His hair in both places was strawberry blonde, like in the song my brother liked to sing about this man Casey waltzing.

When we got to the U.L., which is in the basement of a hotel on 72nd Street, my father acted very different. He waved hello to everyone, real friendly, with a big smile. He was very handsome when he smiled, my mother said. The room was smoky on account of the cigarettes and cigars from the men who sat at the folding tables playing cards, waving their arms as they signed and making grunting noises. There were only a few women. They looked up when my father took me around. The deaf people always asked the same questions. This time it was Mr. Fiorini who asked, "Can sign?" meaning me.

"A-s-k," my father said, meaning he should ask me, so he did.

"I can sign," I told him.

"Wonderful!" Mr. Fiorini said.

I never knew why they thought it was such a big deal that I could sign, just because I could hear. My father looked awfully happy.

We went over to a table where Mr. Weisbaum, Max Cohen, and Mrs. Klepp were sitting right under a fluorescent light, the kind with long tubes. Mr. Weisbaum was wearing his yarmulke, of course. He and my father made jokes in Hebrew, which I didn't understand. They said the Hebrew out loud (I don't know if you can even sign in Hebrew), reading each other's lips. Both of them were bar mitzvahed, which my Uncle Sol said was really something, because they were deaf.

Max Cohen and my father went to the horse races together sometimes. Max Cohen bet a lot, my mother said, and was always in trouble with his wife, Mrs. Cohen. One year he didn't go to the U.L. because he was in Florida, hiding from the bookies.

Mrs. Klepp was one of the few women who went to the U.L. She got in because her husband was a member, but Mr. Klepp wasn't there. "How g-a-m-e?" she asked my father, meaning baseball.

"Not hear," my father said, meaning no one had told him the score. When Sidney was home, he listened to the game on the radio and told my father what was happening.

As Mrs. Klepp signed, smoke came up from the cigarette hanging out the side of her mouth. When the cigarette was between her fingers, smoke came all around us, because she waved her arms a lot.

"You millionaire," my father teased her, about the money she spent on cigarettes.

"Me win poker, can a-f-f-o-r-d smoke all day," she said, and then they both laughed.

I never saw my father laugh at home. He sat down at the table and I sat on a chair next to him and watched Max Cohen deal the cards. I knew a little about poker but not enough to play. I looked over Mrs. Klepp's clothes. She had on a beige cardigan and a black straight skirt, like a high school girl. My mother wore dresses with flowers on them, unless they were pastels. She said Mrs. Klepp was a show-off, but I couldn't figure out what she meant, unless it was the high heels.

After a while I got up and went to the buffet table to get a slice of American cheese, which I ate real fast. My father didn't like me to eat it without bread, for some reason. Mrs. Jacobs got some paper and pens for me to draw with from the office. I wasn't very good at drawing, so I wrote a story about a boy and his dog. The dog runs away, so his father hits him and says it's the boy's fault, but later the father buys him another dog. I knew my father wouldn't ask me to show it to him.

At four-thirty my father had to leave to go to the post office. He wanted Mrs. Klepp to walk him to the subway but she wanted to play more poker, so she stayed. I had to stay, too, since she was taking me home.

They got a sub for my father in the game, Mr. Fiorini. He teased me about being a great poker player like my father. "A-l-b-e-r-t b-e-s-t," he said. "Me g-l-a-d he leave."

I saw my father take all the coins off the table, so I knew he'd won.

When they were done playing, Mrs. Klepp lit up a cigarette. She asked me, "How brother?" and when I said fine, "How sister?" Then she wanted to know what my mother was doing that afternoon. I shrugged.

I thought we were going to leave when she got up, but she

had me walk her over to another table, where Mrs. Gertzner was. She was a friend of my mother's although we didn't see her very often. She lived in Brooklyn, near the Steeplechase, with a blind and deaf husband. He could read the sign language by feeling your hand when you signed. My mother said Mrs. Gertzner went to the U.L. to get away from her worries.

Mrs. Gertzner asked me how my mother was. "Home?"

"Fine," I told her. "Ironing."

Mrs. Klepp said, "R-u-t-h my daughter. See, same dimples. Me her mother."

Mrs. Gertzner said, "You wish."

"You fresh?" Mrs. Klepp asked.

"You hungry A-l-b-e-r-t," Mrs. Gertzner said, meaning my father.

Then Mrs. Klepp said, "I smack your face."

"D-a-r-e," Mrs. Gertzner spelled out slowly. "You d-a-r-e."

And Mrs. Klepp did. Mrs. Gertzner smacked her back. Then they started pulling each other's hair and clothes, until the men stopped them. Then Mrs. Klepp took me home.

On the subway ride to Dyckman Street, Mrs. Klepp told me how fresh Anna Gertzner was. "You see yourself. Fresh. Say me hungry A-l-b-e-r-t."

"Maybe true," I signed, suddenly feeling like I couldn't breathe. My heart was pounding so fast I could hear it over the roar of the train.

"You fresh," she said. "I tell your father."

"I tell my mother," I said, looking right into her eyes, which were like blue marbles.

We went the rest of the way without signing.

When I got home, I wanted to tell Melva, but I decided not to, so I told Mary. She said I should apologize to God for being fresh, and I did. I said that if He didn't let Mrs. Klepp tell my father about it, I'd do good things for people when I grew up, like become a nurse.

The next Saturday my father said he couldn't take me to the U.L. because Mrs. Klepp had a dentist appointment, so there wouldn't be anyone to take me home. I nodded, trying not to show him how happy I was, but I felt like bursting. He looked at me real funny. For a second I wondered if he could read my mind, like he was God.

Behind his back I shouted, "Mrs. Klepp is ugly and stupid!"

My father turned around very suddenly. That really scared me, but he didn't say anything. I started to skip out of the room. "She's ugly and stupid!" I shouted again.

"Ruth!" he roared, real loud. He only yelled that loud when he was very angry. When I turned, I saw him waving at me to come back. I crossed my toes and walked slowly toward him. He reached into his pants pocket and took out a quarter and gave it to me. A nickel was what he usually gave me on Saturdays.

"You love father?" he asked.

I nodded.

"Show me."

I threw my arms around him and hugged him. He gave me a kiss that made a big smacking sound on my cheek. "You good girl," he said.

I took the quarter and put it under my blouses in the dresser drawer, then got my skates. Tommy Shanahan was already on the stoop when I got there. He dared me to skate Nagle.

"You're crazy," I told him. "You can get killed on Nagle from all the trucks."

So we went around the corner and skated Sherman Avenue until eleven-thirty, which is when Sidney and Melva got out of Temple.

On Monday, when I was coming home from school, I saw a police car in front of the stoop. When I got almost to the fourth landing, there was a policeman standing in our doorway. Next to him I saw my father and then another policeman in the foyer, and my mother holding a bloody handkerchief over her nose. The cops seemed very glad I was there to interpret.

"Ask your mother if she wants to press charges," one cop said.

I made the sign for "press" like in "iron" and "charges" like in "price." I knew that made no sense, but I didn't know what "press charges" meant.

My mother stopped crying. She signed, "Go jail."

"I think my mother wants him to go to jail," I said, not looking at my father and trying not to move my mouth very much, so he couldn't lip-read me.

He looked pretty sick when they made signs like he had to come with them. I grabbed onto his leg. "I'm sorry," the policeman said to me when he took my hands off.

When they left, my mother told me how my father had pushed her down on the kitchen floor and beaten her up. She thought our neighbor, Mrs. Cafferty, must of called the police.

"Who s-u-p-p-o-r-t me and children?" she kept saying. Then she answered her own question. "S-t-a-r-v-e," she said, meaning we'd all starve with my father in jail. I couldn't help crying. I was afraid I'd never see him anymore.

When my brother came home from working in the cleaners, my mother told him to go to the police station and get my father. "Change mind," she said to tell the police.

"Sonofabitch," Sidney said. "It's one thing when he picks on me, but using his fists on a woman . . ."

While he was gone, Melva came home from baby-sitting. "Oh, God!" she said when she saw my mother's swollen face and the bruises on her arm. "Stay jail," she told my mother. "He should rot there," she said to me. "He deserves to die for every rotten thing he's done."

My brother came back alone. He told my mother that after my father got out of jail he decided to go to the U.L.

"Funny, not work," my mother said.

Then Sidney called the post office to tell them Mr. Zimmer had a toothache and to charge it to sick leave.

We all sat around the kitchen table after that. My mother was knitting a sweater for me. Sidney had the *Daily Mirror* open in front of him on the table but he wasn't really reading it. Melva was saying terrible things about my father and sometimes she'd start to cry, which made me cry.

"Sonofabitch," my brother said again. "I could kill him. Just pick up a knife and let him have it while he's asleep. He'd never hear me coming."

"Sidney!" Melva said. "You better ask God to forgive you."

When my mother asked what we were talking about, all Melva said was "Daddy." Melva told Sidney and me she should be the one to kill him, though, because they weren't so tough on girls. "They might put me in reform school for a while," she said, "but you'd have to go to jail." She meant Sidney.

That's when I got the idea. They would never suspect me if I did it. For one thing, I wasn't a grown-up. For another, I was my father's darling.

That night I woke up when I heard the double locks open on the outside door. Mary and I lay in the dark, listening, while my father went through his whole routine, kissing the mezuzah on the door, leaving the sink water running, and then going to bed. I told Mary not to worry, and then I got up real carefully, so as not to wake Melva, who's a real light sleeper. I didn't have to worry about waking up Sidney. I could hear him snoring as I went past his hide-a-bed in the living room on the way to the kitchen.

My mother came in while I was looking through the kitchen drawer for the big knife. I forgot that the light always wakes her up. It shines into the hallway mirror and into her bedroom.

"What d-o-i-n-g?" she asked me.

"Hungry," I said. "Make sandwich."

"Big girl," she said, but she made the sandwich for me, shmeering some peanut butter on rye bread.

After I ate it, we both went back to bed. I thought a lot about what to do next time. It got light out before I fell asleep.

The next day was Rosh Hashanah. My mother made a big dinner, with chicken soup and matzo balls and potato pancakes. She and my father weren't speaking, though. Her eye was still swollen and there was a little scar under her nose. After dinner my father didn't go to work because of the holiday. He and my Uncle Sol went to the Orthodox synagogue. Sidney and Melva went to the Reform. My mother and I hung out the window. When she went to the bathroom, I ran and got the knife from the kitchen and put it under my pillow.

As soon as she came back to the window, she asked, "What wrong?"

"Nothing," I told her.

"Devil?" she said.

"No," I said, but she looked like she didn't believe me.

It was hard staying awake after everyone went to bed. I told Mary a lot of stories I remembered from the books I read from the 207th Street Library. When I heard my sister breathing like she was asleep, I took the knife out from under the pillow and went to the other bedroom. I had to stand in the doorway a while, until I could see in the dark, then I went over to the bed.

My heart was pounding so loud that I thought I might have a heart attack and die. I told myself to hurry and get it over with. I jabbed the knife in my father's back, over his pajama top. Nothing happened, except he made some funny sounds before he started his regular snore. I tried harder. This time my father jerked and his arm slapped my mother, who woke up. She saw me right away. I dropped the knife on the floor and kicked it under the bed before she came around to where I was. "Sick?" she asked me.

"Headache," I told her, but she couldn't see what I said, so we went over to the window where there was moonlight. I signed, "Headache," again.

We went to the bathroom and got a Bayer's. In the kitchen she looked in the drawer for the big knife to cut it in half. "Funny, gone," she said. She used another one and gave me half to take. "Go bed," she said. "Me stay read. Can't sleep, think too much A-l-b-e-r-t."

On my way back I remembered that my mother dusted with the mop every morning under her bed, so I couldn't leave the knife there. I went to get it, but I couldn't see where it was in the dark. While I was down on my knees feeling around, my father got up. I rolled all the way under the bed, practically dying. When he went to the bathroom, I grabbed the knife and ran back to the bedroom. I could hardly breathe I was so scared.

After he flushed the toilet, I heard him go through the living room. I put the knife under my pillow and went to the hallway just outside the kitchen and peeked in the mirror.

My father was kissing my mother. Real kissing. On the lips, which I'd never seen him do. He was bending her slightly back over the kitchen table. Their arms were around each other, like in the movies. For a second I thought he might be trying to smother her, but then they stood up straight.

"Bed?" my father asked her.

My mother nodded.

He started walking out of the kitchen. Just before she pulled the light cord, I saw her stick her tongue out at his back.

I ran for dear life through the living room and almost squashed Mary when I jumped into bed. In a little while I heard funny noises coming from the other bedroom. I was scared my father was beating my mother again, but I didn't hear her crying or anything. I put the pillow over my head and Mary's and we fell asleep.

In the morning my mother was in the kitchen, so I couldn't put the knife back. I hid it in the dresser drawer where I kept the quarter my father had given me. When I came home from school, my mother was ironing my father's shirts.

"Make u-p," she said, meaning she made up with my father. She was smiling kind of funny.

I wondered how come. "Daddy pray sorry?" I asked her.

She shrugged. "Brother uncle advise," she said, meaning my Uncle Sol had told my father to do it. "Not believe pray."

"Not believe G-o-d?" I asked her, to make sure.

"Good teach children, that a-l-l."

"S-i-n not believe," I told her, which is what Melva had told me.

"Shh," she said, placing a finger over her lips. "N-o tell Daddy."

I put a finger over my lips.

She gave me a shirt of my father's to hang up. Carefully, I buttoned the top button, like she taught me once. "You very d-a-r-l-i-n-g. A-l-b-e-r-t l-u-c-k-y," she said.

I burst out crying but I wouldn't tell her why.

"You sorry see me hurt," she said, pointing to the large reddish purple mark on her upper arm. "D-o-n-t worry, will better," she said, telling me that she and my father were going to the movies later and my sister would baby-sit me. Then she squeezed me against her soft round belly and big bust.

Later I got the knife back into the kitchen drawer, but I couldn't figure out what to do with the quarter. Mary said I should give it back because I didn't deserve it.

On Yom Kippur, when everyone was in Temple except my mother, who was hanging out the window to see what people were wearing, I did something I'd never done before. I kissed the mezuzah. It wasn't easy, because it was way up high on the doorjamb. I had to jump up a couple of times to reach it and I didn't know the right prayer. I told God I was sorry and that if He could forgive my father, maybe He could forgive my mother, too, because she didn't mean Him any harm. I was going to promise not to skate in the street anymore, but at the last minute I thought of something better. I told God I would bury the quarter in the garden. If it was still there on my next birthday, that would mean I was supposed to have it.

"Hungry o-r f-a-s-t?" my mother asked when I went to the window.

"F-a-s-t," I said. "You?"

She nodded.

"Why? You not believe."

"You devil, t-o-o many nosey," she said, but I could tell she wasn't angry or anything.

After I got dressed I went down to the stoop and climbed over the wrought-iron on top of the little brick wall around the garden. I buried the quarter in the ground where we fed the sparrows sometimes, between the middle two bushes, four steps from the building.

As I was climbing out, my father came up the stoop. "Why there?" he asked.

"Play," I said.

"Not play today. Religious holiday," he said.

Behind him, Melva and Sidney were walking up the first level. Sidney was in his good suit and Melva was wearing a coat she got secondhand from our Cousin Rona in New Jersey. But she had on her new shoes, with high heels and straps across, like Mrs. Klepp's.

"What me say?" my father signed to me, real gruff.

"Uh oh, she's gonna get hers," Melva said, loud so I could hear.

"Not play," I said. "Sorry," I told him.

When my father started coming toward me, Sidney rushed up. I guess he thought my father was going to hit me, but all he did was kiss me on the forehead. Melva gave me this look, · like she was real disgusted.

My father turned and saw them. His face got all cranky. "Not think sister, bring Temple," he said to them, meaning they should of taken me with them to synagogue. I could see Sidney getting angry back. "Jesus Christ!" he said out loud.

"Be careful," I told them, without moving my lips.

"Shut up!" Melva said to me, without moving hers. "We know what side you're on."

By this time my father was yelling so that everyone on the stoop could hear him. I kept my eyes on the ground, even though I could feel Melva looking daggers at me. Later she would do an imitation of us talking like ventriloquists and Sidney would imitate my father yelling and we'd all get hysterical, but right then I stood there with my face burning, wishing myself dead.

❦ Begin the Beguine

THE day before my Cousin Rona's wedding, my Aunt Sadie called from New Jersey. "Tell Mother she shouldn't bring anything," she said.

My mother was by the window sewing. I had to stomp my feet a few times before she felt the vibrations and looked up.

"S-a-d-i-e telephone," I told her in sign language.

My mother got up all excited and knocked the picture frame off the table. "Stupid, hurry," she signed. Of course, she couldn't hear her slippers crunching the glass.

She stood next to me by the phone the whole time I was interpreting back and forth.

"What n-e-w-s?" she asked me to ask Aunt Sadie.

Aunt Sadie said my Uncle Ben was more nervous about the wedding than Rona. Then my aunt asked how everyone was feeling. Then she asked what everyone was doing. I told her my mother was hemming the coat she sent us which used to be

Natalie's. It had a mouton collar and cuffs on account of my Uncle Ben being rich from his car business. I didn't tell her my sister wouldn't wear the sweater from Rona, which my mother said was foolish.

Finally Aunt Sadie said, "I only wish your grandmother was alive. Not in her wildest dreams, darling, I can tell you . . ." I didn't know what she meant about the dreams, so I just interpreted the first part to my mother.

After I got off the phone, my mother said, "M-i-s-s, sorry never see you." She pointed to the picture of my grandmother in the frame she'd knocked down. "W-i-g," she reminded me. My grandmother kept her head covered and she had to meet my grandfather through a matchmaker on account of being Orthodox. He always wore a yarmulke, but in the picture he's wearing a top hat. He came to America by himself the first time because my grandmother didn't want to go, but he went back to get her and my mother and my Aunt Sadie.

"Plane?" I asked my mother, even though I knew the answer.

"N-o plane, old-fashioned ship slow." She told me again about getting off the big boat in New York. When the men questioned them, she hid behind my grandmother's skirt to pretend she was shy. They didn't allow deaf-mutes into America for some reason, but she got in.

My mother swept up the floor and took out the pieces of glass that were still stuck in the frame.

"Why n-o other picture Grandma?" I asked her. We had lots of pictures of everyone except her. My sister told me once there was some big secret why, but she made up lots of stories, so you never knew.

My mother shrugged. She looks funny when she isn't telling everything. She pressed her thin lips together and raised her eyebrows. "Nothing," she said, and then to get my mind off it she pointed to the wedding picture of her and my father on the other side of the frame.

"Handsome," she signed slowly, like she was remembering.

She always says that about the wedding picture and the pictures of my father playing basketball at the Lexington School for the Deaf. But this time she told me something I never knew before: she almost married another man. She said he was a Socialite, which I guess means a big deal. On account of his being very rich. But the reason she didn't marry him was that he could hear.

She imagined what it would be like when they were out with his hearing friends. "Think me stupid, deaf, d-u-m-b," she said. She figured he would leave her home most of the time.

"Very rich?" I asked her.

"Millions," she said. "Family high c-l-a-s-s."

"Why like you?"

"P-e-a-r-l teeth," my mother said, which was really silly. She was always telling me how white her teeth used to be when she was young. Everyone called her Pearl, instead of her Jewish name, Chana, or her American name, Hannah. "Think me beautiful," she said, about the Socialite.

As a bride my mother looks pretty nice, with the flowers around her head and the long white veil and dress, and she has a real big smile that shows her dimples, but I wouldn't of said she was beautiful. In some of the other pictures I've seen, she's even a little fat or looks like a tomboy, especially in the middy uniform she wore for school. She didn't go there long because her family was so poor her father made her go to work as a seamstress.

"Why marry Daddy?" I asked, even though I knew the answer.

"Talk smooth. Dimples like actor G-a-b-l-e," she said.

She told me again how the lady at the knitting store on Delancey Street where she got all her wool introduced them. "No good marry, father advise," my mother said, because he was always playing pool instead of helping his family in their dairy store.

"Enough look back," my mother said. If she finished hemming the coat we could go to 207th Street and get new glass for the frame. I went to get my ruler to measure it. When I brought it, she was looking out the window, not sewing. She didn't feel the vibrations of my footsteps. Finally she saw me. "T-o-o late, sorry," she said, about marrying my father.

The space where the wedding picture went was eight inches across and ten inches high, although the picture was smaller than that. My mother and father look really happy in it. I wish they could of stayed that way.

My sister tried on a dozen outfits before she decided on the black dress for Rona's wedding. My mother tried to tell her she shouldn't wear black to a wedding because it's bad luck for the bride, but Melva had made up her mind. It cost her a whole paycheck for the dress but she said she didn't care, she was making up for all the hand-me-downs we got from Rona and Natalie. I hated wearing Natalie's dress to Rona's wedding, even though it came from Lord & Taylor's, but all I had were the awful things my father had bought in the wholesale factory that made me look like some freak.

I swear it took Melva three hours to do her hair and face. When she walked into the kitchen, my father said, "B-u-m," meaning she looked like a tramp. She did have a lot of pancake makeup on and too much black eyebrow pencil, but anyway men usually thought she was gorgeous, like Jane Russell.

"Shame," my father said.

I thought Melva was going to curse him under her breath like usual without moving her lips so he couldn't read them, but she just made her green eyes tiny like little emeralds. Then she took out a brown bag from under the counter and put it over her head. "Better?" she signed. She left it over her head until the phone rang. She messed up her hair she was in such a hurry to take it off, in case it was Jeff Feinberg.

"Crazy," my father said about Melva when my mother came in, all dressed up. She had on my favorite, the red and white check dress, with a necklace that had lots of strands of teensy red beads. Her hair was in a big wave on top and pulled back on the sides. The rest hung down to her neck.

"Who telephone?" my mother asked me.

I got up and went into the foyer to listen for a second. When I heard Melva saying, "Uh uh," really soft, I knew it was Jeff.

"Boyfriend," I told my mother.

Then my brother came into the kitchen with his new brown suit. "Melva looks like a *shiksa*," Sidney said, meaning a woman who isn't Jewish. While we waited for her to get off the phone, we looked at the *Daily Mirror*. Sidney said he was going to vote for the Democrats because most of them came up the hard way.

We took the subway downtown to where the synagogue was. A lot of the wedding was in Hebrew, but my brother explained it to me. At the end the bridegroom steps on a glass on the floor till it breaks, because it has to do with when the Jews were killed in Jerusalem. It's supposed to remind you to keep your promises or your marriage will be very unhappy.

Rona's gown had a long train in back and pearls sewn in all over. My mother said it must of cost a thousand dollars. "Can a-f-f-o-r-d," she said about my Uncle Ben. Sidney said the wedding was a good investment because the Zuckermans, who were the bridegroom's family, got in on the ground floor of the washing machine business and were millionaires. Melva said that could be the only reason Rona was marrying Morty because he was ugly as sin.

I didn't think he was so ugly, except for all the holes in his face. I counted thirty-three. He wore a tuxedo, like my Uncle Ben and the men who walked down the aisle with the bridesmaids. They had light orange dresses—organdy, I think. My Aunt Sadie cried a lot, but later, when she was dancing with him, she told Sidney the day was her crowning glory.

We got a ride from the synagogue to the Capitol Hotel in two different cars. The hotel was very fancy, with chandeliers as big as the ones in Radio City Music Hall, even in the ballroom, where the orchestra was playing. While we were looking at the ice sculptures of fish and birds on the long table with all the canapés, my mother stuffed a bunch of the orange matchbooks, which had "Rona & Morty" on them in gold, into her pocketbook.

"Plenty time, dance," my mother said, about the couples on the dance floor. She told us to help ourselves to the cana-pés so we wouldn't get hungry before dinner.

There were three women we didn't know sitting at our table. One had a big picture hat and the other two had little hats with veils and fur stoles, a silver fox and a sable, which Melva whispered was the most expensive kind. I guess they could tell we were talking about them because they started to talk to us.

"May we introduce ourselves? We're from the Philadelphia branch of the bridegroom's family," the sable lady said. "I pre-sume you're related to the bride."

I'd never heard anyone talk that way except in the movies. Even my father's family, who were rich, Aunt Lois especially, didn't talk like that.

"So glad to make your acquaintance," said the woman who was wearing the silver fox.

"S-i-l-l-y hot," my mother said, about the furs, but after a while they took them off, even though they kept their hats on.

Everything was hunky-dory until the dinner, which started with the chopped liver. After Melva started eating it with her spoon, the sable lady picked up her small fork and said, "I think this is the implement you want, dear."

"Who do you think you are?" my sister said to her, real loud.

All of a sudden I wished we hadn't gone. Sidney started to say something but changed his mind. I put my big fork down and picked up the small one, which made Melva say, "Don't be a phony baloney," which she said to me when I started trying to talk like Jean Simmons in that movie with Stewart Granger.

During the chicken soup Rona came to our table. She hung

over Sidney's shoulders like she was flirting with him, showing a lot of her capped teeth. "My mother-in-law, Morty's mother, gave me a Jewish cookbook," she told us. "I'm going to learn to make matzo balls as good as those," she said, meaning the ones in our soup.

When I signed it for my parents, my father told me to tell her she would make Morty a good Jewish wife.

Rona went all around the table to show off her wedding band with lots of little diamonds. My mother mouthed to her that her engagement ring was beautiful.

Around the big diamond were sapphires. "Birthstone," she mouthed to my mother. My mother shook her head like she couldn't get over it.

After Rona went to the next table, my father said to Melva, "Why not learn you cook?" She just glared at him. He used to smack her when she looked like that, but after she graduated high school and got a job he stopped hitting her.

Under her breath Melva said, "Some joke, Rona's gonna have a maid to cook."

"D-o-n-t teach fresh," my father said to Melva, but of course he didn't know what we were saying. "Stubborn, o-l-d m-a-i-d."

"O-n-l-y twenty," my mother said. "Still young." She had been twenty when she got married, but she was trying to make peace.

"Not worry, you get r-i-d o-f me," Melva told my father, which surprised me. I didn't know she was planning to marry Jeff Feinberg. She was always fighting with him because he wanted her to go all the way. My mother had no idea, so she kept telling Melva that Jeff would make a good husband because he worked steady in his father's tie factory.

When Melva went to the ladies' room, my father said to my mother, "Never cook, never marry. Stubborn." When my mother tried to argue, he said, "You know nothing," reminding her about Ronald Cohen, who had taken Melva to the high school prom. Melva didn't date him after that because she said he looked like a mama's boy.

"Nothing, b-a-b-y f-a-t," my mother told her. "Important b-i-g heart. Learn grow l-o-v-e." But Melva got furious and said she just wasn't attracted.

While she was gone, Melva's roast beef got cold, which got my father all upset. That's when I wondered what the Socialite would of been like if he'd of been my father. I mean, if he had a bad temper, or was the kind who might have taken us to restaurants with tablecloths and to the Music Hall. Since he was rich we could of sat in the loge and even lived in my most favorite building in the world, 1025 Fifth Avenue, which I was sure had an elevator. You could see the air conditioners from the Fifth Avenue bus, and the doorman.

Melva came back to the table with a whole lot of lipstick on. She didn't eat anything except the peas, which she mashed with the back of her fork. She kept making cracks about the noises my father made chewing. I had to agree with her. The Socialite wouldn't of eaten like that. He would never of used the knife for a toothpick either. My mother pretended like she didn't see. Anyhow, it was her fault for marrying him.

All this stuff was going on but you'd never know it when the photographer showed up to take our picture. When he said, "Cheese!" we were all smiles, our heads all together and our arms around each other. Then he took a picture of the three women just before Uncle Ben came over and introduced himself to them.

"Darlings, are you having a good time?" he asked them.

"With Rothstein's you can't miss," the lady with the sable said, which I didn't understand.

"The roast beef is always lean," said the one in the picture hat. "You can count on it."

"Uncle Ben, you went all out," Sidney said.

Uncle Ben nodded. "My daughter only gets married once," he said, handing him and my father cigars, even though my father didn't smoke and Sidney smoked Pall Malls. "When's your turn coming up, darling?" he asked Melva. "Are you going steady yet?"

She stood up and looked at him kind of funny. "When hell

freezes over," she said, her eyes like slits. After she signed she was going home, she left. Just like that.

My father shook his head, disgusted. My mother told me to tell Uncle Ben she was sorry.

He stuck his hands out like you do to see if it's raining. "Tell her naturally Melva's jealous," which I did. "Between you and I, she never had nothing," he told Sidney and me, which we didn't mention, with my father sitting right there. "When the right fella comes along . . ." he started, but he didn't finish. Instead he told us some jokes, one in Jewish, which Sidney understood.

He made a sign with his fist like he was drinking, and got my mother to go with him for a little schnapps. When he brought her back, she was acting silly, laughing at nothing. "Feel g-o-o-d," she kept saying, over and over.

Uncle Ben gave a real big sigh. "Be happy. God bless you, Hannah." He said, "God bless you," again, exaggerating the way he moved his lips, so my mother could understand. He leaned down and kissed her on the forehead.

When they brought the parfait, my mother asked my father to dance.

"Know not interested. Why ask? Make trouble?" my father said.

"Forget self, good time," my mother said, like she was try-ing to convince him.

"Your relatives stink," he told her. "Think wonderful? Why sit table b-a-c-k? Ashamed deaf?" he said.

My mother shook her head. "N-o, n-o."

Suddenly my father got up, shoving the chair into the table with a bang, and walked away. My mother was pretty sure he was only going to the men's room.

"Why does he always have to be such a killjoy?" Sidney said. *Meshugge*, he called my father, which means crazy.

A few minutes later Sidney took my mother to dance and I was sitting there by myself, except for the three women across the way. The one in the fox stole asked me the usual questions about my parents, how come I could hear and all that. I tried to be polite. The one wearing a big picture hat thought it was so wonderful my mother could dance, which was really stupid. My mother was very graceful and a good follower. She and Sidney were doing the fox-trot with dips and everything. They were still dancing when my father came back.

He said my mother's family were all snobs, especially Aunt Sadie. What could I say? My mother said his family thought they were too good for us. I knew my Aunt Sadie didn't like him because of his beating up my mother. "Thanks God he's civil to you," she told me once. "Maybe because you're the baby." It took me a while to find "civil" in the dictionary because I thought it started with an "s."

"Nice m-u-s-i-c," I told my father, to change the subject. Just then, though, the orchestra stopped so the emcee could introduce three girl singers all in pink, even their hats, long gloves, and high heels. One of the women across the table said it was a famous trio and it must of cost a fortune to hire. I didn't tell my father.

My mother came back without Sidney. He was talking to some people, she said. She was giggling again because she had another schnapps. It was funny to see her like that because the only time she and my father ever drank was on New Year's Eve, when they had cherry herring. I tasted it once when they didn't know. It was like cough medicine, which could make me vomit.

After they cut the giant wedding cake, which had different colored layers in vanilla, chocolate, and green for pistachio, Sidney came back to the table with a very tall blonde named Delores. She had on a shiny aqua dress cut low in front so you could see the top of her bust and a huge bow almost on her behind.

"Look Protestant," my mother signed to me about Delores.

I almost died when Delores nodded yes to my mother. She knew sign language, it turned out, because her mother and father were deaf, too. My parents didn't know them, though, because they lived in California. Delores explained she wasn't living with them because she was going to college in New

Jersey, which is how she met Rona. But she was still going and Rona wasn't, since Rona was going to be a housewife now and have babies.

I liked Delores right off. My mother did too because she knew the sign language, but my father acted real peculiar. Sidney told Delores I was in a special program on account of my I.Q., which she thought was great. She asked me if I liked to read and what my favorite book was.

A Stone for Danny Fisher, I told her, and then wondered if I should of. I read it while baby-sitting at the Dorfmanns.

"My God!" she said, "did you understand everything?"

I nodded, but I remembered this one part where Miriam is afraid on her wedding night.

"That was real sad," Delores said, putting a cigarette in her mouth, which my brother lit. "I like the part where Miriam's mother tells her she better be sure that she loves him because she'll have to live with her decision the rest of her life."

It was as if Delores had read my mind. "It was awful," I said, about Miriam. Delores asked if I'd read *Gone with the Wind*, and when I said no, she told me she would get it for me. She meant to keep. All I had were Nancy Drews, which I got from Natalie and Rona. Everything else came from the library because my father didn't give my mother extra money. My mother always said he was saving up his overtime from the post office to buy a gold brick for his headstone.

Then the orchestra leader announced that by special request of the bride they would play "Begin the Beguine." Rona had taught me to play the melody with the right hand on her accordion. Rona was terrific on the accordion. She played at bar mitzvahs and weddings, even though she didn't need the money. Rona and Morty got up to dance, and then my Aunt Sadie and Uncle Ben, and then Natalie with a real cute boy, probably from her class, but he didn't dance very good.

"This one's ours," Sidney said to Delores.

She put out her cigarette. "You took the words right out of my mouth."

It was like watching the movies when they were on the

dance floor. Her long blonde pageboy spread out like a fan when he twirled her, as they did the box step, and at the end they did a dip so low the ends of her hair touched the floor.

I was real sorry when Sidney came back without her, but in a few minutes she showed up again. She was holding the centerpiece from her table that she won. Orange and white gladiolas, which she handed to my mother. "You sweet woman," she signed. "Nice meeting you," she said to my father, but he just nodded.

On the subway my father let Sidney have it. He told him he couldn't ever see Delores again.

"Why? Why?" Sidney asked.

"Not Jewish," my father said.

For some reason, that made me feel very nauseated. I bit the inside of my cheek to keep from crying.

"J-u-s-t go with," Sidney told him, meaning he was just going to date her, not marry her.

"N-o!" my father spelled and barked at the same time, so that everyone in the subway train turned to look at us. "N-e-v-e-r again."

I thought about the book she promised me, but it wasn't just the book.

"Like dead, marry not Jewish," my father threatened, before we got off the train at Dyckman.

When a Jew marries someone who isn't Jewish, Sidney explained later, everyone sits *shivah* on wooden crates to mourn them, just like they were really dead.

"Are you going to see Delores again?" I asked him, even though I didn't know whether it would be worse for him to say yes or no.

He messed up the top of my hair. "She's taller than I am," he said, "and besides, New Jersey is a helluva commute."

It was almost one o'clock in the morning when we got home and Melva wasn't there. My mother pulled the door to our bedroom shut right away when she found out, so my father would think Melva was asleep already. She told me not to say anything, but she was plenty worried because it was a work night. Sidney wanted to call up her friend Toni, in case she was there, but my mother said it was too late.

When Melva finally came home, it was light out. She woke me opening the bedroom door, but I kept my eyes closed. After a while, when I wondered what she was doing, I peeked and saw her staring into the mirror. She kept staring and staring. Suddenly she spun around and said, "Stop pretending. I know you're awake."

"Where were you?" I asked.

"Swear to God you won't tell anyone, I mean anyone?"

She made me swear, with my pinkie to my lips, and then she said, "With Jeff. Do I look different to you?"

She looked kind of white without the pancake makeup, but I said, "Not really. Why?"

She held her forehead like she had a headache. "I did it. I went all the way."

I thought I was going to be sick on the spot. I sat up in bed but I didn't say how nauseous I was. "Was it okay?" I asked, like it was no big deal.

"You know what an orgasm is?" she said.

I nodded.

"What is it?" she said, testing me.

I had to tell her I didn't know.

She looked happy for a second because I didn't, then she looked moody again. "You ought to know. That's what happens at the end when you play with yourself."

I think I was blushing. I didn't know she knew I did that sometimes after I thought she was sleeping. "You mean, like a climax?" I asked her. After reading the book at the Dorfmanns, I finally figured out what a climax was.

"Yeah. It's another name for it. Orgasm. Well, I didn't have one." She started crying.

"Maybe next time?" I said. I couldn't figure out exactly what going all the way had to do with it.

She shook her head. "It's chemistry," she said. "Jeff and I don't have it."

"Don't cry," I said. "It's not the end of the world, is it?"

"I'm not a virgin anymore. Don't you understand?"

I didn't know how bad a sin it was, really. It wasn't the sort of thing you could ask the hygiene teacher or a rabbi. I was trying to think of something to say.

"I'll have to marry him," she said. "Oh God!"

It was awful to hear her sobbing so hard.

"You don't have to do it, go all the way, I mean, very much when you're married, do you?" I asked her. The book said couples did it twice a week. I didn't know how long it took, though.

For some reason, this made her laugh. It wasn't the normal kind of laughing but the kind she used to do when she would pretend to be Peola, who was a thousand years old, just to scare me. It was the way she laughed when later she had to stay in the Shady Grove Sanitarium. Real haunting.

My mother came in to wake me up for school. She took one look at Melva and knew she had spent the night with Jeff. I don't know how she knew. She told her not to say anything to my father.

"What me stupid?" Melva asked her.

"Careful you not pregnant," my mother said.

Melva didn't say any more about how it was after that first night, although all through November she spent a lot of nights with Jeff. One morning in December, when it was snowing real hard, she came home and looked like she wanted to tell me something but she only giggled and kept looking at herself in the mirror. I wondered if it had to do with the orgasms.

Sidney spent a lot of money making phone calls to New Jersey from the drugstore, so they wouldn't show up on the phone bill. He didn't get to see Delores a lot, just once every other week, and not Thanksgiving because she went to California. She was always studying. At the beginning of my Christmas vacation he brought her up to the apartment when my father was at work. She had a couple of packages with her, in gorgeous gold paper and green bows. One was toilet water for my mother and when I felt the other one, which was very heavy, I knew it was *Gone with the Wind*.

On New Year's Eve, Melva and Jeff got engaged, but Sidney and Delores broke up. It was terrible on New Year's Day, trying to look both happy and sad in the same apartment. I kept changing from room to room.

Because the drugstore was closed, Sidney called Delores from our phone, after he made Melva get off. She had been talking to Jeff for two hours straight.

Right away Sidney started yelling. "What'd'ya mean you don't wanna be poor all your life?" he said to Delores. "You think I won't get promotions? I ain't gonna be a sales clerk forever."

When Delores hung up on him, he started cursing. "Goddam women! All they care about is money!" That night he filled up two ashtrays with the butts from his Pall Malls.

Melva and Jeff went down to the Diamond Exchange on 47th Street the next Saturday to get her an engagement ring, but the place they were supposed to go to was closed, on account of the owners being religious. Then they were supposed to go during Melva's lunch hour, but Jeff never showed up. Later he told her he got a terrible stomach upset at the last minute. That week she screamed at me and Sidney a lot, especially when we asked her when she was getting the ring.

"T-o-o b-a-d, t-o-o b-a-d," my mother kept signing, but I only realized later what she meant, after Melva came home early Friday night from her date with Jeff. She went into the bedroom and slammed the door. I heard her crying and tried to go in but she yelled at me to get out.

I went in when it was my bedtime and she started talking to me in the dark. "He doesn't want to marry me," she said, just like that.

"Really? Why not?"

"First he said his father wouldn't let him because I went all the way and if I did it with him I'd do it with some other boys. Some crust! Are you listening?"

"Of course."

"Then I got him to admit he doesn't want to. He says he's too young to settle down."

I went over to her bed, sitting on the edge. From the moonlight coming in the window, I could see the outline of her, like a sarcophagus in the museum.

"Don't worry, you'll marry someone else," I told her. "That jerk will be sorry." He wasn't really a jerk. He was good-looking and had a good sense of humor, but I didn't know what else to say.

"Who'd marry me? I'm not a virgin now."

"Lots of women aren't when they get married," I told her. The book at the Dorfmanns said so.

She didn't contradict me, so I thought she agreed, until she said, "I can't live without him." She kept saying she wanted to die and telling me how wonderful he was, until I fell asleep on her bed. She woke me so I could go back to my own bed.

In the morning when I woke up she was hanging out the window already. She hadn't slept all night. For the first time in ages she went to synagogue and then came back and hung out the window again. That's all she did Sunday, too, and she didn't go to work Monday. When I got home from school, she was still looking out the window. My mother and I went to the store and when we got back there were police cars in front of the building and a crowd was looking up to the fourth floor, where Melva was sitting on the windowsill, her feet dangling down, and she was laughing.

We let the policemen into the apartment and they grabbed her from behind and took her to the hospital for observation. That night I was still awake when my father came home from the post office. When I heard my mother go into the kitchen, I tiptoed across the living room where my brother slept on the hide-a-bed. I stood in the foyer, looking into the mirror that reflected into the kitchen. My mother was telling my father what had happened with Melva. I could hear him muttering to himself like he does when he says his prayers under the mezuzah.

"Fault, your mother," my father said to her. At first I didn't get what my grandmother could of had to do with it. But when he said, "Inherit crazy," I figured out her mother had gone crazy. So that's why there were no pictures of her after Russia.

"Not, not," my mother said.

"Why lie? You know true," he signed. He was starting to make gruff sounds, which scared me, so I ran back through the living room into my bedroom. It seemed very lonely without Melva there for some reason, even though she usually went to bed after me. Still, if she had been there I couldn't of told her what I found out.

I heard my mother go to bed but not my father. After a while I got up and looked in the foyer mirror again. I couldn't believe my eyes. His head was down on the newspaper and his body was jerking like he had the hiccups. I'd never seen him cry before. All he ever used to do was smack Melva around, and when he finally stopped doing that he said sarcastic things all the time. Maybe he was sorry, I thought, which meant Melva must of been worse than Sidney told me.

The next weekend my mother and father brought Melva home. She was kind of quiet but she looked okay. She spent all day reading, so I didn't get to talk to her till supper. She showed me a poem she said was the most wonderful one she'd ever read, by a man named Catullus who lived a very long time ago. "'I hate and I love,'" she recited, real dramatic, stopping to explain it was exactly how she felt. I was afraid to ask her anything, like if she still wanted to kill herself.

When Sidney came home from work, he and Melva started talking in the kitchen. When I came in, they said it was private. I tried to hear what they were saying in the other room but I couldn't. They talked for hours. Usually they didn't even get along. I didn't mind, really, but I was just curious. Finally they came out with their arms around each other. I wish I had a picture of that because I could hardly even believe it myself.

No one wanted to come with my mother and me to New Jersey. Melva and her friend Toni were going to a dance that night on Fordham Road in the Bronx to meet boys, and Delores was coming into the city. She and Sidney made up after he sent her a dozen roses for Valentine's Day that cost him a fortune. Just my mother and I went, on the bus from the Port Authority.

My Aunt Sadie came hurrying down the front steps of their house as we were coming up the walk. She spelled out to my mother that Rona was there. She said Rona was getting a divorce. My mother had been knitting a little blanket because Rona was going to have a baby. She asked what was wrong, but Aunt Sadie just shook her head and pressed her lips together, the way my mother did. I wondered if it was because Morty was clumsy on their wedding night like Scarlett O'Hara's first husband. It was creepy just to think of it. Anyway, Aunt Sadie said not to mention anything to Rona.

I went upstairs, first to Natalie's room, which had pink curtains made out of the same material as the bedspread, and dozens of dolls lined up on the shelves my uncle had made. Natalie said she was busy doing a project for Girl Scouts, so I went back down.

My Uncle Ben was coming up. "How's my niece?" he said. "I'm real glad you and Mother could make it out here." He didn't look very glad. Just the opposite. "They're in the rec room," he told me, so I went all the way down to the basement.

Aunt Sadie was telling my mother about the bar they had just put in, with a real sink. There must of been a hundred photographs on the walls, each one with its own frame. The walls were orangey wood, shiny like they'd been shellacked.

"What'd'ya think?" Aunt Sadie asked me. "Quite a remodeling job, *nu?*"

"Very nice," I said.

Rona was sitting on the high stool at the bar and when she turned around I saw how big her stomach was. Her eyes were sunken in like a skeleton's, and under them her olive skin was even darker than usual. With her long red hair she looked like Rita Hayworth. She waved at me to come closer, and when I did she put my hand on her stomach. "Just hold it there a while, you'll feel the baby kick."

It didn't take very long. I felt it. I couldn't get over it. I told my mother, but she wasn't very excited. I sat next to Rona on a high stool and Aunt Sadie gave us sodas to drink from the little frigidaire. After a while I got up to look at some of the pictures. A lot of them were of my aunt and uncle playing golf, Natalie playing tennis, and Rona playing her accordion. I recognized Rona and Natalie when they were little, and even my family, when I was much younger. There was the exact same picture of my grandfather and his family in Russia that my mother had, and a brown and white picture of a couple dancing that I thought was my Aunt Sadie, but I knew the man wasn't my uncle. Uncle Ben had a fat round face and a big nose and the man had a long face and a thin nose.

"Who's the man?" I asked my aunt.

She came over to look. "Darling, that's the man who was courting your mother when she met your father."

And then I realized the picture wasn't of her but my mother. "The Socialite," I said.

"She told you?"

I nodded.

"Your mother gave me the picture because she was afraid your father would tear it up. Darling, if she had only married that man! How he loved to dance!"

All of a sudden I felt the tears in my eyes. They burned. I said I had to go to the bathroom and I ran up the stairs.

When I came back, Rona's accordion was resting on top of the bar because her stomach got in the way of carrying it and she was playing a song I didn't know.

I stopped in front of the picture and took a real good look. My mother had bangs and a long plain sundress, but I think that's what they used to wear for dressing up. She had on high heels and her head was tilted back. Her smile was phony like, but I liked it. His head was tilted back, too. They were turned slightly away from each other, with their arms crossed in front, holding both each other's hands. In back of them, other people were dancing the regular way, face to face. When I noticed my mother watching me from across the room, I said, "S-o-c-i-a-l-i-t-e."

"Call me P-e-a-r-l," she said.

Aunt Sadie came over with another soda for me. At home we didn't have sodas, except in summer. I noticed she had the same bangs my mother had in the picture. "What are you thinking so hard? You'll wear out your brain," she said.

"He could of been my father," I said, like it was something to brag about.

"What're you talking? In biology you'll learn it takes two sets of genes, your mother's and your father's. With a different father you wouldn't be the same Ruthie," she said. I'd never thought of that before.

While Rona played the accordion with her back to us, I saw Aunt Sadie spell out to my mother that she was going upstairs to see how my uncle was. She didn't know many signs so it took her a while. "H-e-a-r-t-b-r-o-k-e-n," she said, about Uncle Ben, then put her finger on her lips, like it was a secret.

"Sorry," my mother said.

I got up next to Rona again and sang songs with her. Then she started playing "Begin the Beguine." We sang that one, too, until she got to the line about swearing to love forever and promising never, never to part. She stopped suddenly and started sobbing.

My mother came over. "D-o-n-t cry," she told me to tell Rona. "Man not worth."

Soon my Uncle Ben came down the stairs and right off started dancing with the cigar in his mouth which wasn't lit. "Play a rhumba," he told Rona, and he danced around the room by himself a while, with one hand on his midriff and his other arm in the air, until he got my mother to do it with him. They must of danced three or four different numbers before my mother said she was tired and had to sit down.

"Can you dance?" he asked me. I told him Sidney had

taught me all the dances when I was little. He was real surprised, I think, because I even knew the obeebo. He pushed and pulled a lot harder than Sidney, so he was real easy to follow.

"Tell your mother you get your grace from her," he said, and I did.

"Fair," my mother said, because she thinks compliments spoil you.

Uncle Ben spoiled me a lot that afternoon and taught me this step where you pick up one leg and rest it against the back of the other one while your partner bends your body way to the side. It was terrific! Finally he said it was intermission and he went around the counter.

"Bar's open," he said, and gave my mother a glass of schnapps. He drank his really fast and then had another one. He opened a jar of all cashews, which are the expensive kind, and a huge box of pretzels. "Enjoy," he said. "Later we'll go to the country club for dinner. How's that?"

I was sure Melva would be sorry for not coming to Jersey with us. She'd never been to a country club. After they first joined, my aunt told my mother all about it. That's where the golf course and the tennis courts were, and a swimming pool besides. She and my uncle were the first Jews who got in, in New Jersey.

Uncle Ben started telling us jokes which were hard to translate to sign language, so I summed them up, which wasn't the same, of course. When he did one about a Frenchman, Rona played the Can-Can. He got this idea to roll up his pants so you could see his hairy legs, and he started doing the kicks, just like the Rockettes. I got up and did some kicks, too, but not very high, because I had a dress on.

When Natalie and my aunt came down, we formed a conga line and snaked around the whole basement, except for my mother who watched. Rona kept playing the music faster and we had to go faster and faster. We were yelling, "One, two, three, KICK," and bumping our hips into each other so hard we almost knocked each other down. Tears were rolling down our cheeks we were laughing so much.

Finally my Aunt Sadie said to my uncle, "Enough, before you get a heart attack." So we stopped.

While she was wiping the sweat that was dripping from his forehead, my mother signed to me, "Terrible, s-a-d," but I didn't want her to say that. As far as I was concerned, the afternoon had been pretty terrific and there was no telling what was going to happen later, especially if there was music at the country club. With violins, maybe. Or better yet, maracas.

2. Retracings

☆ Relics of Stars

USING the full length of their arms, the two women sitting on the bench closest to the entrance of Chasen Center wave at the silver-haired man shuffling back and forth past them. Lost in thought, he is looking down at the sidewalk and does not see them. Discouraged, Trudy Berkowitz drops her arm to her lap, smiles tolerantly while Marian Lowe continues to wave, making grunting sounds which no one except the blind lady sitting on the next bench over can hear. The others taking their morning air just now in front of the brown brick building for the disabled are deaf-mutes.

As Albert gets within reach, Marian leans forward and taps his arm. He stops with a jerk. "Look me," she signs. "Dream too much."

He looks from her to Trudy and back again, juts out his chin as if to say, What is it?

Marian points to her watch. "Late?" she signs.

"N-o, n-o, n-o," he spells out, his fingers making sharp motions to indicate his displeasure. "Know R-u-t-h here, eleven-thirty, s-u-r-e," he says, about his daughter.

Marian holds her hands up, palms facing him, meaning, Take it easy. As he resumes his shuffle, she signs to Trudy, "My sweetheart, r-e-s-t-l-e-s-s." Marian follows Albert with her eyes, approving of the whiteness of his sharply creased polyester pants. When he moved to Chasen Center after divorcing Hannah, it was she who explained to him about the washing machines, how much soap they took and when to use bleach. "Bright, pretty," she says to her friend about the shirt she picked out for him.

Trudy shrugs. "Like t-e-n-t," she says of the green and yellow stripes.

"Jealous," Marian accuses.

"Make me laugh," says Trudy, thinking of how Albert has been trying to get a date with her for years. She let him kiss her once, but because of Marian she has to refuse him.

Albert doesn't see their conversation as he continues pacing. His thoughts are elsewhere, on what he is going to tell his daughter who has flown all the way from Portland for his eightieth birthday party. He must be sure to tell Ruth about Dr. Gomez at Beth Israel giving him the thumbs-up sign after his prostate surgery, instead of using the hospital's interpreter. And about Bess Goldman's stroke and how her multi-millionaire brother Barry, of Goldman's Shoes, won't let him see her because he's such a snob. And his weekly visits to Aunt Lois's office and how she always asks about Ruthie. Last time she wanted to know if Ruth was seeing anyone steady.

"Maybe ex-commissioner," he wrote down on the notepad for his sister, who never learned sign language.

"Port-land," she mouthed to him, carefully forming each syllable. "How do you know?"

"Finish term, get divorce," Albert told her. "Ruth wrote me." He imagines the ex-commissioner is still a popular man and must have made a lot of money from all his connections. He volunteered the fact that he wasn't Jewish.

"That's o-kay," Aunt Lois said. "Ruth is not a young woman." She had to write it down because Albert couldn't lip-read "young."

Thinking about age makes Albert look up now. Trudy will be seventy-six at the end of the month but she looks so much younger than Marian, who is seventy-three. But Marian dresses better. Albert likes how neat she looks in her blouse with the big bow and a skirt. He doesn't know why Trudy has to wear dresses that hang sloppily. He's told her a couple of times, but all she says is that they're comfortable and she's too old to change.

Time is passing so fast, Albert thinks. He's sure the world must be spinning a lot faster.

He looks up the street but sees no sign of Ruth. He turns around and toddles toward the benches on the far side where Meyers and Riley always sit because they smoke. Then he sees Irving Gold and spins around, almost losing his balance. He doesn't want Irving to get the idea he's trying to make up with him after their fight. Irving had some nerve telling him not to give Trudy advice.

Marian points to Albert, says to Trudy, "Look, s-o excite, think too much, daughter," just as Albert shuffles toward them.

"You jealous," Trudy says. "Me catch you."

"N-o, n-o," Marian says, grunting. "His business, hands o-f-f."

When Albert checks his watch again, it is eleven twenty-five. He stops in front of Marian and Trudy. "Maybe t-r-a-f-f-i-c," he tells them.

He doesn't see a cab pull up at 14th Street and Avenue B. A tall woman with red hair, perspiration stains on her lavender blouse, scrambles out, slams the door, but doesn't close it, so she opens it and slams again, then starts running down Avenue B. Deftly, she dodges children, old women with shopping carts, steps around a puddle of vomit, ignores a man leaning up against a boarded store window who hisses at her, keeping her eyes on the cracked cement to avoid twisting an ankle like she did the last time she visited New York. Her heel catches and she walks out of her pump.

Sheepishly she returns for it, thinking, I'm still afraid of him. Afraid to be seen taking a cab, afraid to be five minutes late. She slips her foot into the shoe, asking herself, Would Wendell run? A man who knows his own importance? He'd run down the street only if his life were in danger, and maybe not even then. She starts moving again, not running, but at her usual brisk pace.

Rounding the corner onto 12th Street, she sees her father right away, notices the brightness of his shirt, not one of the ones she sent him. His back is to her. She feels a lurch in her stomach, wishes that seeing him could be a pleasure instead of duty.

As Ruthie crosses the street toward them, Marian starts waving vigorously, grunting, "Uh uh," but when Albert doesn't see her, she stands up, taps him on the arm, and points.

His mouth open with surprise, he toddles toward his daughter, both arms outstretched. They embrace. She is prepared to let go when she realizes he is still hugging. When her mother was alive, he never hugged her so hard. Still in his embrace, she pats him on the back, squeezes gently until their bodies separate.

"Look good," she signs. He swells with satisfaction. The picture of health, she thinks, wiping the sweat off her forehead with the back of her hand. She'd forgotten how hot New York is in June.

He stands there, his arm outstretched toward Ruthie, as if he's presenting her. Ruthie's smile freezes when Marian, in a green two-piece outfit, comes forward. Letting Marian hug and kiss her, she keeps striving to feel neutral, aware her father treats Marian so much better than he ever treated her mother. Trudy advances on her next, her shapeless navy dress hanging lower on one side. She hugs Trudy with enthusiasm for resisting her father's overtures.

All signing among the deaf people on the benches has halted. Ruthie steps back, waves hello. She recognizes Mrs. Kahn and Emily Levy from Fort Tryon Park, where Ruthie's mother took her to play most afternoons throughout her childhood. She remembers Mr. Mazzoli who taught her the breast stroke in Brighton Beach, where she went with her parents in the summers to swim and watch fireworks. She wonders if Mrs. Mazzoli has died, then recalls her father writing her that she became senile and had to be put in a nursing home. Mr. Mazzoli asks how long the plane ride took. Mrs. Kahn wants to know if the weather in Portland is very cold. Ruthie's cheek muscles ache from continually smiling.

Her father moves closer. "Finish eat b-r-e-a-k-f-a-s-t?" he asks. When she shakes her head no, he looks at Marian. "Know her w-a-y-s." He turns back to Ruthie. "Come, me t-r-e-a-t."

Buoyed by the thought of coffee, she tries not to show surprise. Her father hooks his arm around hers and they wave good-bye to everyone.

"Enjoy eat," Marian says, looking wistful.

As they cross the street, their backs to the building, her father speaks in his guttural voice instead of signing: "Tell you something, not want see." When he doesn't tell her, she realizes he means at breakfast and wonders where they are going. He holds her arm tightly as they slowly navigate the rocky sidewalk of Avenue A. A couple of times he stumbles slightly. She doesn't recall his balance being so shaky. Just last year he used to walk all the way to Columbus Circle once a week by himself.

"Dirty," her father signs, wrinkling his nose at the sight of shattered glass on the pavement. "Worse, worse," he says.

To her the neighborhood looks the same. Olive-skinned men in undershirts congregate on the corners. Above the stores, robust women in floral patterned blouses hang out the windows. Her father must be comparing it with the Inwood neighborhood where she grew up, at the other end of Manhattan. Inwood, the way it used to be . . . By the time her mother died, it had changed. Not nearly as dirty or noisy as here, though, she observes.

"Why stay?" she asks him, knowing what he'll answer.

"High r-e-n-t all over," he tells her. His rent in Chasen Center is subsidized, which makes up for living in an area that he says "stinks."

It does stink, of rotting fruit, soggy cardboard, leather from the shoemaker's, beer from the tavern, and when they get to Giorgio's Coffee Shop, of rancid fat. She tries to breathe through her mouth, to avoid smelling the grease, as they edge past the people crowded in front of the donut counter to the orange vinyl booths in back.

The waitress in an orange uniform saunters over, points to the sign in back of her advertising the $1.39 special: juice, eggs, toast, coffee. Before Albert nods, she writes on her notepad.

"My daughter," he says in his guttural voice to the waitress. She looks up, smiles, and points to the yellow sign again.

"I'll have the same," Ruthie says.

"You can hear!" the waitress exclaims. "But isn't he your father?"

"He had meningitis that made him deaf. It wasn't inherited."

The waitress nods, looks sympathetically at Albert. "He's such a cute man. Is he on disability? He always dresses so neat."

"Him? He's retired from the post office."

"Tell, you work p-o," Ruthie signs to her father.

"Thirty years," he barks.

"Thirty years," Ruthie repeats.

The waitress shakes her head as though this is remarkable, turns away. In a flash she's back with two plastic glasses of orange juice, smiling benevolently at him as she sets them down.

The fan in the back wall tousles Ruthie's short wavy hair, but the breeze is hot. She feels sweat running between her breasts and accumulating on the backs of her thighs. She drains the warm juice, amusing herself with the thought that the entire breakfast costs what she paid for a glass of freshly squeezed orange juice when she took her father to breakfast in Portland. She is sure he got the idea to take her out because of all the meals she bought him during his visit there. At least he learned something, she thinks, even if Giorgio's is not exactly her style.

Albert drinks his juice. "What new?" he signs.

"Same," she says. "Busy, write a-d-v, different people, most p-o-l-i-t-i-c-i-a-n-s." Her fingers feel rusty, spelling out such a long word.

"Good money?" he asks.

She nods, regretting she can't tell him she works only part-time now on a free-lance basis because she is trying to write a novel. "What new you?"

"Every day eat s-e-n-i-o-r c-e-n-t-e-r. Good food. Crowded. Fifty cents."

She nods politely. He told her about the senior center when she last saw him. Periodically he mentions it in his letters. He tells her now about yesterday's menu and how he took some cartons of milk and packets of sugar home with him. She remembers how she had to stop him from taking a handful of sugar packets from the posh Trattoria Paolo. The thought of it makes her cringe. Her friend Barbara tried to suggest that he didn't know any better because he was a deaf-mute, but Ruthie set her straight. Her mother never slurped coffee, as he is doing now.

Albert sets the cup in the saucer. "Show you," he says, reaching into his shirt pocket. He takes out a plastic baggie, extracts a slender chain, and puts it down on the orange formica table. There is a little pendant with a tiny scrolled initial "E." "Save for you," he says, his eyes shining.

She looks quizzically at him, since none of her names starts with "E."

He explains he spotted it lying on the counter of a telephone booth he passed. "Don't want give M-a-r-i-a-n, keep for you," he says, looking at her expectantly.

The nausea comes upon her, not from the smell of the food that the waitress is setting in front of them, or the grease swimming under the eggs and on top of the toast. It always happens when she sees him, even after years of therapy with Dr. Dessein.

She thanks him with a forced smile, wondering what presents he's been getting Marian, or finding for her in the street. She cannot recollect anything he ever gave her mother, except a necklace with a silver chain and a red glass pendant, when they lived in Brighton Beach, before Ruthie was born. It's her only evidence that at some time in their lives there was love between her parents.

Putting the baggie in her purse, she sets about eating her eggs, being deliberately slow, in contrast to her father's rapid shoveling. When he sets his fork down with a clatter, she asks, "What you want tell me before?"

He thinks for a second, then nods. "Want T-r-u-d-y B-e-r-k-o-w-i-t-z."

Ruthie sighs, motions to the waitress to refill her coffee.

"N-o g-o-o-d, too much coffee," her father says.

Ruthie nods, but drains her cup anyhow, as he talks about Trudy.

"I explain her, me old, can't waste time," he says. "T-r-u-d-y n-o me, afraid M-a-r-i-a-n angry."

Ruthie already knows the entire story. She lets him continue about asking Trudy to go to the Poconos with him. Ever since Trudy moved into Chasen Center, he's been asking her to go to the Poconos. Once more he tells her about the poem he wrote to Trudy.

Ode to a Jewish yearn, Ruthie thinks to herself. Blotting her toast with a napkin, she watches the yellow liquid ooze onto the plate, decides to focus her thoughts on Wendell. How tender he is with her, a contrast with his public persona, the cold, overbearing executive. The way he laps at her in bed like a pet dog, her shoulders, her breasts, how he gloms onto her nipples like an infant.

When her father stops recounting his fruitless pursuit, she says, "T-o-o b-a-d."

He concentrates on eating his toast while she resumes thinking about Wendell and his lapping, amused when she realizes the crotch of her panties is wet. She looks up to see the Greek cook behind the counter eyeing her. He purses his thick lips. She looks back at her father, trying to think of something to say. "M-a-r-i-a-n present shirt?" she asks. "Nice."

He shakes his head. "Me buy. Help pick. Shop two s-u-i-t, three pants, four shirt, a-l-l new bathroom, curtain, towel, f-u-r-n-i-t-u-r-e."

"Buy a-l-l new?" She thinks it odd that he's buying a wardrobe and furnishings at this age, after a lifetime of such stinginess that her mother used to say, "G-o-l-d b-r-i-c-k," meaning he was going to have a gold brick for a headstone.

"Show you."

When the waitress refills her cup, he says, "Enough, not healthy," and without asking, hands her cup to the waitress to take away.

Ruthie tries to tell him she's in good health, but he waves at her to stop. "Coffee, coffee. N-o g-o-o-d," he spells out for emphasis.

She imagines smashing a plate on his head, then erases the image by telling herself he's just an old man set in his ways. She steals a furtive glance at her watch. Only twenty-five minutes have gone by.

He picks up the check, studies it, seems to think of something he wants to say, puts it down. "Deaf talk, why can't see stars?" he tells her.

"What?"

"S-h-u-t-t-l-e up explode, stars gone," he says, meaning the space shuttle has caused the stars to explode and disappear.

She laughs, realizes he's serious, and shakes her head. "N-o, n-o," she signs, explaining that in New York you can't see the stars because of pollution.

"What mean p-o-l-l-u-t-i-o-n?" he asks.

Startled by his not knowing, she makes a clumsy effort to define it, settles for giving him a picture of its effects: "Cloud, from dirt, s-m-o-k-e from f-a-c-t-o-r-y and cars," she tells him, making a sign to show smoke rising. "Can't see, fault cloudy."

He disregards her explanation. "Deaf think why, why. Can't understand."

She imagines telling Allison, "It's not as if he isn't highly intelligent. He follows current events and sports and always wins at poker. But if he doesn't know *that,* what else doesn't he know?"

After putting a quarter on the table, Albert heads for the cash register up in front. Ruthie lingers, slips a dollar onto the table, hears the waitress behind her say, "Thank *you.*"

Thank Dot, she thinks, who was a generous tipper, leaving five- and ten-dollar bills at a time when a dollar bought dinner. Dot must have been Ruthie's age now when Ruthie was ten. It strikes her odd that the adult she admired most for so many years was a hatcheck girl.

She catches up with her father at the register where he is bantering with Giorgio, who, with his dark mustache and beefy shoulders, looks like the man who drove Dot and her kids and Ruthie to Bear Mountain. To this day Ruthie still has the clown decoration from the ice cream parfait, and that was eons ago. Where is Dot now? Where are Glory and her stepbrother Nelson? What is it they used to call him—Hopalong Cassidy?

"Will raise p-r-i-c-e," her father tells her Giorgio said.

"Such a nice man," Giorgio says to her, winking, before she follows her father out the door.

Outside, it is even hotter than in the coffee shop. She feels the heat from the sidewalk rising under her skirt, the blazing sun baking her wet clothes onto her back. Her father still looks fresh and crisp. "Where now?" she asks, knowing what he'll say.

"Home, show you."

She sneaks another look at her watch as they make their way arm-in-arm down 14th Street. Less than an hour has passed since she emerged from the taxi. Who says being a dutiful daughter is supposed to be fun?

Marian and Trudy are standing in front of the building when Ruthie and Albert return. Again Ruthie greets everyone, including Irving Gold, who walks by.

"No!" her father barks. "Don't talk him, mad," he mutters, grasping her hand, pulling her toward the entrance.

She feels the nausea once more, despising herself for letting him control her. She doesn't like being rude to the deaf people, especially on account of his quarrels with them. Besides, Irving Gold was a close friend of her mother's.

Albert waves at Marian to come with them. In the elevator he tells Ruthie about the fight with Irving, how Irving told him not to give Trudy advice on where to go for a vacation. Ruthie feels embarrassed for Marian, who watches without comment.

Marian steps through his apartment door first, turns on the hallway light, points to the carpet. "Taste good?" she asks Ruthie.

"Very nice," Ruthie says. The rust plush looks expensive. She wonders what's gotten into her father. Perhaps he's decided not to leave her a dime. Not that he has a fortune, but since he never spent anything she is sure he has saved twenty or thirty thousand dollars.

Like a tour guide, Marian stands at the entrance to the combined living room-bedroom, making a sweeping gesture with her arm. Ruthie silently inventories the new acquisitions: sofa, studio bed at the other end, armchairs, a new dark wood dinette set with captain's chairs, a lamp with a wheel for a base. A nautical theme, she realizes, even before Marian points it out. She follows Marian around the room as Marian directs her attention to prints of schooners, a barometer, a framed saying Ruthie finds ironic: "Love thy neighbor as thy self."

Marian sees her glance at the framed pictures of her brother and sister. "Must f-a-i-r, a-l-l three," she explains. "You not o-n-l-y c-h-i-l-d."

Ruthie notices that the picture of Bess Goldman, the woman her father used to be crazy about before her stroke, is gone.

As Marian fluffs a pillow and tells her to sit down, Ruthie calculates that her father has spent five thousand dollars on his new furnishings. She and her father sit in the armchairs, with Marian on the sofa opposite. "Nice?" he asks her, about his purchases.

"Very nice," Ruthie says, pleasing him.

He and Marian look at each other. Marian nods, then he turns to Ruthie. "You move N-Y, me give what you want, a-l-l new f-u-r-n-i-t-u-r-e, any."

Marian bobs her head. "S-w-e-l-l."

Ruthie smiles automatically while she figures out how to answer. Once, when she refused his suggestion that she move back to New York, he stopped speaking to her for a couple of months. Her mother finally cajoled him into making up. At the time, she was married to Aaron, which made his suggestion even more ludicrous.

She waves her hand now. "My j-o-b, P-o-r-t-l-a-n-d." She doesn't say that it's really her friends that keep her there, knowing he would resent their importance to her.

"Must have boyfriend," Marian says to him. To Ruthie she says, "Marry?"

Ruthie shakes her head. "W-e-n-d-e-l-l not want marry. Like free. Me same."

Her father tosses his head with annoyance, twisting his jaw from side to side, which he often did around her mother. "You get j-o-b easy. Many n-e-e-d s-e-c-r-e-t-a-r-y."

She sighs. She thought she'd made him understand that she wasn't a secretary when she showed him around the advertising agency in Portland that she used to direct, especially after she introduced him to her secretary. "Me writer now, not s-e-c-r-e-t-a-r-y."

"Look j-o-b, me give you plenty, comfort live."

She thinks about the $1.39 breakfast. Not even enough for two espressos. Even if he gave her enough to breakfast at the Plaza, it wouldn't solve her fundamental need to keep a great distance between them.

"Sorry," she says. She waits for his anger to explode, imagines not going to his birthday party after all, the relatives asking about her . . .

After a long silence Marian starts talking about baseball. Albert nods but says nothing.

"Your father angry," Marian says out loud to her.

Ruthie waves to attract his attention, intending to ask him what team he's supporting, but he doesn't look at her. She surprises herself, walking over to his chair and leaning down to hug him, even more surprised when he doesn't pull away. "Please," she says. "D-o-n-t mad, can't help."

He nods almost imperceptibly, closing his eyes as if he has a terrible cross to bear.

Ruthie returns to her seat as Marian gets up to turn on the baseball game on the TV. Ruthie jumps up to reduce the volume.

"L-o-u-d," Marian says, putting her hands over her ears.

"Think you hearing person," Albert teases.

"Me can hear," Marian jokes, telling him the game's score, which has just flashed on the screen.

As Marian and her father watch the game, Ruthie wonders what he sees in the woman with tight bluish-gray curls framing a very long face and crepuscular neck. Her mother had such beautiful skin, virtually unlined except for crow's-feet around her eyes from so much smiling. She wonders if Marian still suffers from her gallbladder and if that's why he wants Trudy to go on vacation with him. If just once he'd taken her mother on vacation, she thinks, before telling herself to stop it.

Totally bored, Ruthie begins watching the game. The Mets' catcher lets the ball get away from him, causing a batter to get on base. Her father slaps his knee. Marian hits her head, saying, "Ohhh," audibly. The catcher throws his mitt down.

Her father threw a baseball mitt across the living room once, breaking her favorite vase, with the Chinese lady embedded in its front. Her brother had stolen the mitt after her father refused to buy him one. She recalls the sound of Sidney's shrieks while her father beat him with the strap, and the picture of her father's face, sweaty and triumphant, as he emerged afterwards from the bathroom.

And that's my father, she thinks, as he pounds on the arms of the chair, watching the runner get to third base. Such a cute little man.

During the next commercial she announces she has to leave to meet a friend. Marian rises to hug her, and her father walks her to the elevator. A roach wobbles along where the wall meets the floor. The corridor smells of insecticide and feels like a furnace. She wonders why, on a post office pension plus Social Security, her father feels he has to live here.

At the elevator he embraces her, holds her tightly, apparently resigned to her not moving to New York. When finally he lets go, he says, "Restaurant, twelve-thirty," meaning she should be there by then for the birthday party. He reminds her of the address.

She nods, looking into his pale blue eyes, eyes that remind her of Wendell's. Alone in the elevator, she shivers, her clothes clammy with sweat. A wave of anxiety sweeps over her. Her thoughts flit to the window in the hotel that has no bars and opens, then to why being with her father makes her even think of suicide. She recites Dr. Dessein's telephone number to herself, in case she needs to call him, finds herself chanting it like a mantra as she waves good-bye to the deaf people on the benches.

Walking up 14th Street, she tries to think about how she'll spend the rest of the day, but her attention is diverted by the masses of people rushing past her, past seemingly endless cubicles offering merchandise and food. No one walks in Portland, except downtown or at a mall. No one jaywalks, she thinks, crossing the street now against the light in a crowd that includes a policeman. She counts the different accents she can hear on the block between Second and Third avenues, stops counting when she hears two young men with what could be a Bronx accent, not nearly as strong as Aaron's was. She finds the standard English of Oregonians as uninspiring as the homogeneous population: there are few Jews or Irish in her neighborhood; mostly childless WASPs. Still, after divorcing Aaron, she remained.

Was it because she enjoyed the distance it gave her from the past? she has to wonder. Or how easy it was to find work that paid well, even if ultimately she found "good government" disillusioning? Unlike other politicians she knew, Wendell made things happen and without any pretense to altruism. She's attracted to him not because he reminds her of her father but because he's so much her opposite. Wendell, as she likes to tell her friends, amuses her and gives her a measuring stick in the bargain.

She buys an Italian ice from a sidewalk vendor and strides uptown, walks the entire distance to the midtown booth that sells half-priced tickets. After an hour in line she finds that the play she wants to see, about the reconciliation of an estranged family, is not listed on the boards, so she settles for a musical in its sixth year. Something Wendell would enjoy.

Impulsively she takes a cab to the Empire State Building. Rationalizing that Vince will have limited time to see her, she calls him from the lobby.

"Wait for me," he says without missing a beat. "I'll be right down."

Instead of waiting, she buys a ticket and rides up to the observation tower. Of course, while she lived in New York she never went there or to the Statue of Liberty either, she muses, wondering if this officially makes her an out-of-towner. The wind whips at her hair and blouse as she walks around, studying the skyline. Tower upon tower, but where are the people? she asks herself, recalling the rhyme Melva taught her about the church and steeple, playing the game on her fingers. Ruthie pushes away the sudden sadness.

In the lobby she sees Vince striding up ahead, follows him

until he spins, reaches for her hands. As if poised for a square dance, they face each other. He apologizes for his yellow linen jacket with a brown shirt and purple paisley tie. "Didn't know I joined the mob?" he jokes.

"Let's say, Covello, you have panache." His hair and eyes are blacker than she remembered. An inner voice warns: *Don't. Don't fall in love with him again.*

"For panache I'll buy you a drink," he says, steering her outside.

Breathe, she tells herself, racing to keep up with his long stride, not quite able to focus on his nonstop stream of chatter, stealing sideways glances at him. What was it her friend Emily used to call him? My *sheyner goy.* Emily had the world's biggest crush on him and he never knew it, never thought a beauty such as Emily would go for the likes of him, which only added to his attractiveness.

The cocktail lounge is dark, empty, so much smaller than bars in Portland. Here space is at such a premium, she thinks.

"I apologize for the lack of ambiance. A trade-off for privacy," Vince says, plucking some stuffing from the slit in the vinyl covering of their booth.

"It's okay. I've given up my attachment to the so-called good life."

"Let's talk about that, but first I want to say, How come you called? I thought you were still mad at me."

"Maybe. But I wanted to hear a familiar voice from my past," Ruthie says.

"That hard-up for friends in New York?" He orders them another round of Courvoisier.

She tells him about her father. Everything. That's one of the things about Vince, she thinks. She can breeze in and talk about anything, the deepest hurts, even the ones he's caused . . .

He takes her hand, gently squeezes her fingers. "I hope to hell I know who *my* kids are, and that I've let them know who I am," he says.

Just as she's aware that something in her is rebelling, she

hears herself say, "Do they know their father screwed around with another woman?" Coolly she studies his reaction, a flash of anger followed by defensiveness. "Sorry," she says, "couldn't resist. I'm sure you and they know each other better than most."

He drops her hand. "How's Wendell?"

She picks up his. "How's Bibi? Still modeling?"

"She's gone back to school for a master's in French. Now that the kids are grown she's thinking she can work more hours . . ."

The kids are grown. Ruthie fights that glimmer of hope that springs from who knows where. She hasn't given him up. Not entirely. When she tunes back in, he's describing a trip he and Bibi took together, without the kids, to Europe. A timely reminder: not only is he not free but he is attached. Happily attached.

"All through the trip," he says, "I carried this around with me. I wrote it one night in Amsterdam. I even tried to call you from the hotel lobby." He takes out a poem crumpled inside his wallet and flashes it briefly, reads the poem:

> "It was better than the memory
> Better even than how he'll tell her
> It was. Sweet, almost to hurting,
> Bitter, nearly to loving,
> So brief, and yet forever.

"It's about us," he says.

"I know," she says, struggling against a sudden rush of feeling. "Still, we had no right . . ."

"Ruthie, if Bibi hadn't found out . . ."

"But she did, and we risked her finding out, by even starting . . ."

He brings her hand to his lips, kisses the tips of her fingers. "Can't we be friends—loving friends?"

"Without romance?"

He crinkles his brow. "*With* romance."

She throws her head back. "Oh," she says, starting to laugh. "I'm so obtuse. You want . . ." She leans forward, whispers, *"Coucher avec moi, n'est-ce pas?"*

"Isn't that why you called?" he says.

She considers. Was it the memory of his long, beautiful body slanted above her, riding her as if he were on an invisible surfboard? Or what she said, that he was the only happy connection to her past in New York? Most likely, that she never admitted losing the competition to another woman.

"Why?" he prods her. "Not because we went to junior high together?"

She looks at her watch. "I've got an hour and a half, if you want to come to my hotel." She thinks it won't hurt anything to go to bed with him, that maybe it will free her of the wound. At the least it will keep the wedge she needs between her and Wendell.

In her hotel room he drapes his clothes neatly over the chair. "What are you waiting for?" he asks, and when she doesn't move he efficiently strips her of all her clothes.

They lie side by side on the bed. After a few open-mouthed kisses, he rolls on top of her. She doesn't understand why she feels only the sensation of contact at various points, but no excitement. She strokes his back and head methodically. When he grabs a nipple and pinches it, she cries out.

"You liked that last time."

"So brutal?"

"You liked it, I tell you, or maybe you just pretended. Tell me what you do like."

"Spontaneity," she says, knowing it's eluding them.

He pumps away while she thinks about her father's limited world, what she'll say to Dr. Dessein, why Vince didn't leave Bibi for her. When he grabs her hair and fastens his mouth on hers, lifting the rest of his body off her, like she remembers, she has a flicker of erotic feeling and then he climaxes.

"Did you come?" he asks.

"What difference?"

"Did you?" he asks insistently.

"Did *you?*" she mocks. She feels contemptuous of his ignorance, of the ignorance of most men, making an exception for the married lover she sees occasionally in Portland who uses his tongue on her to her satisfaction because he ejaculates prematurely.

"A dinero for your thoughts."

"Obscene," she says, going to the bathroom. When she returns, he is half dressed.

"Have you been back to the neighborhood?"

She shakes her head. "I want to, though. It was such a special place."

"*Was* is right. Now it's . . ." He shakes his head. "Did we just imagine how beautiful it was?"

He looks boyish, the way she remembers him in junior high, when he sat behind Alan Goldfarb, with whom she was infatuated from the fourth grade on, right up until she went to high school. Her first one-sided relationship. How early the patterns are set, she muses.

As if he can read her thoughts, he says, "I got a letter from Alan. He's become the executive director of the Miss Young America contest."

She squeals, "Those poor baby lambs!"

"I never thought he was that good-looking," Vince says wistfully.

"Guess he wasn't your type."

"He was yours?"

"I've always been a sucker for charm. No matter how shallow. The ex-commissioner is a case in point. Mr. Charm," she laughs to herself.

"Ex-commissioner. That's like saying he's out of commission, isn't it? You're in love with him, or what?"

"Definitely or what. It's therapeutic dating an emotional tightwad. Usually I get taken in by men who talk convincingly about love," she says, thinking Vince a prime example.

He frowns. "You're just being glib."

"Yeah," she says, suddenly not wanting to admit that she told him the awful truth. She wonders why she always finds herself at a distance from her men, thinks of the chasm between her and her father. Another matter for Dr. Dessein. Only, on her part-time earnings she doesn't have the fifty-five dollars an hour he charges, or used to charge when she last saw him.

When Vince leaves, she starts the shower. A loud knock brings her back to the door. "I forgot to ask you about your book," he says.

Damn him for caring, she thinks. "Not much to say. I've just started it."

"It's about Inwood, right?"

"I told you that?"

He grins. "I assumed."

She nods. "My nostalgia trip."

"It's more, though. You're trying to preserve something outside your memory. A world worth preserving . . ."

She stands on tiptoe to kiss him on the mouth. "You're a sweetie, but I have to go or I'll be late." She closes the door and steps into the tub, her tears mingling with the stream of shower water.

Seeing all the couples in the theater, Ruthie feels a little sorry for herself. Before the show she surveys the men sitting by themselves, makes eye contact with one, but as the lights dim another man sits down beside him. At least she's away from the anxiety that the men from her life in New York have provoked, she thinks, trying to focus on the frenetic dancing and sparkly costumes of the opening number. She pulls her sweater around her, glad she anticipated the powerful air conditioning. After a while the songs and dances of the first act blur. She knows the idea of being there is better than the real thing, but she's not unhappy.

During intermission she glances at the playbill, catching the name Ione D. Opals. Ione? From 46 Arden? Ruthie's mother baby-sat Ione when Mrs. Opals took Iris and Ivy to their lessons: singing, dancing, elocution, anything that might groom them for show business. Ruthie tries but fails to pick Ione out from the tap dancers in the second act, all wearing skintight caps and bodysuits. It's been seventeen years since Ruthie left home to marry Aaron; Ione was still a little girl then.

Ruthie smiles to herself as she makes her way backstage after the show, remembering how Iris once taught her to walk correctly. Iris, the oldest of the Opals sisters, was her good friend, playing with her in their cramped living room whenever she found time between lessons. Ruthie can see Iris with a Bible on her head, walking carefully past Ione's crib, enunciating her instructions: "It's really important to keep your chin parallel to the ground. That gives you a high carriage." Right then the Bible fell and hit the baby in the forehead.

Should she be looking for a little scar? Ruthie wonders, as she moves unnoticed through the dressing room, a flurry of bodies taking off and putting on clothes, packing duffel bags. Should she call out Ione's name? *Paging Ione Dixie.* When she glimpses the curly blonde hair and pouty lips, she fights the sudden urge to flee. She approaches Ione and introduces herself, relieved when Ione swings around from her dressing table to exclaim, "Ruthie Zimmer! My God! I can't believe it!"

Within a few minutes Ruthie learns that Mr. and Mrs. Opals just sold a fragrance boutique in Palm Beach, where they live now. Iris is in Hackettstown, New Jersey, married to a former football player she met while she was Miss Washington Heights. "My sister makes more money selling real estate than Jim does sporting goods," Ione tells her. "She's just like my dad." It's then Ruthie recalls that her brother wrote once about Mr. Opals' having sold some property in Inwood that no one knew he had—for half a million dollars. That was after the Opals had already moved to Central Park West. When Ione goes on and on about Iris, Ruthie interrupts to ask about the middle sister, Ivy.

Ione digs into a purple vinyl bag with metal studs. "Ivy's

just gone back to school to get a degree in vocational rehab—rehabilitation, you know—but . . ." She extracts a wallet, flips it open to show Ruthie the pictures.

The first ones are easy to recognize, even though Iris has gained a lot of weight. Ruthie fastens on the midriff bulging under the sweater, wondering if her memory is deceiving her. Wasn't Iris the diet-conscious one of the family, continually teasing Ivy, who loved to eat? She studies Jim. No mistaking the ex-football player in his beefy build and thick neck. Their two teenaged sons are wearing football jerseys.

In another photo Mr. and Mrs. Opals are wearing linen sportswear that Ruthie thinks belongs in *Travel and Leisure*. "Memorial Fountain," she says, recognizing the landmark from when she and Aaron honeymooned in Palm Beach, so long ago. Except for Mrs. Opals' gray hair, she looks exactly the way Ruthie remembers, with the high cheekbones and perfect nose of a model, which she'd been before her marriage. Mr. Opals is a little thinner, stooped.

When Ruthie comes to a picture of a pudgy blonde with ratted hair, she says, "Ivy?"

"Ivy's daughter, Yvette," Ione says. Before Ruthie can digest this, Ione flips to the next picture. "And Yvette's baby, Sam." She waits for Ruthie's reaction.

"I don't get it. How can Ivy be . . . how old *is* her daughter?" Ruthie looks back to Yvette's picture.

Ione grins. "My mother refuses to believe it, still. You might as well know. Ivy ran off and married at sixteen. Like mother like daughter. Yvette's seventeen now and Sam is six months tomorrow. Here's Ivy in the Bahamas. Some grandma!"

Ruthie exhales. "Not grandma? Grandma? She's a grandma!" Ruthie says, trying to make the word sink in. She studies the slender brunette in a black mesh bikini while searching her memory. "Ivy would have been in college when . . ."

Ione snickers. "Never went to college. She threatened to kill herself if my dad forced an annulment. Would you believe it?"

Ruthie's eyes tear up all of a sudden.

"Oh God! I'm sorry," Ione says. "I forgot your sister . . ."

". . . it's okay. It's been quite a while . . ." Ruthie remembers the arguments with her sister. Melva was certain Ivy would be famous someday. Ruthie said Iris was the one with the talent; by high school she already spoke several languages. What was it Mrs. Opals used to say? "A natural mimic"? Although Ione modeled a great deal as an infant, Ruthie and Melva wrote her off when she turned into a homely little girl. Actually, Ruthie thinks, she's grown up to look like Brigitte Bardot.

Not waiting for Ione to ask, Ruthie tells her about herself, mentions that she divorced Aaron, that Sidney died of an aneurism, that her mother died a couple of years ago, what she does in Portland . . .

"It's cold up there," Ione says, "isn't it!"

As Ruthie explains about the mountains that trap the rain clouds, she sees Ione tune out. "What happened to your middle name?" she asks. "I used to envy all of you because you had middle names." And more, she thinks.

Ione turns back to the mirror, rubs cream on her face. "My agent, who I swear by, says Ione Dixie sounds like a Southern bubble dancer." She pulls the black fringes from her eyelids. "My father calls these centipedes. He's still the greatest!"

There's a long silence. Ruthie tries to think of something to ask. "Have you been back to the neighborhood?"

Ione shakes her head. "Not on a bet. Although a lot of actors are moving up there now cause they can't afford to live anywhere else. Not me. I need my beauty rest." She sees Ruthie's questioning look. "Radios all night long. Cars being dismantled, clank clank clank, in the wee hours. No thank you."

Another silence. "Well!" Ruthie says. "It's been great to see you. Would you give my love to everyone?" She puts her business card on the dressing table. "Weingartner is my married name," she explains, "my ex-married name."

"I'd love to have cappuccino with you or something but I'm supposed to meet my friend Bill. He's in *Winters* so we only get to see each other after eleven . . ."

Winters was the play Ruthie had wanted to see. "No problem," she says.

"Here." Ione writes down a name and number on Ruthie's playbill. "My agent," she says. "He always knows where I am." She stands up, hugs Ruthie, getting cream on her face and hair. "God, I'm sorry," she says, dabbing at Ruthie with a tissue. She points to the jar. "This cream is dynamite for the skin."

Ruthie notices the crow's-feet around Ione's eyes as she puts up her hand to wave. Unable to find any more words, she turns around, inhales, and heads briskly to the exit. Outside, she hails a taxi, feeling confused about her evening, about the whole day. As the taxi speeds toward her hotel, she finds it ironic that of all the people she misses from Arden Street, Ione is the one she knew the least.

Albert knots his tie, the blue one that Marian helped him pick out, wondering if the face he sees in the mirror looks old to his daughter. Eighty, he thinks. Where did the time go?

His glance travels to the framed picture of his son on the dresser. Sidney made a nice appearance in a suit, Albert thinks. Everyone liked Sidney. They didn't know how stubborn he was—like Hannah. If only Sidney had listened to him, he might have been a success!

After straightening his collar, Albert puts on his gray sports jacket, realizes he isn't wearing cuff links, but before he puts them on, gets distracted thinking about his nephew. He hopes Dan will bring Terri to the party because she's always been so sweet to him, interpreting what everyone says by writing him notes. So what if Dan is much older and she's not Jewish? Dan bought her such a beautiful house in Long Island—a palace big enough for ten people. Maybe that's why she converted.

He looks for his watch on the nightstand where he sees

Melva's picture, wistful that his older daughter never married. Her shape was like Jane Russell's, Hannah told him. He used to worry for Melva when she wore those tight sweaters. Then Larry spoiled everything, scaring her with his epileptic fit after they got engaged. He made her crazy.

Albert remembers he left his watch on the sink. As he passes by the mezuzah nailed onto the doorjamb, he kisses his hand and places it on the scroll. He mutters the Mourner's Kaddish for Melva and Sidney, which his older brother Sol taught him as a boy. He puts on the watch, notices he's forgotten to put on a belt. When the belt is buckled, he returns to the dresser, kisses the tips of his fingers, and touches them to the top of Melva's head in the picture. He remembers how he used to pray she would keep taking her medicine. He kept telling Hannah to watch her. Yes, yes, Hannah told him, but he knows she lied. Ruth sided with her anyhow. When he tells Ruth how Hannah lied, she will understand finally. He decides to tell her before she goes back to Portland.

He toddles to the kitchen, checks his watch against the clock, wondering why Marian hasn't come down yet. From the cabinet under the sink he gets out his shoe polish kit. He bends down a little farther to make sure that the jars of coins are still there. Almost a thousand dollars in quarters and half dollars. He buffs his brown shoes with an old towel, the way Vera used to do when he visited her in the afternoons while Otto was at the printshop. She said Hannah didn't take care of him right. Then when Hannah found out about Vera, she told Otto. What a joke, he thinks, Otto wanting to put him in jail. That pansy! Albert could have knocked him out cold right there in the U.L., but he didn't—for Vera's sake. He wishes she hadn't moved away.

The light near the ceiling flashes. He gets up quickly, feels dizzy, puts his hand down on the formica-topped table to steady himself, but it starts to tip. He lunges toward the stove to regain his balance, then rushes to the door.

"Waste time," he barks at Marian when he sees her. Suddenly remembering the kitchen cabinet he left open, he pushes Marian toward the living room, rushes to the kitchen, shoves the cloth and polish kit into the cabinet, and closes the door. Marian waits patiently as he goes to the bathroom, looks for his wallet, fills his pocket with change from the nightstand, and finds a handkerchief. "O-K?" he asks her, meaning, how does he look.

"Cuff links," she tells him.

He opens a dresser drawer. Should he wear the gold ones that Sidney got him? He lingers on the silver ones that Ruth gave him for Father's Day, decides on the ones with green stones. Maybe Vera gave them to him, he's not sure. Once again he checks himself in the mirror. Before he dies, he would like to visit Vera. He could see his cousins in Las Vegas, take a trip to Lake Tahoe to see Vera, then visit Ruth in Portland, maybe surprise her. He'll go in the spring for sure if there's a bargain in air fares.

Again he preens for Marian. She comes toward him to kiss him, saying, "Happy birthday," in sign language, but as she gets close he holds his hand up. "Careful, messy," he says, meaning he doesn't want to muss his appearance. "Come," he says, "T-r-u-d-y downstairs wait."

Ruthie arrives at the restaurant, finding only her father there with Marian and Trudy, learns that the party isn't supposed to start until an hour later, but he wanted to be certain everything was okay. The waiters are still setting up the tables, two long rows of them, with pink tablecloths and black chairs, black ashtrays, and vases with pink carnations. Much nicer than Ruthie expected, actually. The four of them sit on chairs along a mirrored wall, trying to make conversation. Daddy's harem, she thinks.

Half an hour before the party is to start, a large group of deaf people arrive in a van from Chasen Center, and then her relatives arrive, followed by a contingent of deaf people from Brighton Beach. Ruthie moves through the clusters of her father's friends, now standing with cocktails in their hands, almost tipping them over as they sign to each other. Because her father is across the room talking to his favorite nephew, she greets them as though she were the hostess. None of her other cousins could make the party, her father said. She wonders if she would recognize them if she passed them on the street. Since she left home, she hasn't seen them or the playmates of her childhood. But it's her friends—not her relatives—she's been longing to see.

"N-i-c-e party," Mrs. Kahn signs to her. "F-r-e-e drinks," she says, tilting her head like this is something very special.

Mr. Mazzoli nods vigorously. "S-w-e-l-l," he says.

Ruthie sees Marian and Trudy surveying the arrangements, questioning if there are enough chairs at the table. "Fifty," Marian signs.

"A-l-b-e-r-t say invite forty-eight," Trudy argues. "You a-s-k," she says, pointing to him.

Ruthie looks over, sees him asking his nephew where Terri and the boys are. Dan mouths the words, which even she can understand from across the room. "Home. Baby has flu, high temperature." Ruthie sees her father's crestfallen expression.

She finishes greeting everyone and finds herself on the side where her relatives are. Uncle Sol leans against a black column, its marbled pattern clashing with the bold black and white checks of his linen jacket. The jacket dwarfs his small figure. Sol's head comes up to Lois's shoulder. She stands erect next to him, in green flowing silk, holding her cigarette by a gold filter. She stubs out the cigarette as Ruthie approaches.

Aunt Lois says, "I've been telling Uncle Sol about the ex-commissioner, dear. What your father shared with me. Am I giving away secrets?"

Before Ruthie can answer, Sol adds, "Can he afford to keep a wife in style? To put a fur coat on you?"

"Portland's too warm for furs, Uncle Sol."

What was it her mother used to say about her father's family? "Cold. Think, think money. Not like my sister, cousin, warm heart." Even Sadie and Ben, Ruthie thinks, had warm hearts plus a lot of money. The rest of her mother's family just scraped by, but they were always generous. She wonders if she'll ever see Rona or Natalie, cannot imagine going to New Hampshire, especially after the last letter she got from Rona on the virtues of Richard Nixon.

Aunt Lois is talking about the usefulness of fur coats. When Ruthie doesn't encourage her, she says, "A raincoat with a mink zip-out lining would be very practical, if you can't afford a fox."

Ruthie finds it strange that she once modeled herself after Aunt Lois, drawn by her huge house, the largest house she'd ever visited until a few years ago when she attended a fund-raiser for a gubernatorial candidate. Aunt Lois had real—not plastic—flowers in every room, even the bathroom. And the colors were muted, only one or two colors per room—not the hodgepodge of the apartment Ruthie grew up in. Now she realizes that it was the WASPish aspects of Aunt Lois's life-style that she wanted to emulate, almost laughs when she tunes back in and hears Aunt Lois say, "Tell me, is this fellow you're dating a six-figure man?"

"He owns an industrial park," Ruthie says, "so probably."

"And you're keeping steady company?" Sol asks.

"Oh no, we're not in love." She looks into his gray eyes, hardly visible beneath the dropped lids. At eighty-two he looks so much older than her father. He looks as though he's suffered.

"Darling, a woman needs to be married," he tells her as her cousin comes up to them.

"Not anymore," Dan says, winking at her as though she's some hot number.

"That's what my Davida said, may she rest in peace, but that doesn't make a woman happy. That makes her used goods."

To distract him from his daughter's suicide, Ruthie asks,

"How're you feeling? All right?" She finds herself thinking about the suicide. Does it run in families? Sol was on the verge of moving to Cleveland, where Davida lived, but after she died from monoxide poisoning, taping a note to the windshield, he moved to Boca Raton. Davida's book was published posthumously, with the intimate details of how her parents made her crazy. Ruthie wishes she had such courage. Public relations of a different sort, she jokes to herself.

Aunt Lois turns to her brother as he reaches up to pat Ruthie's shoulder. "Hasn't she turned into a beautiful woman!" she says. "The spitting image of Albert. I'm so proud."

Ruthie refrains from joking about how she couldn't be the spitting image because she had surgery on her nose. With her Instamatic, she goes across the room to get her father to pose with his relatives, since it may be the last chance to capture all three of them together. He insists on having a picture with Marian and Trudy first, then on Ruth's joining them. When she gets him to the other side of the room, he insists on one just with Dan. Finally Ruthie manages to get pictures of him with his sister and brother. Then her father toddles back across to Marian and Trudy.

"Marvelous!" Dan says, "the way the women hang on your father. At his age!" He adjusts his diamond-studded tie bar.

"The girls were always crazy about your father," Aunt Lois says to her. "Did you know that?"

Ruthie strives to keep her tone neutral. "I remember the affair he had while I was growing up."

"Listen, darling, your mother, God bless her, was not the easiest person to get along with . . ."

"No excuse!" Sol cuts her off. "A man who has honor keeps his word, doesn't cat around like *goyem.*" He catches Dan's expression, says, "You should excuse," in deference to Dan's non-Jewish wife, Ruthie supposes. "Lousy," Sol says. "No other word for it."

She follows him to a chair, where he sits down. The others move with them. "You were the one who called family meetings to straighten things out," she tells Sol, wondering who picked out his loud jacket. It wasn't his sedate wife, who didn't come to New York for the occasion. Anyway, her father didn't like Elsa because she always had a housekeeper. "I remember," Ruthie adds, "the time you told my mother she should divorce him."

Sol looks pleased. "You remember? Such a little girl then. So grown up, always interpreting for Albert and Hannah. I felt sorry for you."

"Excuse me," Lois says. "The main thing is that she turned out so well. Albert must have done something right, God bless him, even if she isn't so grateful . . ."

Ruthie holds her tongue, takes a drink off a waiter's passing tray. Someday she will tell them all the things they don't know or don't want to know about her father. If only he could've died before her mother. She misses her mother so much. Ruthie had planned to throw a big party for her eightieth birthday, but she died two years short of that. She remembers her mother's face in the coffin, so tiny, so smooth, and how cruel her father was before the service. She wishes she could tell his relatives *that.* How dutiful is a daughter supposed to be? she asks herself.

On a signal from Albert, people seat themselves. Albert, flanked by Dan and Ruthie, then Sol and Lois, are at the end of one table. Marian and Trudy sit at opposite ends of the other. The rest of the places are occupied by Albert's deaf friends.

Everywhere Ruthie looks, arms are waving or heads are bobbing, faces contorting to complement the signing. Only four of us can speak, she thinks, and none of us is talking. Finally Dan brags about a cruise he and Terri plan to take. "The Star Pacific is supposed to be the crème de la crème," he says.

"It's pretty good," Ruthie says, "but I've been on better."

"You've been on it?" When she nods, Dan says, "Someone take you? Or you were writing about it?"

She laughs. "No, just for pleasure. They had a lot of different jazz musicians, all kinds of lectures . . . I travel a lot, on land usually . . ."

"Writing must pay well," he says, sounding dubious.

"Not like a manufacturer's rep, but I do okay," she says.

"Good for you! I'm glad one of Albert's children has made it."

"Dan!" Lois remonstrates. She lights a cigarette. "When I think of Melva, that beautiful girl . . ." She squeezes Ruthie's arm, her eyes tearing. Ruthie sees Sol's eyes also tearing. Great, Ruthie thinks, we're all going to cry now. Aiming for a light tone, she says to Dan, "Some family history!"

"My uncles deserved better," Dan says, putting an arm around Sol and his arm on Albert's sleeve. His diamond pinkie ring catches the light.

"Your cousins deserved better," Ruthie counters.

Her father gestures as if to say, What's up? about Dan's display of affection. "Nothing," she tells him, "j-u-s-t like you."

Seeing the waiters with trays of chicken soup, Albert stands up. "Wait, wait, me speech," he signs, meaning no one should start to eat. Those who saw him signing tap the shoulders and arms of those who didn't. Ruthie knows the worst is coming, the embarrassment he always causes her, the inevitable nausea. She tells herself that in two hours it will be over and none of it will matter.

"Today," Albert begins, "most happy day o-f my l-i-f-e. I very l-u-c-k-y alive, healthy . . ."

Ruthie interprets for the relatives, none of whom understands sign language. She puts in the articles and prepositions and tenses that the deaf people she knows omit when they sign.

"Me happy you celebrate with me this day: my nephew from L-I, my daughter R-u-t-h, plane from P-o-r-t-l-a-n-d, my sister here N-Y, brother from F-L, good friends from C-C and B-B . . ."

Ruthie explains he means Chasen Center and Brighton Beach.

"Not think old, advise all you. Me eighty feel like k-i-d. Me thank G-o-d you all alive. Stay well, happy, long l-i-f-e. Eat, drink, b-e m-e-r-r-y, tomorrow . . ." He pauses for emphasis. ". . . w-e live."

He sits down to applause.

Aunt Lois wipes her eyes. "I'm so proud of him," she says. "He's remarkable. I tell you."

Dan rises and makes a show of applauding him, mouthing, "Terrific, terrific!"

The cute little man did okay, Ruthie thinks. More than okay, she concedes. Why wasn't he so eloquent or charming at home? she wonders. Wouldn't he have been if he could? She answers her own question, reaches into her purse for aspirin.

When the waiters roll the birthday cake in on a cart, she snaps more pictures. Her father demands one of the cake by itself. "Name," he instructs her, meaning she should be sure to get the yellow and pink buttercream swirls that say "Happy Birthday, Avraham," his Hebrew name. He poses with Marian and Trudy, then sends them back to their table so he can have a photo of just himself cutting the cake, and then one of Dan beside him. Dan takes the picture of her with her father cutting the cake.

"Nice?" her father asks her about the cake.

"Very nice," she tells him, forcing a smile. He never gave her or Melva or Sidney a decorated cake for their birthdays— or anything else. She feels pleased with herself for controlling her resentment, for having done her duty, even if Aunt Lois thinks her lacking in appreciation.

Albert blows out the sixteen candles: one for every five years and one for luck. As everyone applauds, a wave of sadness sweeps over Ruthie, thinking about her father having to order his own eightieth birthday party.

At their breakfast in Giorgio's Coffee Shop the next morning Albert gives Ruthie a sheet of paper containing a list he made of his birthday presents. She scans the first few items:

Mr. Mazzoli – $5 cash
Mrs. Kahn – $10 check
Trudy & Marian – toaster
Lois – tie clasp
Sol – $100 check
Dan & Terri – bathrobe

"Nice," she tells him. "Get my present?"

"Thank you," he says.

At least he didn't criticize her, she thinks. She gave him two books on coins, an 8″ x 10″ color photo of herself in a silver frame, and stationery engraved with his name and address. Usually he tells her she's gotten him something he doesn't need. It amuses her that he doesn't realize how expensive her gifts are. Exceeding her duty gives her pleasure. After all those years of giving her no birthday gifts, he now gives her either five dollars or ten—she never knows how he manages to decide.

Giorgio's is even hotter than it was two days before. Her bra and panties cling like a wet suit. Her father doesn't look so crisp either. His muted plaid sportshirt—one of the ones she sent him this spring when he had the prostate surgery—is limp.

"Hot today," he says, wiping his forehead.

This time she eats quickly so they can leave, but after he finishes he starts talking about her mother. "Mama p-o-i-s-o-n your mind, S-i-d-n-e-y mind, M-e-l-v-a mind," he says. "Always tell children hate me."

"Mama love you, always love you," Ruthie says, wondering why he is bringing this up now, with her mother gone almost two years.

"N-o!" he barks. "Why with another man?"

"What?"

"Sneak h-o-t-e-l, I catch, think me stupid."

"H-o-t-e-l another man?" Ruthie repeats. An image of a little smiling woman with breasts and stomach stacked like two beach balls, trysting with one of the deaf-mutes, seems implausible. Comical.

"Y-e-s," her father says, sticking out his chin. "Sneak, B-B. Why move M-a-n-h-a-t-t-a-n?"

"Don't know."

"That why."

She gropes for bits and pieces of remembered conversations with her mother. How Albert hit her the first time when she was pregnant with Sidney. Before Ruthie was born. How she walked along Brighton Beach, contemplating throwing herself in the ocean. Did he hit her mother after he caught her with the man, or did she go with the man after he hit her? Was there even a man? Was there an innocent explanation for why her mother might have been there? Was she there? Ruthie berates herself for believing anything of what her father is saying.

"Me stupid, not i-n-v-e-s-t young," her father tells her now, claiming her mother kept him from buying stocks that would have made him rich at an early age. "T-o-o l-a-t-e, buy s-t-o-c-k," he says. She knows he has some stock from seeing envelopes from brokerage houses in his apartment but never gave it much thought.

"You follow s-t-o-c-k?" she asks him now.

He nods. "L-u-c-k-y g-u-e-s-s," he tells her, "money grow like itself."

She thinks about this while he starts complaining once again about Irving Gold, who courted her mother after Albert divorced her. "I-r-v-i-n-g n-o g-o-o-d," he says, "collect S-S-I, always poor . . ."

Her heart thumping, Ruthie interrupts. "What difference? You your friends, Mama hers." The last time she confronted him she was seventeen and he had ordered her to stop seeing Aaron. "You wonderful father," she had signed. "Honor father," he said, and smacked her across the face. Shortly afterwards she moved out. Melva and Sidney were at home then, Sidney recovering from the end of his first marriage, Melva between stays in the mental institution.

What is her father thinking now? He is staring past her shoulder. After a few minutes he asks, "Like new rug?" as if that's what they'd been talking about all along. She tries to reassess him. Was the lion always a pussycat? Just a bully? Or has he mellowed? Soon he is back on the subject of her mother. She should have known.

"Not right children bring up," he says.

She knows if she walks out of the coffee shop it would mean a permanent rupture. Why doesn't she? Signing with sharp motions to indicate her displeasure, she says, "Forget. Finish. Mama dead."

Her father looks off into space, seeming to be at a loss.

New resentments displace old, Ruthie thinks. Why is he doing this to her? Her mother cannot defend herself. He has insinuated doubts, clouded her images of her mother, whom she cannot defend now—not with certainty.

The waitress returns, coffee pot in hand, but looks to her father as if to ask his permission to refill Ruthie's cup. "I'd like some more coffee please," Ruthie says, a pronounced edge in her voice.

As she drinks the refill, her father watches her, not with irritation but acceptance, an oddly gentle stare. How can he not know what he does to me? she wonders. Why did she think her mother's death would free her from conflicting loyalties? Ruthie had sided with her mother, but always there was resentment for not being free to love her father. Not that he'd earned her love, not after what he did to her mother and to Melva and Sidney. Still, she needed to love him. If only her mother had understood that . . .

"Come," her father says, "show you something downtown."

They take a bus that is not air-conditioned up First Avenue. She feels faint from the hot air blowing on her face from the bus's open window. When they change for the crosstown, she says, "I p-a-y t-a-x-i," but he shakes his head vehemently.

"What f-o-r? Waste money," he says, making a beeline for the connecting bus. They get off at Madison and as they walk arm-in-arm across the street, he points. "My b-a-n-k."

She follows him inside, wondering why he has to show her where he keeps the money, since the passbook undoubtedly has the bank's address, in case something should happen. They don't go to the lobby where the tellers are, though. He ushers her toward a circular stairway down to the vault. They descend slowly into the cool gray marble. Her father brushes back a shock of hair from his brow.

"Hello, Mr. Zimmer," the guard says as he unlocks the gate and lets them inside. Albert salutes him with two fingers.

"N-i-c-e man, same many years," her father tells her, then signs the register.

"Does he come here often?" she asks the guard, knowing the answer when he goes to a box, puts in a key, waiting for her father to catch up and put in his own key.

"Every week," the guard says. "You must be his daughter. He told me you were coming."

Albert and Ruthie are seated across from each other at a long table in a spartan little room, the door closed. Albert takes the lid off the long metal box. "Show you," he says.

He takes out a handful of watches with silver, gold, and leather bands, puts them on the table. He takes out another handful, explaining, "Found, street. Finish sell many." He holds up an odd shape of almost translucent pink stone. "Know what?" When she shakes her head, he says, "L-a-m-p." A finial, she realizes. "Worth much money. A-n-t-i-q-u-e." Then he returns the watches and finial to the box, points to a long row of envelopes neatly stacked on their edge like index cards. He grabs a fistful and puts them on the table, picks one up and points to a little mark like a *1* on the front, no bigger than a quarter-inch high. "See?"

She nods, although she doesn't know what he's getting at.

He opens the envelope and takes out a thin pile of crisp bills. "Count," he says to her.

She looks at him, uncertain.

"Count," he signs again.

She takes the bills, all fifties, and counts.

"How much?" he asks.

"Twenty."

"How much?" he asks again.

She multiplies in her head. "One thousand."

He nods. "Satisfied," he says. He takes the bills from her, straightens them out, slips them into the envelope, which he places at his far right on the table, then hands her the bills from another envelope. "Count," he says.

The significance of the little mark on the outside of the envelope becomes clear. She eyes the envelopes still in the box, trying to gauge how many there are.

The second, third, fourth envelopes all have twenty crisp fifties. Then she counts one with ten hundreds. She counts and counts and always the total is a thousand dollars. This is crazy, she thinks to herself, but keeps counting. More than an hour later she has counted all the envelopes. He has neatly restacked the money in each one and lined them up in the box. Now he pushes the long metal box toward her. "Count," he says, meaning the number of envelopes.

"How many?" he asks her.

She counts them. "Two hundred fifty," she tells him. Two hundred fifty thousand dollars, she says to herself. A quarter of a million. She chants it almost, trying to make it real.

"I-f me die, you very l-u-c-k-y." He looks at her expectantly.

She notes the unintended irony, plans to tell her friend Allison when she gets back. Allison has a good sense of irony, being the poor little rich girl. "Me not l-u-c-k-y you die," she tells her father, a frown on her face to show he's said the wrong thing.

"Save for you, worry your future."

She tries to look appreciative, wishing she had the courage to spit in his face. With a shock of white hair over his eye, he could pass for an elderly Hitler.

As they walk down Fifth Avenue to the bus stop, several inner voices advise her: *Don't do anything rash. Show him your gratitude. Keep the status quo. Call Dr. Dessein.*

In between the voices she catalogs examples of her father's miserliness: the breakfast in that greasy hothouse; the cartons of milk and sugar packets he filches; the fleabag he insisted on staying in when he visited her . . . until she forces herself into what she calls neutral. A funny image for someone who doesn't drive a car, she muses. Why doesn't she drive? Is it a sign she hasn't grown up?

At 14th Street they get off to transfer to the crosstown. Taxis speed by. A quick death, she thinks. A truck would be more certain. *World Wide Movers*. An ironic death, she thinks of telling Allison. Then she sees the bus coming from the intersection. A voice inside her says: *Now. Now or never. Do it.*

Then another voice says, *Bloomingdale's.*

As the bus rolls into the stop, she looks at her father, the picture of a contented old man. She hardens her resolve to go on a major shopping spree. When they get out at Avenue A, she is about to leave him on the pretense of having to catch her plane, but he asks her to come back to Chasen Center with him.

"Important," he tells her. "D-o me f-a-v-o-r."

She marvels at his asking, instead of telling. She suspects what he wants to show her is financial in nature. "O-K," she says, holding his arm as they navigate the rocky sidewalk. In another hour she'll be on her way, free to deal with her mounting anxiety. Silently she chants Dr. Dessein's number again until they get to the building.

Once in his apartment he sits in the armchair, not saying anything. After a few minutes she asks, "What want show me?"

He searches his memory, gets up, walks over to the closet. He takes down a box, places it on the coffee table in front of her, tells her to open it. For a moment she thinks it might be a present for her but realizes her foolishness when she takes out a blue and gray velour robe, the one Dan and Terri gave him for his birthday.

"Nice?" he asks.

"Beautiful," she says.

He takes it from her and puts it on over his clothes. "O-K?"

"Very nice," she says, feeling her jaw ache. She unclenches her teeth.

Carefully he folds it up and places it in the box, beaming. He puts away the box, returns to his chair. "Happy you like."

She waits a few moments. "Finish show me?" she asks.

He nods, like he's satisfied, gets up when she does. In the middle of unlocking his door he stops and beckons her to the kitchen. He points to the little formica-topped table against the wall, a table big enough for one. "Nice?" he asks her. He starts to remind her how he got it, but she cuts him off, says she knows. She moves toward the door, biting her tongue hard enough to make it bleed.

After he undoes one of the two locks, he beckons her back to the kitchen, opens the lower cabinet doors, telling her to look. She sees the giant glass jars filled almost to the top with coins, coolly wondering how she'd ever get them to the bank.

He motions her to the living room, where he takes out a telephone book from the bottom of the bookcase. It is ten years old. He opens it to show her pages of stamps tucked in the back. "Very v-a-l-u-a-b-l-e," he tells her. "Remember, i-f anything happen."

Then he takes her to the dresser by his studio bed and points to the bankbooks in the bottom drawer under a pile of towels. An inch of them. On the dresser Ruthie sees the picture of Sidney in Fort Tryon Park, looks away and sees Melva in the picture on the nightstand. Remembers a word that Vince liked to use a lot: ineffable.

Finally they are in the corridor outside her father's apartment. He double-locks the doors, stands there as if he's trying to think of something. "Know," he says, after a moment. "Want ask you. Deaf a-l-l ask, why n-o stars? Think maybe s-h-u-t-t-l-e explode."

At the elevator he hugs her a long time. "I love you," he

mutters into her ear. When she steps back, he says it again out loud, not signing it. He reaches inside his back pants pocket and hands her an envelope. "For birthday next month." She sees his eyes glisten but doesn't feel guilty having lied to him about the time of her return flight. "S-a-f-e plane," he says.

She waves to him through the little window of the elevator. Outside, she hugs Marian and Trudy, who are sitting on their favorite bench, waves good-bye to the others. She walks over to 14th Street, turns around to be sure her father hasn't followed, hails a cab.

As the taxi speeds along, she opens the envelope. There is a hundred-dollar bill, no, several hundred-dollar bills. Keeping the envelope cautiously in her lap, she counts. Ten bills. A thousand dollars. Enough to pay the airfare and hotel for the week, so at least she's come out even. Then she thinks about what Dr. Dessein will cost and knows she's behind. Suddenly it hits her that today is the first time her father has ever told her he loves her. A man can change, she tells herself, even at eighty.

At Bloomingdale's she floats through the designer rooms, tries on many items from the sale racks, but is unable to buy anything. She walks out, goes to an expensive Chinese restaurant, orders extravagantly, but finds she has no appetite. After drinking two vodka tonics, she pays the bill and leaves.

Outside, the sky has darkened. The air is heavy. When she hears a clap of thunder, she doesn't immediately hail a taxi. Big drops of rain splatter on her and the sidewalk, and still she keeps walking down Third Avenue toward her hotel. When the downpour starts, she doesn't change her pace, aware her clothes are getting transparent as they cling to her body. She smells the funny metallic smell from the rain on the sidewalks she remembers from her childhood. The rain is so hard now she cannot see what the traffic signal says. She starts to cross when a car suddenly rounds the corner. She jumps back, her heart pounding violently at how close she's come to getting hit. Only a moment later does she realize the car has splashed her. As another car nears the deep puddle in the street, she stays put, feels the water run down her legs. She studies the muddy streaks on her yellow skirt. She knows she is acting like a crazy woman, but somehow it feels good to be drenched. Punishing.

The social worker waves at the old people in front of Chasen Center, signs, "Hurry, hurry," as they board the bus for their free trip to Atlantic City. Albert lets Marian and Trudy board in front of him. By the time he's navigated the high steps and toddled up the aisle, he finds Marian and Trudy sitting together, which is not how he imagined it would be. He had pictured Marian next to the window, himself next to her, and Trudy across the aisle. But it is he who is across the aisle and Trudy is by the window on the other side. He cannot even see her without leaning forward. He likes the blouse she is wearing, hopes she wore it because she knows he likes green.

"B-i-g gambler?" Marian asks him now, about what they will do in Atlantic City.

"Me follow you," he tells her. "Bring lots money?" he jokes, thinking he will give them each five dollars worth of nickels and ten for himself.

Trudy leans forward to sign, "Me like o-c-e-a-n air, that a-l-l."

Albert thinks that if Trudy doesn't use her nickels he'll put them in a slot machine for Ruth and send her half the money if he wins big. He wonders if everything is okay with her and when he will hear from her.

The bus starts moving and he leans forward to get a glimpse of Trudy, who is looking out the window. Tomorrow, when Marian is visiting her son, he'll talk to Trudy again about the Poconos. Maybe she would like to see the colors of the trees in the fall. Ruth said it was very beautiful in the country in fall. He doesn't know why she didn't show more appreciation for the money in the safe-deposit box. Too quiet, he thinks. He can never tell what's on her mind. Lois says she's a proud woman. Lois can talk to her because they both can hear. He's glad Lois loves Ruth so much. She's always telling him to be proud of his daughter. If only Ruth had made him a grand-father, he thinks, before he dozes off.

On her last day in New York, Ruthie takes the bus up to Fort Tryon Park, a long ride she took many times as a girl just to see neighborhoods different from her own. The bus travels along Madison Avenue with its designer boutiques and chic little restaurants, through decaying neighborhoods in the 90's and beyond, around the northern edge of Central Park and Upper Harlem, which seems to have moved north into Washington Heights, once populated by German refugees but now heavily Hispanic.

She gets off the bus at the last stop on Fort Washington Avenue, walks a block to the south entrance at the top of the park, aware that the area is curiously deserted, before recalling a *New York Times* article about drug-related crimes. Wonder-ing if she can get to the Cloisters safely, she starts into the park, sees a couple of menacing-looking teenagers duck be-hind some bushes up ahead. Quickly she retraces her steps, her heart thumping. Deciding to visit her old neighborhood down below, at the foot of the park, she goes to the elevator, and while she waits a policeman happens by.

"You shouldn't be here alone," he says sharply.

"Then how do I get to Broadway?" she asks, realizing it's a silly question.

"Look, I'm just telling you for your own safety. We've had a few rapes in the last few months here."

She thanks him for the warning, trying to integrate her new sense of danger in Inwood with her memory of its safety. The policeman rides in the elevator with her, then walks with her around the deserted bend to Broadway. This time she thanks him profusely.

"Ma'am, just doing my duty. We don't need more negative publicity."

No more rapes or no more negative publicity? she wants to ask him. Has everything become a matter of public relations? She reminds herself that even she is involved. Image enhancement of the worst kind—for politicians.

Walking along the Broadway boundary of the park she recalls the autumn she fell in love with Aaron, at the tender age of thirteen. On her way to high school in the mornings she would crunch the fallen leaves with her shoes, thinking about how awful it would be to die before she and Aaron had slept together. Hearing castanets, she looks up, realizes it's the chatter of Hispanic women. She is in a stream of light brown-skinned women and children moving toward a long, low white building that apparently has replaced the A&P. The sign tells her it's the welfare office.

Her sudden anger surprises her. All these people on welfare, draining the economy! At fourteen her mother made dresses in a sweatshop. Immigrants and immigrants, Ruthie thinks, distinguishing between those who get jobs and those who collect welfare, those who learn English and those who try to make everything bilingual. With a shock, she realizes that if there had been welfare in those days her mother might have been able to remain in school. And what about Grandpa? an inner voice asks. He never spoke anything but Yiddish!

At the northern tip no elderly people sit on benches, no baby carriages are parked in front of young mothers. The benches have been spray-painted with graffiti; many are missing slats. Except for a few Hispanic children on the swings and one chasing pigeons, no one is in the block-long playground. How full it used to be in the afternoons when she was there with her mother for f-r-e-s-h air! The pool is dry, the fountain spigot gone. She and Robin Reinstein bathed there in the summers. Robin was the first to wear a two-piece bathing suit. Ruthie smiles, remembering one of the few times she exerted her will as a child, refusing one day to swim anymore unless she had a top to go with her swimming trunks. She and Robin used to skate on the cement around the leafy trees, trees almost bare now and spindly. No deaf people sit on benches around the sandbox, arms waving in the air as they sign.

She takes out her notebook, jots some notes, then for the next hour walks back and forth the length of Dyckman Street, still the commercial center of Inwood, but now Hispanic. Her eye catches the eye of the few Caucasians who pass by. We're outnumbered, they seem to say to her. On her last tour of the street she keeps stopping to record her impressions:

DYCKMAN STREET

- Nedick's (First air-conditioned store. Sidney took me for orange drinks.) Gone!
- Dr. Howard Schlusser (Mama's optometrist. Mama said he died of a heart attack a few years ago.) Gone!
- Five and Ten (Later Woolworth's. Mama took me for hot cocoa with marshmallow creme during blizzard, I was 6? A very big deal!) Gone!
- Fish market (Metal bins on sidewalk with chopped ice & walleyed fish on top. Never knew why sawdust on floor inside.) Gone!
- Miss Marguerite's Dance Studio (Tap & acrobatic lessons w/Glory. Dot made Spanish costume for spring recital, bought me maracas.) Gone!
- Nick's Fruits (Crates on sidewalk. Mama never trusted his scales.) Gone!
- Bakery (Name??? Mama sent me for rye bread, no seeds sliced.) Gone!
- Loew's Theatre (20¢ double feature w/cartoons, newsreel; vending machines w/nigger baby candy & nonpareils.) Gone!
- Schiffman's Toys (Ballerina marionette I named Mitzi, coveted more than anything else in whole childhood.) Gone!

DYCKMAN STREET NOW

- Discount stores (15' wide; plastic shoes, gilt-painted religious statues, assorted *tsatskes*)

- Prostitutes (young teens, black teased hair, pink minis & boots, hustling truck drivers, one hanging off cab, bare ass showing)
- Pimps (bright tank tops, black leather caps & pants)
- Latin-Chinese restaurant (neon sign—*cerveza fria*)
- Bodega (green bananas in window)
- Young curly-headed boy, like Hopalong? (Sees me writing and asks if I'm a "welfare bitch.")

At the corner of Dyckman and Nagle she puts away her notebook and steels herself for Arden Street. Before she gets there she passes the place where Mahmoud's Garden flourished briefly, smiles at the thought of Mr. Mahmoud lusting after her roly-poly mother, giving her a bargain on his plastic flowers. Then she remembers her father's claims.

On Arden Street she strides past clusters of Hispanic men, ghetto-blasters at their feet, skinny young children scampering on the dirty sidewalk. She feels the eyes of the men on her, realizes her attempt to be inconspicuous by wearing a khaki-colored ramie suit has failed. Its simple design looks expensive. She keeps her eyes focused straight ahead, but cannot help turning to see two girls half reclining in a doorway, their eyelids drooping, a syringe lying at their feet.

The sweat on her back turns clammy. Her feet feel leaden as she forces them along the sidewalk toward her old building, diagonally crossing the little street, passing two cars without fenders, tires, or doors. The odor of garbage wafts in the air from a green plastic bag that has burst, its contents strewn along the curb in front of the alleyway where the vendors used to sharpen knives and men used to sing for coins. How many times did she call up to Melva or Sidney to throw down her skate key or her Spaulding! On the first landing of the stoop are four Hispanic girls jumping rope, with pigtails like the ones she wore as a child, but she never wore jeans. They make no effort to stop or move as she squeezes between one of the rope turners and the wrought-iron grill at the edge of what used to be the garden but is now only dirt, barren of plants or shrubs. On the second landing she checks the garden on the other side and wonders who found the quarter she once buried. Black, spray-painted graffiti cover the bricks around the windows at the top of the stoop.

She looks up at where the Opals' windows used to be, then at the Silbermans' windows, which were in the center building on the ground floor. There are wrought-iron bars on all those windows now. She walks to the entrance of 38 Arden, where she lived with her family, for her first seventeen years. She studies the names next to the panel of bells outside the door. Martinez, Delgado, Ruiz, Sanchez, then Reinstein. She can hardly believe the Reinsteins are still there, especially because they lived across the court, but she rings the bell anyhow, hears the buzzer, and opens the front door.

Garbage is heaped in the center of the lobby, cans and cereal boxes strewn near the door of the apartment where her friend Glory lived with her stepbrother Nelson and their mother, Dot, who taught Ruthie there were other worlds beyond Inwood. Ruthie walks along the shredded rubber runner, passes the mailboxes, three of them dangling by their hinges. She walks up the marble steps, avoiding the concave dip in the middle. She finds herself counting, as she used to do as a little girl, nine steps in each half flight, two flights to Apartment 3G, the one just below 4G, where she lived.

She rings the doorbell. After a while she realizes the bell isn't working, so she knocks, hears the peephole cover moving aside, then the chain, sees the door open a couple of inches.

"Who is there?" a German-accented voice says.

"Mrs. Reinstein? I used to live upstairs. Ruthie. Ruthie Zimmer."

"I don't buy anything," the voice says.

"Upstairs!" she shouts. "Remember my mother, Mrs. Zimmer?"

"Gott in heaven!" The door slams, the chain lock rattles,

and Ruthie is looking at a stooped figure with a jutting jaw, wisps of gray hair over the ears and forehead. A skeletal face, all bone and sunken dark eyes.

"Mrs. Reinstein?"

"You're not Ruth," Mrs. Reinstein says. "Who are you?"

"Yes, it's me," she tells her. "I look different."

"Different? You look like an actress. Come in, come in. What did you do to yourself?"

Ruthie tries to take a deep breath but can hardly breathe at all, steps into a dark hallway with the odor of mothballs, then into the kitchen, which has yellowed, the dumbwaiter painted shut. Mrs. Reinstein waves at her to sit down, puts some water in a teakettle on the gas stove to boil, and sits down herself, running her hand over her sparse hair. "Turn sideways," she says.

When Ruthie does, she says, "A nose job?" Without waiting for an answer, she adds, "And you dyed your hair. Very becoming. The red looks natural."

Ruthie grins. "No one else noticed. My father never said anything, the people I went to school with never noticed . . ."

"My Robin used to ask me ten times a day how to get a nose like yours, like a Roman goddess it was . . ."

Ruthie tells her she must be dreaming this. There was a year she almost killed herself because she didn't have Robin's cute little nose. Fortunately her brother made her throw up all the aspirin by forcing black coffee down her.

Mrs. Reinstein makes her instant coffee. "I would have baked a cake if I knew you were coming, *bubeleh*. How are you? I'm sorry about your mother. She was a wonderful woman."

Trying not to feel anything, Ruthie says, "My father lives on East 12th now."

"Him don't mention, please." Mrs. Reinstein makes a pretense of spitting. "Ptooh!" She leans forward and grabs Ruthie's hand. "Mrs. Cafferty called the police twice on him. What would have happened to your mother if she didn't?"

After Ruthie chokes up, Mrs. Reinstein hands her a hankie, but she finds tissues in her purse.

"Have some Sara Lee. It'll lift you," Mrs. Reinstein says, getting an aluminum foil cake pan out of the refrigerator. She stands over the cake, knife paused, to tell Ruthie that Mr. Reinstein died five years ago from pneumonia, that her son and his wife moved into this apartment and she moved in with them, then her daughter-in-law had a baby and they moved out. Ruthie barely remembers Howie. Was he the one Melva had a crush on? Still standing, the cake uncut, Mrs. Reinstein tells her about their house in Hempstead and Howie's wonderful job in accounting with the federal government.

"Just a little piece," Ruthie says, to turn her attention on the cake. It works. She gets a fat slice and Mrs. Reinstein puts the pan away, sits down, her head tilted back as if she's remembering.

Afraid of what she might hear, Ruthie asks about Robin. Mrs. Reinstein scrunches up her wrinkled mouth, making her cheeks even more hollow. She sighs, gets up, leaves the kitchen. When she returns, she hands Ruthie a photo album. In it are pictures of Robin and Nairobi.

"Two million children in New York and my daughter has to go to Africa to teach," she says. "She hates me so much?"

Ruthie tries to say reassuring things, studies the pictures. Robin looks very much the same, dark and slender, her inquisitive eyes bulging, her nose still short and straight. After a while she says, "I wonder if you'd mind if I walked through your apartment. It's like ours was upstairs and I want to remember . . ."

"What's to remember, *bubeleh?* A hole in the wall. Your mother died here. I'll die here." But she gets up to show her.

The wooden floors are still in good condition. Ruthie thinks Mrs. Reinstein sweeps and polishes them as much as her mother did. The bedrooms are as airy and light as she remembered, facing onto Arden Street, which doesn't seem so far down, but then she's one floor closer. How many hours did she and Melva and her mother spend leaning out on the sill, watching whatever was going on in the street? The summer when Sidney was washing cars for money she and Melva used to sit out on the fire escape. There was no heavy iron bar across the window in their apartment. They'd just lift the lower sash and climb outside.

"They come in from all over," Mrs. Reinstein says, meaning robbers. "Like the roaches."

"I have to use the bathroom," Ruthie tells Mrs. Reinstein, so she can see it alone, uncertain if she wants to see it at all. Only because it's her last chance, she thinks.

She stands with her back to the door, surveying the white tiles, brick-shaped ones on the walls and the tiny octagonal ones on the floor, now cracked throughout. How many thousands of times had she been in the bathroom just upstairs?

She has a flash of her mother's naked body, breasts hanging to her rotund belly, stepping out of the shower . . . the times she herself lay on the cool tile floor, face down, squeezing her legs together until she achieved that strange, scary sensation that made her heart pound . . . the nights Melva pretended to be Peola, a creature who was a thousand years old and who wanted to kidnap Ruthie and turn her into someone named Petunia.

Ruthie moves to the narrow window, runs her hand over the bumpy surface of the frosted glass, tinted blue-green. She imagines Melva standing there shedding her pajamas, opening the window, climbing up . . . How did Melva manage, she was so heavy then from all that starchy food in the hospital? Did she sit on the ledge and push herself off, like from a diving board? Or did she plunge headfirst?

Mrs. Reinstein knocks on the door. "You all right?"

"Fine. I'll be out in a minute," Ruthie says, opening the window quietly. She leans out far enough so she can see straight down, into the alley. She imagines Melva's body sprawled on the cement, naked. "I know you're happier now," she says softly, then closes the window.

When she leaves the building, the girls are still playing on the stoop. Spanish music blares from an upper-story window. The girls are running in two concentric circles, except for the tall dark one who is dancing around the outer circle. Ruthie asks her what they're playing.

The girls look at her and at each other, talking in Spanish. The one she asked says, "What's it to you, lady?" and the rest of them start to giggle.

As she walks down to the bottom of the stoop, something hits her back. She turns to find a wadded-up Snickers wrapper. The girls are staring at her expectantly.

"*Adiós,*" she says, blowing them a kiss. She turns up the street toward what used to be the fanciest building, where Linda Lindemann lived. It had an elevator and Linda had her own room, she recalls. The windows on the ground floor are boarded up. The gray stone is almost black with graffiti. She remembers the cool marble steps inside where she and Aaron used to make love late at night because in those days there was nowhere else to go, not if you weren't married. She imagines teenagers on the steps now shooting up or nodding off, marvels that she's old enough to have seen a neighborhood die.

As soon as she turns onto Sherman Avenue, a wave of nausea sweeps over her. She steps to the curb, retching helplessly. When she is done, a boy on a bicycle stops at the edge of her pool of vomit, says something, but his accent is so thick she cannot understand. A woman comes rushing up beside her, yelling in Spanish. The boy yells back and rides away.

"He asks if you want the dope," the woman says. "I tell him, 'Not her, she a lady.'"

"Thank you," Ruthie says weakly. Great! she thinks. Two skirts ruined in two days, this one splashed with salmon flecks. Ruthie wishes she had bought something in Bloomingdale's.

"You wait," the woman says, disappearing into a bodega. She returns with a wet paper towel and helps Ruthie wipe off her skirt.

"I'd like to give you something," Ruthie says, reaching into her purse. The woman holds up her hand, backs up toward the grocery. Ruthie follows, thanking her. Deciding to forego her bus ride, she heads briskly toward Broadway to catch a cab.

As the cab lurches and speeds along the West Side Highway, Ruthie recalls playing Actress with her friend Glory on the stoop, using the scarves and jewelry and makeup that Glory's mother gave them. Dot was always transforming everything around her, including herself. Afternoons she sat under her big dryer in an orange chenille robe, polishing her nails or sewing clothes with sequins and beads. Unless it was her day off. In which case, she would pull her hair into a ponytail and put on a loose tunic over pants. None of Ruthie's other friends' mothers ever wore pants then. Dot would take her kids and Ruthie to places that Ruthie never dreamed existed. Once she took them to Washington Square for an outdoor art show. Once Dot's boyfriend drove them all to Bear Mountain. When Dot and her kids moved to Westchester, Ruthie was devastated.

In the past year Ruthie has placed ads in New York magazines and papers, trying to find Glory, although the ad wasn't so specific: "For a book about 38-42-46 Arden, I would appreciate hearing from anyone who lived there in the 40's and 50's. Ruth Zimmer Weingartner." She received one reply, from a woman who lived at the other end of Arden Street and didn't know anyone she knew, and vice versa.

Perhaps Glory moved to Hawaii to be with her father, Dot's second husband—a wrestler named Tiger Joe. Ruthie imagines Glory wrapped to her underarms in batik, her dark shoulders sloping gracefully to arms that lean on a lanai overlooking the waters of Kihei. "I'm sending you a message, Glory," she says to herself, her eyes closed. "Hear me."

"Lady, do you hear me? Six forty."

Ruthie reaches into her purse, hands the cab driver a ten, and says, "Keep the change," slams the door, but it doesn't close, so she slams it again. At the newsstand she buys a magazine because she likes the picture of Vice President Rockefel-

ler. With graying hair, it could be Wendell. Handsome. The
thought of being alone in her hotel room drives her into the
cocktail lounge where she sits on a stool at the bar, orders a
drink. In a short while men sitting on either side of her com-
pete for her attention. One is a computer software salesman
from Raleigh, blonde, rather nice looking, smooth. The other
edits a trade magazine in Boston, is awkward, with shy dark
eyes that keep looking away every time he starts to talk to her.
She decides on the shy one, gives him most of her attention.
The salesman moves to a table in the lounge near two gabby
women. She finds out that, like her, the shy man used to be in
city government and also doesn't like President Ford. He
seems very interested in her writing for political candidates.

After a few drinks he loses his shyness and asks her to his
room. When they get there, they lie on the bed and embrace a
couple of moments. "I'm very nervous," he says, sitting up.

Quite tipsy, she laughs and unzips him. "Everything is going
to be very fine," she says. She fondles him while he undresses
her and wonders if she can keep her promise. When he starts
to apologize, she shushes him, takes his penis in her mouth.
Once she is sure of his erection, she pushes him back down on
the bed and mounts him. As he thrusts inside her, he caresses
her, but so unimaginatively that her mind begins to wander.

"Oh, God!" she says all of a sudden, surprised when he
says, "What?"

Oh, God, she thinks again to herself. The lost interest. On
two hundred and fifty thousand dollars she's lost twenty-five
thousand dollars in the past year alone, more than enough for
her to live on comfortably.

"I can't believe it," she mutters as he comes.

No one meets her plane in Portland. She realizes it's irrational
to be wistful, but she's wistful nonetheless. She hadn't asked
anyone to meet her, not Wendell, not Allison, not Barbara,
not any of the people who offered. She takes the airporter to
downtown. The clusters of tall buildings seem both very famil-

iar and strange. They make her think of Aaron. When they divorced, he was writing a paper on the psychology of people who grew up in the midst of skyscrapers. How ironic, she thinks, that while she's seen her old neighborhood die she's also seen a town grow into a major city. What Wendell likes to call "countervailing forces." Still, she envies Aaron for having gone back east, hopes he is doing well at the college in Virginia—or is it Maryland?

From downtown she takes a taxi to the Northwest area. Her taxi moves evenly along Burnside, like most streets in Portland at night, deserted. Soon the gland that produces her adrenalin will atrophy, she thinks, and she will no longer miss New York.

In the morning, she calls Dr. Dessein's office.

"Is this an emergency?" the receptionist asks.

"I don't think so," Ruthie says, regretting her honesty when she gets an appointment two weeks off.

Over the next several days she is listless. She sleeps a lot, drinks too much coffee, even by her own—not her father's— standards. Both of her closest friends are too busy to see her. Allison has to meet a deadline for a magazine. Barbara has a new man in her life. She puts off seeing her married lover. Wendell doesn't call. It takes her twice as long as usual to crank out brochures and speeches for her clients. She feels guilty for charging them twice as much, settles for charging only one-and-a-half times what they would normally cost. When no one objects, she considers raising her rates.

In response to a letter from her father, addressed as usual to Mrs. Aaron Weingartner, and with its usual closing, "Love from Trudy and Marian," she starts to handwrite an innocuous note filled with the usual summary of the latest weather (cloudy and mild), her health (always fine), and how busy she is (always busy), but tears it up. She drinks a pot of coffee, circles her living room, makes another pot of coffee, goes into her study, puts a piece of paper in the typewriter.

"Dear Dad," she types.

"I know you won't understand why I am writing this litany of complaints . . ."

She stops, realizes he doesn't know the word "litany," crosses it out, and yanks the sheet from the typewriter. She puts another one in, decides to write in her own words any-

Dear Dad,

Thank you for the $1,000 birthday gift and for your inten-tion to give me what is in your safe-deposit box and bank ac-counts, etc. I know you won't understand why I've written this letter and you will go to your grave thinking your daughter is ungrateful. "N-o a-p-p-r-e-c-i-a-t-e," I can see you signing. "Mean. Stupid," you will say about me. Still, since Mama, Sidney, and Melva are not here to confront you for what you did to them—and to me—I've taken the responsibility upon myself, even knowing my efforts will be futile.

I'm sure you wanted me to tell you I was impressed with your having made all that money—a deaf man without much edu-cation. The truth is, seeing the money made me sick. It en-rages me that you used your supposed lack of money to deprive us. It deranges me to think of how even the tiniest portion might have made a tremendous difference to our family.

You gave Mama barely enough money to pay the bills. She was an absolute genius, feeding us with flour and potatoes. Fab-ulous soups, blintzes, crepes, knishes, knödle, pancakes, kugel! But you never praised her, and you continually criticized. You left every household chore to her, refusing to hire help, even though she had heart trouble. On the pretext that you didn't have money to take her along, you left her at home while you went gallivanting to conventions of the deaf, and to all your relatives around the North American continent. After you di-vorced Mama, you had the *chutzpah* to complain about Sidney's taking her to Hawaii for a vacation instead of you!

Do you remember the catcher's mitt you didn't buy him? Too much money, you said. Unable to play on the team, he took to hanging around with juvenile delinquents, and when they went joyriding in a car, he wound up in jail. You said that proved he was "rotten." In spite of your example, he was always kind and generous. Thanks to you he lacked any sense of self-worth, and being in jail even for a few days finished him.

As for Melva, she had too much pride to wear hand-me-downs, you wouldn't even give her money for a dress for the prom. Mama had to borrow one from Alexander's, which Melva wore with the tags tucked inside. Why couldn't you imagine how Melva felt? I remember your once giving a blind stranger on the subway a dime for his pencils, telling me how sorry you were for the man. How much sympathy have you ever had for your family?

On your salary from the post office (never mind the stocks) you could have paid for art school for Melva, but you said you couldn't afford it. You forced her into being a secretary, which she hated. You of all people! Because of limited opportunities for the deaf, you were forced to take a job in the post office, although you had the brains to do more challenging work.

And while I'm on the subject of opportunity, I recall how you fought my going to college. You wanted me to work full-time after I graduated from high school, to pay you room and board, so I moved out of home. You never knew I'd worked nights when I was fifteen, using a false Social Security number. That money plus scholarships plus working summers got me through college. Do you remember you forbade Mama to see me because you disapproved of my having moved out at seventeen? You said I was a "b-u-m," meaning tramp.

All because you wanted me to give you a few dollars you didn't even need. How can I begin to understand? Not that you fooled us. We knew you were a miser. We just had no idea to what extent. And though I'm mainly giving you examples of the money you *didn't* spend on us, what you really hoarded was your self.

Besides being a miser with your money and love, you were, as Melva used to call you, "the world's biggest hypocrite." You sat *shivah* for Sidney when he married out of the faith, weeping in front of your brother Sol and your sister Lois and even your god. At the very same time, you were in the midst of an affair with your own *shiksa*.

Even with a quarter of a million dollars you cannot buy a new past. You cannot erase my memories of your beating

Mama, using the strap on Sidney, breaking Melva's nose. You cannot make me feel sorry when I see the scars on your neck and back from the time you attacked Mama at the stove and she threw a pot of boiling water at you. I confess that few things have made me happier.

And while I'm confessing, let me mention the trick I played when you visited me in Portland. You loved being entertained by me so much you told me that you would move to Portland if they had a good deaf club. So when you asked me to take you to the club, I found a roundabout way: what is normally a twenty-minute bus ride took hours. I regret deceiving you, but I regret even more the necessity.

The truth is, three thousand miles between us is exactly the right distance. Emotionally we could not be closer if we were nose to nose. You profess to love and miss your daughter, yet you haven't a clue as to who or what I am. What's worse, you haven't the desire to find out. You have always been and will continue to be concerned exclusively with your own wants and needs, just as you were at Mama's funeral.

While I was trying to greet the mourners, you showed up at the chapel with both your women friends, and then demanded to see me privately. In the room next to Mama's open coffin you told me what was so urgent: you wanted to be sure I gave you Mama's formica-topped kitchen table. When I recall such a moment, I think it is a miracle that I haven't flung myself under a truck long ago, or hacked someone to death, maybe you. I didn't express the rage I felt just then, but stunned by your insensitivity, I hesitated before answering. And what did you do? You admonished me, "Think first father."

To make a long story short, I will keep your birthday present and buy something extravagant—something with no useful purpose—with the money you should have given me for college. I want nothing else from you. Not a penny. Find someone else you "love" and make her or him your beneficiary. With Melva and Sidney dead, you are now childless: the sole survivor.

Ruth

He'll never understand this, she decides, not even if she could manage to write it all in his vocabulary. She imagines telling him in sign: "You terrible father, you selfish . . ." She feels she has to send the letter, that something of the message might penetrate. Just maybe. Maybe not. Probably not. She imagines her father crying to Marian, saying his daughter is mentally ill ("mind wrong"). She sees him under the mezuzah asking God why she hates him, after he has offered up to her everything he has.

She takes the letter to the mailbox, but doesn't mail it. She spends the evening trying to unearth the happy memories of her family, jots each one down: a short list, and never is her father in the picture.

The next day the letter sits on her dresser while she lunches at Orvio's, an extravagance she used to enjoy when she was director of press relations for the mayor. The host recognizes her, asks why she's been away so long, exaggerating his displeasure. She banters with him, throws back her head, laughs, suddenly glimpses Wendell's silvery hair across the room. Wary of what she'll see next, she's relieved when it's a man in a gray pin-striped suit.

After she is seated, Wendell sees her and comes to her table to say that he's been out of town and will give her a ring. She never noticed before how stiffly he moves, the way elderly men do, even though he's only forty-seven. The immaculate cut of his suit can no longer hide his paunch.

She watches him discreetly, taking childish pleasure in recalling their intimate moments. She doesn't recognize most of the people who stop to talk to him. All of them share a look of exhilaration when they come away from having talked to him. Wendell's gift.

She has cold scallops and a celery root salad with mustard dressing, one glass of wine, the bill for which is twenty-seven dollars. She envies Wendell's money, thinks she deserves more than he to eat in such places, since his taste runs to baked

ham and mashed potatoes. She's had fantasies of raising a
child by him, one that he would generously support. For a
while she tried to get pregnant without telling him, justifying
it by the fact that he once said he wanted a son.

Later, having completed her work for her clients, she
stretches out on the sofa, a glass of wine in hand, and listens
to a Chuck Mangione tape that she played the last time she
and Wendell made love before she left for New York. She
recalls how the whole time he crouched over her she held
onto his hairy forearms, arms exactly like her father's. He
asked her to sink her teeth into his shoulder, claiming it didn't
hurt him, pressing her to do it harder. She could only do it at
first by pretending he was a baby cub being held by its mother.
Then she began to enjoy it, testing his limits and hers, cli-
maxing when he moaned with a mixture of pain and pleasure.

"As long as we're to-ge-e-e-ther," she sings along with the
tape, as the phone rings.

"I decided to have a party on the boat," Wendell says, without saying hello. "Thirty good friends. Saturday. Can you
make it?"

"Yes," she says, reluctantly. He's given her such short
notice. Did someone else cancel?

"I'll come get you at five. Make it four-thirty."

After hanging up she realizes he didn't ask how she is or
how her trip was. Wendell's manners, she thinks. But it's more
than that. He denies her existence except in connection with
his. Like her father. And the two men she was involved with
before Wendell. Aaron was so much the other way, continually asking what she was doing, what she thought, how
she felt. Invasive.

Please, God, she thinks now, isn't there some happy middle
ground?

Even knowing Wendell will be late, Ruthie is ready at four-
thirty on Saturday, dressed in a green silk dress and matching
sandals that together cost nearly a thousand dollars. He arrives
at five, doesn't comment on her appearance except to say she

has stilts on, high heels that make her an inch taller than he is.

"I expected you to be ready," he huffs while she puts on lipstick, ignoring her explanation that she wanted to kiss him without getting it all over him. A wasted gesture, she thinks, when he doesn't kiss her.

"Your hair's as shiny as foil," she tells him, wondering if he had it touched up, not daring to ask.

"What there is of it," he says. "Can we get going?" His tone is colder than usual. It amuses her to think of how he will melt later in her arms or between her legs.

As their elevator descends to the parking lot, she puts her arm behind his jacket, running her hand down the silky white linen over his buttocks. She feels him tensing, but not in a sexual way. Is it age, she wonders, that makes him so different from Scott, the first lover she had after her divorce? Scott was willing to do it anywhere, anytime, in an elevator once, even in his station wagon one night at Portland International after he'd met her plane. Too bad she could never talk to Scott.

Wendell backs up the Porsche with a screech, takes off at a scary speed down her street, nearly rear-ending a car at the stoplight. "The best brakes money can buy," he says gleefully, before pulling out and around the car and zooming down the street.

She checks her safety harness, puts her foot out to brace herself, realizes she isn't as ambivalent as she'd thought about wanting to live. She used to enjoy Wendell's flirtations with danger. "Wendell . . ." she starts to say. She stops, knowing his response would only be to drive faster. She vows to get a driver's license so she will never again be at anyone's mercy.

As soon as she and Wendell step on board what he calls his "boat," an eighty-one-foot yacht, it sails away from the dock. Wendell is obviously enjoying the flurry of attention from his guests, many of whom comment on what a beauty the yacht is, with its mostly wood construction. "A ratio of one to four," he boasts, meaning crew to passengers. Ruthie recognizes Freddie, who tended bar at Wendell's last party, at his home, and Diane, who is playing piano. She wonders where he dug up the harpsichordist plucking away at the strings, a fixed smile on her face, pleased probably at playing for a man who could be the state's next governor. Ruthie waits patiently as the female guests hug and kiss him, looking over his shoulder to size her up. She recognizes some of the last names—a banker, a developer, the secretary of state—but doesn't know anyone except Lucinda Bratt, who sashays up to them. Art director of a major architectural firm, Lucinda is one of Ruthie's nonpolitical clients, a referral from the mayor for whom Ruthie used to work.

Lucinda kisses Wendell on the mouth, wipes her purple lipstick off him with her hankie, which she then flips saucily before his face. "Ruthie, how green you look!" she says.

"How variegated *you* look!" Ruthie returns, with a glance at the mélange of leather and satin swatches, tulle flowers attached to a gray jersey tube.

"I can't even spell *vara* whatever, but I don't have to," Lucinda says, her eyes on Wendell. "Is she always correcting your grammar, darling? Writers are such sticklers." She turns to Ruthie. "Is he giving you grief? He's getting handsomer all the time." She pats his paunch. "The health club for you, darling, *tout de suite.*"

Apparently amused by their consternation, Lucinda runs her hands through her masses of permed blonde hair and does a sudden turn, like a fashion model on the runway, and is gone.

Wendell jabs Ruthie with his elbow. "Bratt's beard scratched my chin."

"Poor baby!" Ruthie says. "And how will you describe me in years to come?" She realizes "years" may be stretching it. Always she thinks each date with him is her last, that he is only a bulldozer of women. At least she did not become involved with him while he was married, which Lucinda did. No hell like an affair with a married man, she reminds herself, as her eyes meet those of an attorney to whom Wendell introduced her earlier. She stares pointedly at the man's wedding band, turns back to Wendell.

"My Jewish wine," he says, referring to her last name.

"With or without an 'h'?" Ruthie jokes.

As they complete their tour around the deck, Ruthie cannot escape the feeling that she is the object of a lot of curiosity. Even the bartender is staring at her. Deciding she is being paranoid, she drains her drink and starts on another, hoping to relax. There is nothing better than being on the water on a warm summer night, she tells herself, suddenly glad she is there. She thinks her mother would have loved it. Once her Uncle Ben took her mother on a boat ride. For years afterward her mother couldn't stop telling her about it. The pictures must be somewhere in the boxes that Ruthie hasn't had the heart to go through.

"You're far away," Wendell says to her, kissing her on the cheek. "That's a pretty dress. New?"

"Isn't alcohol wonderful!" she says. "Makes us so mellow." She kisses him on his cheek. *He is poison for you. P-o-i-s-o-n,* she spells out in her mind, as though signing it.

The yacht cruises slowly up the Columbia, its guests waving at or lifting glasses to the people on other yachts, suffused with the peach light of sunset. Surprising herself, Ruthie leans back in her chair, puts her head on Wendell's shoulder, enjoying the gentle rocking motion of the boat. When the pianist begins to play and sing "I Get No Kick from Champagne," Wendell springs up. "Don't move," he says. "I'll be right back with fresh drinks."

She is almost unaware of time passing until she realizes that the Chinese lanterns are on, glowing against the inky sky. Everywhere she looks, couples are snuggling together, not because the air is chill or the music (just now it's "Smoke Gets in Your Eyes") romantic, but they can hardly help themselves on a moonlit cruise. She gets up to look for Wendell. He's nowhere on deck. She goes down to the galley, puts on a wrap she left there, and hears Lucinda's throaty voice coming from the other side of the wall, and then, she's sure of it, Wendell's. Ruthie steps into the corridor, finds the voices are coming from behind a closed door. She stands outside trying to hear, but all is suddenly silent. Very silent, she thinks, feeling her anger mount, then bewilderment as to what she should do. It's not as though she's on land and can simply leave.

Back upstairs she chats nervously with the bartender about lemon twists. It wouldn't hurt for Wendell to see her flirting with Freddie, since he's young and good-looking, even if he's not her type: too pretty, too muscular. His chatter distracts her until he asks, "Where *is* the man? I expected him back for a refill long before now."

"Downstairs," she says noncommittally.

His glance travels around the deck. "Don't tell me he's with that cow!"

"Lucinda."

"She the one with the four-inch nails? She'd drive them into Wen's heart if they needed filing."

Wen? She smiles. Feeling reckless, she says, "I'm reasonably certain he is with her. Can I have a refill?"

"Would you mind getting it yourself?" the bartender asks, stepping out from behind the bar. She watches his muscled back disappear down the steps, then fixes herself a strong drink. In a few minutes she hears shouting from down below. She's sure she hears Wendell's voice, even though Wendell never shouts. Moments later he emerges on deck without his jacket or tie.

Now she hears Lucinda's throaty voice rising from below deck.

All eyes are on Wendell, who is pouring himself a straight shot of whiskey. He downs it, turns to face everyone. Raising his hand in an odd defensive gesture, he says, "Just a little spat, folks. Someone had too much to drink."

He steers Ruthie back to where they had been sitting. To be a fly on that wall downstairs, she thinks, what she wouldn't give. Lucinda comes hobbling up the stairs with only one shoe. Her other shoe comes flying after her, making a clatter on the deck. Ruthie sucks in her breath. *Take notes,* she tells herself. *You can deal with him later.* Out of the corner of her eye she can see Wendell's face, a mask of stone. The bartender is back on deck, comes up to them. In a petulant tone that rises above the music of the harpsichord, he says, "Is that your revenge? A homophobic bitch?"

Ruthie bites her cheek, wondering if Wendell knows what the word means. When Wendell turns to look at her, Freddie says, "Not *her*. The cow!"

Lucinda takes her one shoe off, moves toward them, her arm raised to strike. Wendell rises, looking ghostly pale in the moonlight. He lunges at the bartender. Ruthie averts her eyes, hears the thump. When she turns back, Freddie is sprawled on the deck saying, "More, baby. Give it to me."

A couple of men take him by the underarms and half push, half drag him down the stairs.

"Fred's a lunatic," Wendell says, loud enough for everyone to hear, although he's talking to Ruthie. His eyes dart, as if assessing his standing with the others. He points to the Yacht Club up ahead. "Land ahoy!" he says. It crosses Ruthie's mind that by morning the gossip will have traveled the state. Such a small state, and the world of politics even smaller! This could cripple Wendell's run for governor before it begins. She sips her vodka tonic, takes a pickled jumbo shrimp off a passing tray. Before she can stop herself she says, "You've catered your own undoing in high style."

He glares at her. "Why, did *you* want to fuck Lucinda?"

She stands up. "Nice party, Wen. I mean, Wen and his thirty closest friends, male *and* female." She walks away, stops, turns back. "Correction, make that twenty-nine."

She keeps having to unclench her jaw as she waits in the reception room to see Dr. Dessein, rehearsing how she'll begin the hour. The receptionist tells her to go on in. When she enters his familiar office, her rehearsed lines fall by the wayside. His polar bear-like figure moves slowly toward her, one arm outstretched to shake her hand. His soft fleshy neck and jowls make her think of her mother, who, though little, was also soft and fleshy. His eyes seem to ask how she is, although all he says is "Coffee?"

She takes the cup, sits down opposite his desk. He nods encouragingly at her, saying nothing.

She stares a moment, looks away, looks around the office, feels like a cat sniffing around to gain familiarity, but nothing moves except her glance. "I saw my father in New York," she begins.

For a long time Dr. Dessein doesn't interrupt. She talks about the birthday party, seeing Ione and Vince, revisiting Arden Street, and finally mentions the cash in the safe-deposit box. "It makes me want to tell him I'll never see him again," she says.

"Why?" Dr. Dessein asks.

"I want to throw that money in his face."

"Would he understand that?"

"No," she concedes.

"Then what useful purpose would it serve?"

She reminds him of the time she was nine years old and plotted to kill her father, making a couple of comically unsuccessful attempts.

"You wanted to kill him because . . ."

"Because he beat up my brother and sister, because he beat my mother. I've told you all this . . ."

"Your reaction to him . . ."

"I felt I was their defender. Since they weren't able to see that justice was done, it was up to me. No one would suspect me: I was my father's darling."

"And now?"

"I feel I should strike a blow for justice—for my family."

"What would your mother say about your giving up all that money?"

She looks at Dr. Dessein defiantly. "She'd be upset."

"Why?"

"She was always telling me to charm him so that he'd treat me well. It worked. And anyway, I was too chicken to stand up to him the way they did—that's why they were always in trouble. If my father had shown Melva that stash of a quarter million dollars, she would have lit a match to it."

Dr. Dessein appears to reflect on this. "Who knew better how to get along in the world—your mother or your sister?"

Ruthie flashes him a look of anger. "My mother!" She gazes down at her hands, digs a nail into her palm. After a long pause she says, "Why couldn't she have outlived the sonofabitch . . ." Ruthie breaks into sobs. "She could have enjoyed the money *with* me."

Dr. Dessein says nothing. After she's blown her nose, she meets his stare. "It's the guilt, isn't it!" she says, surprised by her discovery. "I feel guilty about enjoying the money without her. Even though she just happened to have a fatal heart attack. Why should I feel guilty for loving him?"

He lets her question hang in the air unanswered before he says, "You want to write. That money will come in handy." He closes his notebook. "Our time is up now. Do you want to meet again?"

She thinks of Wendell, how she blames herself. "I'll call for an appointment." She rises and shakes his hand. Impulsively, she steps around his desk and puts her arms out to hug him, grateful when he hugs her back.

Ruthie heads home, intending to tear up the letter she wrote to her father. Instead, she finds herself thinking about mailing it. She calls her friend Allison, tells her about the debacle on Wendell's yacht. Allison suggests she use it in her novel. "My next one," Ruthie says, "if I haven't forgotten all about him by then." By the time she calls Barbara, she has forgotten about the letter. They talk about what a second marriage will be like for Barbara, which makes Ruthie envious. When Barbara offers to introduce her to a friend of her fiance, Ruthie is about to decline, then realizes that except for her occasional and very married lover, whom she no longer wants to see anyhow, there is no man in her life. "What's he like?" she asks.

More days go by without her having touched her novel. The question of the money still hangs over her. She knows it's crazy but decides to mail the letter to her father. This time she takes it to the post office and drops it in the slot.

A few minutes later she causes a ruckus by trying to retrieve it. The supervisor is summoned, followed by the supervisor's supervisor, and then the postmaster. After questions and explanations, after she shows her identification and signs a waiver, she gets back the letter. She thanks them profusely. They look at her curiously as she tears it up and drops it into a wastebasket.

Before going home, Ruthie stops in at the State Licensing Office to get a learner's permit and signs up for a series of driving lessons. Feeling strapped for money, she remembers the long row of white envelopes, giddily writes the school a check, as though it were an investment in her future.

Exhausted when she gets home, she takes a nap. When she wakes, it is almost midnight. She puts on a Mangione tape, switches to Segovia playing Bach, brews a cup of coffee. She wonders what her father is dreaming about in New York, where it is 3 A.M. Probably the space shuttle taking out the stars. Instead of telling him about pollution, she should have explained about the black dwarfs, the relics of stars that travel through space undetected.

She closes her eyes, sees him making his speech at his birthday party, flushed and happy. Surely every being is entitled to a few moments of happiness, she tells herself. When was he ever happy that she knew? When he was with Mrs. Klepp, maybe. Even for that she should forgive him.

The aroma of French Roast brings her back. She fills her mug, gets out her file from the cabinet, the one that contains notes she's been making for the past year on characters, bits of dialogue, possible situations for her novel, and goes to her study. On the center of the page she types "SOLE SURVIVOR" and ponders a dedication to Hannah, Sidney, and Melva. Seeing her mug is already empty, she gets up for a refill.

The living room, streaked with moonlight, draws her to the window. The stars glitter like the rhinestones Dot once sewed into black wraparound skirts that she and Glory wore when they shook their maracas and stamped their tap shoes in Miss

Marguerite's spring recital. Dot said that while watching them she completely forgot they were in Inwood. Her two little Spanish *chiquitas*, she called them, the Hawaiian and the Jew.

Ruthie decides to add Dot to her dedication. The book will be sufficient, she thinks: her father will never know his darling daughter killed him.

She releases the aluminum catch and slides the window open. If she had the kind that raised up, with a wide sill on which to rest her elbows, she could hang out, as they used to say. Craning her neck, she can see a seven-eighths moon, as silvery as her father's hair, and a sky as dark as Glory's, studded with glitter. *Daddy, the stars are alive and well. If only you could see them.*